THE WRONG FACE

She had first met him in a sweetshop in Grassley the previous winter. She was buying chocolate and he was short of ten pence to pay for his cigarettes. She had given it to him, shy but insistent, and he had taken her home to collect the money to pay her back. His mother invited her to share their supper of spaghetti and red wine and she had fallen in love with Barry that first evening.

THE
WRONG
FACE

Dianne Doubtfire

A STAR BOOK
published by
the Paperback Division of
W. H. Allen & Co. Plc

A Star Book
Published in 1986
by the Paperback Division of
W. H. Allen & Co. Plc
44 Hill Street, London W1X 8LB

First published in Great Britain by W. H. Allen & Co. Plc 1985

Copyright © Dianne Doubtfire, 1985

Printed and bound in Great Britain by
Anchor Brendon Limited, Tiptree, Essex

ISBN 0 352 31646 2

TO JEAN STUBBS
A KINDRED SPIRIT

R

'It'll sting you! For God's *sake*, Nicola!' Robert Slingsby was sitting at the breakfast table watching his sixteen-year-old daughter as she knelt on the window seat trying to make a wasp crawl on to her finger.

'It won't. It wants to get out but it can't find the opening. It knows I'm helping it.'

Robert groaned. The summer sunshine poured through the open latticed window, assaulting his headache as he sat there in a blue silk dressing gown, staring over the rim of his third cup of coffee. The light was like a personal affront, glaring off the white linen tablecloth, flashing on the silver coffee-pot, burnishing the oak-panelled walls. It was his usual nervous headache, he knew that well enough, but he could see no end to his anxieties or to his headaches; both seemed to grow more painful every day. Aspirins had little effect – he had taken four already.

The wasp was now on her wrist. 'I'm warning you – *please*, darling!'

'Stop panicking, Daddy, or you'll *make* him sting me.' She addressed the wasp in a friendly coaxing voice: 'Come on, you idiot, off you go.'

He watched her calm blunt profile silhouetted against the dazzling rectangle of leaves and sky. Her blonde pony-tail was held untidily in a rubber band, and her wispy fringe, luminous with sunlight, kept lifting in the breeze then falling back in front of her eyes. He was taut with apprehension as he saw the wasp crawl along her small curled forefinger, but suddenly it flew away into the bright haze of the August morning, taking to the wide air hesitantly, as if uncertain of its freedom. He returned his cup unsteadily to its saucer.

7

The coffee was gritty and lukewarm. His wife was still in bed, and Ivy the old housekeeper had gone to church.

'There you are, you see,' said Nicola, standing up and pulling a packet of gum from the pocket of her jeans. 'I told you, didn't I?' She began to take the gum out of its yellow wrapper.

'It might easily have stung you.'

'But it *didn't*, that's the point. Barry says you should never say anything *might* have been anything – it's what *is* that matters.'

Barry again. He had heard the name a great many times during the past few weeks: *'Barry says Shakespeare was gay;' 'Barry's mother's got an astronomical telescope;' 'Barry says Britain is a sick society . . .'* Loving Nicola as he did, with a passion that was so much more than parental, Robert could hardly endure the thought of her with a boy friend.

'Tell me about this young philosopher,' he said.

She ignored the quip. 'Nothing to tell. Nineteen. Lives at Grassley. Works in a garage.'

'Where did he go to school?'

'Grassley High.'

'What is he going to do?'

'Doesn't really know. He's mad on cars.'

'But he must have some plans for his future?'

Nicola put the gum in her mouth and began to chew. 'He paints a bit but I think he just wants to stay on at the garage and try to find out who he is.'

'Doesn't he know who he is, then?'

'Do *you*?'

'Nicola, I wish you wouldn't talk in riddles. What's *that* supposed to mean?'

'Oh, never mind.' She threw the gum paper at the hearth. It was a wide Georgian fireplace, decorated in the summer with logs of silver birch. The wrapper landed on one of the logs and stayed there, rocking gently in the breeze from the window. Nicola smiled. It was the pure expansive smile of a child who has just received an unexpected present. 'Look at

8

that!' she cried. 'A butterfly!'

'Your mother won't think it's a butterfly,' he said drily. 'You'd better put it in the waste bin in the kitchen.'

Nicola picked up the wrapper with a sigh and tossed it out of sight behind the logs.

Robert propped the *Sunday Telegraph* against the coffee pot, pretending to read. He had to get through to her somehow, break down this barrier of defiance. He took a deep breath and tried to speak casually: 'Why don't you bring Barry here for a drink sometime? I'd like to meet him.' A lie, but surely she would warm to him for suggesting it.

She shook her head so vigorously that her pony-tail flew from side to side. 'Oh, no – I couldn't do that. He'd hate this place. He can't stand fitted carpets and posh china and things. And he'd *loathe* mother. Sorry!'

'But surely he could manage to put up with a carpet for half an hour or so? And he could come on a Tuesday evening when your mother's out.' This was when Julia went to her Council Sub-committee meetings.

'He goes to carpentry classes on Tuesdays. Never mind – it was a nice thought, Daddy.'

'What about his parents? Don't they have carpets?'

'Old rugs and mats and things. His father's dead but his mother's *super*. She just likes him to be free.'

So she had been to his home. 'Oh, well, I hope he uses his freedom wisely, that's all.'

Robert was relieved that the boy wouldn't be coming to Birch House. His jealousy was easier to bear if Barry remained a disembodied name, one of a vast faceless army of young men in grimy jeans.

He looked at her standing idly by the window – slender, average height, not particularly beautiful – and it struck him, as it had struck him many times of late, that she was old enough to have a baby. Her figure was fully developed although her pale, round little face had hardly changed since she was twelve.

'Your shirt's out at the back,' he said irritably.

'Who bloody cares?'

9

'I do. And don't say bloody.'

'Bloody – bloody – bloody! Lord, don't you *fuss*!'

He thought, she's right – I *do* fuss. It seems I just can't help it . . .

He was a chartered accountant, a maker of lists, a shoe-tree, trouser-press man. His light brown hair, stranded with grey, was closely trimmed, and ten years earlier he had grown a neat moustache to conceal his rather uncertain upper lip. It was at the time when Julia had finally put an end to all sexual contact; telling him that she was 'too busy to bother and had never enjoyed it, in any case.' The big carved four-poster was a fixture in their bedroom, and Julia wanted to preserve the appearance of a happy marriage, otherwise he would have arranged for separate beds or moved to another room.

Dick Benson, the Personnel Officer at Robert's firm, an affable, podgy little man, had said that the moustache gave him the air of a dashing young subaltern. Robert, then in his early forties, feeling middle-aged and believing that his height was his only claim to distinction, had been pleased and flattered.

Now Nicola was tucking the pink cotton shirt into the waistband of her jeans, watching him with her bright, almond-brown eyes. She ought to wear a brassière, he thought, seeing how her nipples pushed against her thin shirt. He looked down at the *Telegraph* and took another sip of cool coffee. That summer he had begun to dream about her – wildly erotic dreams that he dared not allow himself to dwell upon. He would wake in a trembling sweat, trapped with Julia under the red velvet canopy, and lie awake for hours, wondering how to bear the anguish and the secret guilt. And then, next morning, Nicola would be there in all her warm reality, lounging about in tight jeans or little flowered dresses. Did other men feel this way about their daughters? It was something you could never find out. Imagine asking Dick Benson: 'Tell me, old boy, do you fancy that girl of yours?' Not that he'd be likely to, anyway, a great creature like Caroline, with no neck and scowling eyes, but there were millions of men with pretty daughters forever displaying themselves around the house, half-dressed and unsuspecting. Why did he have these feelings? What was wrong with him? And what in God's name could he do about it? He had even thought of consulting his doctor but the idea was ludicrous. Old Fielding had attended Julia when Nicola was born; he would be appalled.

Now she was leaning over him, reading out a headline from the paper, something about a rail strike. Her fringe was tickling his cheek, and he could smell the mintiness of her chewing gum. 'Barry says you can't believe a word you read in the papers. It's all cooked up to put you off the scent.'

'That's rubbish, Nicola. If you choose a responsible newspaper you can be sure of fair reporting.'

'It depends whose side you're on, doesn't it? Barry's on the workers' side. You and mother are always against them. I've never heard you say a strike was right.'

'No, and why should I indeed?'

'They *can* be right – if the men deserve more money or something.'

'You know nothing whatever about it. You know nothing about the problems of inflation, for instance. You think you can simplify all the issues without understanding our economic and political structure.'

'Words!' she said mildly, licking the marmalade spoon. 'Just words. People like you can juggle about with long words and sound terribly wise, but you can't fool me. I'd rather talk to the strikers and believe what *they* tell me.'

Robert's head was throbbing again. Better change the subject. 'Don't you ever comb your hair?'

'Sometimes. Why?' She pulled out the chewing gum into a string and ate it back slowly.

'You've got pretty hair if you'd keep it tidy.'

She looked at him through the maize-coloured mesh of her fringe. 'Tidiness isn't important,' she said.

'What *is* important, Nicola?'

Her pensive brown eyes seemed to be focusing on

11

nothing. An inward dream. Barry, perhaps . . .

'Got to go,' she said.

'Where are you off to this time?'

'Out.'

He said nothing, afraid of antagonising her even more, afraid of knowing. He watched her saunter out of the room; she carried herself proudly in spite of her slovenly appearance. It occurred to him – and he was pleased with his astuteness – that she was proud of her very slovenliness.

He heard the front door slam. Nicola never closed doors; she just walked through them and let them do whatever they did by themselves – bang, close quietly, or stay open. The front door always banged; it was made of solid oak.

R

He stood up and watched through the window for her to appear in the drive. It was not strictly a drive, as it was no longer used for cars; the garage was at the back of the house. It was a straight path to the front gate, fifty metres of fine gravel. On the right was an old apple orchard and on the left a copse of silver birches. The trunks of the birches were gleaming in the sun, bright as aluminium. The estate was surrounded by a high brick wall, and at the end of the drive was a tall wide wooden gate, painted white and topped with spikes. The gate was adorned with handsome scrolled black hinges. Julia had spent some time at an art school in her youth; she had designed the hinges herself and had them forged by a blacksmith in Grassley. She did these things very well. It was a pity, thought Robert, that they gave her so much anxiety and so little pleasure. Not only was the gate topped with spikes, but Julia had had the wall fortified with pieces of jagged glass. Robert could see them now, occasional flashes of vindictive green. He had hated the idea but the house and grounds were a legacy from Julia's father

12

and she argued that the decision was hers.

When Nicola appeared she was swinging her leather shoulder-bag so that it scraped the gravel. The bag had been ridiculously expensive, a present from him – and ostensibly from Julia as well – the previous Christmas. Her shirt was loose again, blowing in the breeze to display seductive glimpses of bare back, and as she passed the orchard she kicked a red apple in front of her, dribbling it like a footballer. After a while she picked it up, rubbed it on her jeans and began to eat it. When she vanished through the gate she left it open, revealing the glitter of fast holiday traffic on its way to Hastings.

Where was she going? Out with Barry, of course. Or perhaps it wasn't Barry; perhaps it was that dreadful Sally Winters.

He sat for a while, staring at the paper until the columns of print swam into a blur. It's no good, he thought, I can't communicate with her. I don't understand people, that's my trouble. It isn't only Nicola and Julia – I just can't make contact . . . It seemed he was only at peace, or comparatively at peace, when he was working at his ledgers. He understood figures. If you handled them correctly, figures were infallible. They were totally obedient, reliable, without caprice.

The French carriage clock on the mantelpiece struck eleven. It had a delicate chime, like the tinkle of a tiny bell. He loved that clock, and especially so because it had belonged to his mother. His parents had been a gentle, undemanding pair, so devoted to one another that when his father died she followed him within a year.

He sighed. Julia would be ready for her bath. He hoped she wouldn't go on again about getting rid of Ivy. They simply couldn't turn her out after all those years. And in any case Nicola would be desolate; Ivy had looked after her since she was two.

He got up slowly and made his way across the spacious hall to the curving, blue-carpeted staircase. That wasp, he thought, she wasn't afraid of it. Not at all. His headache jarred as he climbed the stairs. The prospect of seeing Julia always made it worse.

R

She was sitting up in bed, reading a book. 'Oh, there you are,' she said. She glanced up for a moment, then returned to her book, frowning with exaggerated concentration.

'What are you reading this time?'

'Chairmanship.'

'Oh, yes – I suppose there's a lot you have to know.' She had recently been elected chairman of the Residents' Association.

'I know it already – just checking up.'

She was wearing a green hairnet. Every morning the tight bleached curls had to be pinned and lacquered into their elaborate waves and scrolls. She was a small-boned woman with narrow cheeks and a long thin neck. When she was younger there had been a trim delicacy about her but now at forty-four, she had a pinched look, as if she were perpetually cold. In the large ornate bed with its red velvet drapes she looked particularly drawn and sallow.

'Nicola's amazing,' said Robert. 'Really amazing.' He stood by the window, which looked over the little town of Grassley. Beyond a patchwork of fields and woods he could see the chimneys, blurred and blue in the hazy heat.

'In what way is she amazing?' said Julia at last. She turned a page of her book and continued to read.

'There was a wasp in the breakfast room – buzzing against the window. She made it crawl on to her finger so she could put it out. *Asking* for trouble.'

Julia looked at him coldly. 'Nonsense. You fuss about her far too much. Wasps don't sting unless they're provoked.' She pushed up the hairnet and scratched at the thin red indentation across her forehead.

'Well, she certainly wasn't afraid of it,' he said. '*I* would have been.'

'Tell me something you aren't afraid of, Robert.'

He turned back to the window. He thought, I'm afraid of *you*, damn you. Afraid of your arrogance and your biting tongue and the way you undermine my self-esteem . . . A blackbird was singing on the garage roof; he could see the irregular pulsing of its throat as the notes came bubbling out.

'My work,' he replied. 'I'm not in the least afraid of my work.'

'Yes, you are. You always check your figures three times. You told me so.'

'That's common sense. A mistake could cost the company thousands.'

'But it means you don't trust yourself to get it right first time – even with a calculator.'

'That's not fair, Julia. It's only sensible to double check when your work is as important as mine.' He was chief accountant at Granger Coe, a large building contractor's near Tonbridge.

'But not to *triple* check, surely?' She smiled at him briefly and looked down at the book.

They had had this conversation many times; it was useless to explain. 'What about your bath,' he said. 'It's gone eleven.'

'Where's Ivy?'

'Church.'

'Oh, God – *must* she? That means lunch will be late. Where's Nicola?'

'Out.'

'Out where?'

'She didn't say.'

'That boy, I suppose. What was his name?'

'Barry.'

'Oh, yes. His mother's got a telescope.'

'That's right,' said Robert. 'I wouldn't mind having a look at the moon.'

'If you cultivate Barry you might get invited.' Again that derisive tone that set his nerves on edge.

'He doesn't sound quite our cup of tea.' He said 'our' to warm the atmosphere. 'She was telling me about him.'

'Oh, a confidential chat? What does his father do?'

'His father's dead, but the boy seems to be some kind of a militant. Communist ideas, by the sound of it.'

Her lips tightened. 'Then we'll have to split them up. We can't have her mixing with people like that – drugs and protest marches and God knows what else. I can't risk her getting involved with the police when I'm on the Council.'

'How do you propose to stop her seeing him?'

She shut her book with a snap. 'That's your job, isn't it, if you call yourself a responsible father.'

Robert felt a fresh stab of pain behind his eyes. 'I don't think it'll do any good to interfere. It might make her keener. Remember Sally Winters – they're closer than ever. Live in each other's pockets.'

'Never mind Sally Winters. A boy is altogether different. And if *you* can't handle it, I can. *I'm* not afraid of her.'

'I don't see what you can do – short of a ball and chain.' He gave a dry laugh. 'After all, she's nearly seventeen.'

'It isn't funny. And she won't think it's funny, either, if she goes against my wishes.' Julia threw back the bedclothes and leaned forward, putting aside the book. She wore a pale green nightdress with black lace trimmings, and he could see her drooping breasts through the fine nylon. Her feet were small and shapely, her toe nails painted mauve. He thought how meaningless it was, their marriage. No sex, no laughter, no conversation worthy of the name.

'Would you run my bath now, please,' she said. 'And don't be mean with the essence – I like a lot of foam.'

She was the mean one and he was incensed by this remark. He went into the adjoining bathroom and found himself repeating the words in his head: *Don't be mean with the essence – I like a lot of foam. Don't be mean with the essence* . . . It went on and on, a silent dirge. He often did this with Julia's remarks.

The water plunged into the purple bath and he took the bottle of essence, removed the cap and poured the liquid recklessly into the swirling steam. He stood there trembling as the foam built up in clouds, winking, shimmering, rising above the edge of the bath, overflowing on to the carpet.

'There you are,' he called between clenched teeth. 'You can turn the taps off yourself. I need a drink.'

He did not look at her as he went out but he heard her voice as he closed the door. 'Thank you, dear – that's *so* kind of you.'

Sarcastic bitch, he thought as he hurried down the stairs. And yet she might have meant it; sometimes she was genuine but he never knew for certain.

The drawing room was Robert's sanctuary – blue carpet, dark blue velvet settee, William Morris wallpaper. An old, glass-fronted cocktail cabinet stood beside his beloved Hi-Fi unit, both providing continual solace. He poured himself a large whisky and water and took a gulp as he crossed the room to his leather armchair. The soft squeak of it when he sat down was always a comfort to him. The luxuries of his life – genuine hide, pure silk, the best in recorded music, a plentiful supply of good whisky and wine – helped him to endure the emptiness of his marriage and the torment of his passion for Nicola. How did people manage who had none of these compensations to ease their emotional pains? People who were unemployed or retired on small pensions? He hastily brushed the notion aside. If he allowed himself to worry about the world at large he would suffer even more. There were so many problems on his mind that they almost cancelled one another out, leaving him in a state of blank aching perplexity.

It was Nicola who worried him the most. Where was she now? He closed his eyes and received a mental picture of her spread-eagled in the long warm grass, her shirt undone, her jeans tossed aside in a crumpled heap. She was smiling that wide, curving smile, childish and provocative. Julia was right: they couldn't let her go around with someone like Barry. What was it he had said about the newspapers? 'All cooked up to put you off the scent.' Robert shifted uneasily in his chair. The boy was clearly a dangerous influence. Oh, well, Julia would fix it. Leave it to Julia . . . He got up and hastily poured himself another drink so that when she came down she would think it was his first.

R

He had just returned to his chair when the telephone rang from its table by the window. Who the hell could that be? One of Julia's overbearing friends, no doubt. He waited a moment, hoping she would take the call in the bedroom but presumably she was still in the bath.

'Slingsby here.'

'Oh, Daddy – thank God it's you. Listen, I won't be back for supper. We're going to Hastings and making a day of it. Barry's just got a smashing little sports car – a red one. It's old but it goes like a bomb and –'

'Nicola – *no*! You are *not* to go – I absolutely forbid it!'

'Might be late back so leave the gate unlocked –'

'I said *no*. Where are you phoning from?'

'Barry's place. 'Bye, Daddy – and don't *worry* so. Tell mother I'm out with Sally or something.'

'Listen to me –'

But she had rung off.

When he replaced the receiver his legs were trembling. It was impossible to ring her back because he didn't even know Barry's surname. He downed his second whisky in one draught.

R

There was nothing to be done. He could only wait for Nicola to return in her own good time and pray that she came to no harm. Robert sat stiffly in his chair, clammy with sweat, wondering whether he should have another whisky or some more aspirins. Perhaps he'd just hang on until Julia came down. Then he would have a shower and get dressed; that would make him feel better.

After a while he got up and selected a Mozart violin concerto. He cleaned it carefully, as he always did before he put on a record, set it on the turn-table with the tips of his pink meticulous fingers, and touched the switch. He was already beginning to relax as he sat down and swivelled in his chair to face the speakers.

The wallpaper was blue and green, a harmonious convolution of leaves and stems, but one little section had always reminded Robert of a fearful face with a long nose and screaming mouth. Now it suddenly seemed to stare at him accusingly, recurring in half drops all over the wall. He closed his eyes, trying to concentrate on the intricacies of the music, but the spell was broken. Of course he could never have told Julia about that face, but Nicola would understand. Perhaps he would tell her . . . And then he began to think about the red sports car – an M.G. or a Triumph, he supposed – speeding along those busy roads in the height of the season. Was Barry a careful driver? *Could* he be, at nineteen, fooling about at a garage to find out who he was? It was only the carpentry classes that gave Robert a modicum of reassurance. Carpentry was practical. It involved measurements, accuracy, judgement . . .

The door opened and Julia walked in. She was wearing an olive green dress with short sleeves and a straight skirt. Her hair was immaculate, her face powdered, her thin lips painted a dark plum red.

He got up and switched off the record. Julia had no ear for music. The silence was broken only by the faint hum of traffic; the French windows opened onto a terrace at the side of the house. Beyond the terrace was a large, flat, well-tended lawn.

'Who was that on the phone?' she said, her thin eyebrows raised.

'The phone? Oh, yes. It was Nicola – she won't be in for

supper. She's gone out with Sally for the day. A picnic, I think she said.'

Julia stood very close to him. He breathed the strong French perfume, noted the threads of foundation cream in the frown lines between her eyes.

'A picnic with Sally?' She fixed him with her pale blue stare.

'Yes, that's right. I wish she wouldn't, but there it is.'

'Stop lying, Robert.' Her voice was harsh. 'I listened to the call in the bedroom. She's gone to Hastings with that boy. How *dare* you lie to me!'

'How dare you eavesdrop on the phone then try to catch me out?' It was typical of her sneaky ways, always trying to prove him wrong or to find him out in some small dishonesty.

'*Try* to catch you out?' she exclaimed scornfully. 'I *did* catch you out. No wonder she's a liar herself – "Tell mother I'm out with Sally,"' she mimicked. 'Deceitful little slut!'

His head ached so much that he could have screamed with the pain of it. He was thankful to see the slow, stooping figure of Ivy Jones go past the French windows on her way to the back door. The sight of her gave him a sudden feeling of homeliness and sanity, as the presence of a well-loved dog might do.

'There goes Ivy,' he said, to divert his wife from Nicola. 'Back from church in good time.' He consulted his watch as if to prove his point, and saw that in fact Ivy was later than usual.

'That woman will have to go,' exclaimed Julia. 'She's useless. Moves like a snail – never remembers what I tell her to do. I'll find another housekeeper – someone business-like and energetic. I'll get in touch with the Job Centre tomorrow.'

'But you can't send Ivy away like that,' he exploded. 'She's getting on for seventy – she's got nowhere to go.'

'Yes she has. She's got a married sister in Sheffield. She can go and live with her.'

'But the sister might not want her.'

'She'll have proper notice – she can make her own arrangements. It works both ways, you know. There's been nothing to stop *her* from leaving and I never signed a contract to keep her here for ever.'

'You're hard, Julia – much too hard.'

'It's you that's soft. Soft and weak.' She swung round on the high heels of her green lizard-skin shoes and made for the door. She was an agile woman; her back was straight and she always held her head very high, as if she were straining to look over the top of some obstruction.

'Don't rush into anything – *please*,' he said. 'She's been so good to us all these years. So good with Nicola. You can't –'

'I'll leave it till after lunch,' said Julia from the doorway. And then she was gone.

He knew that in many ways he was indeed too weak. But if compassion was a kind of weakness (was it?) then he was glad to be weak. He cared about Ivy. She was a sweet old girl and she had given them fourteen years of devoted service. She was certainly slowing down a bit on account of her rheumatism, and sometimes she was forgetful, but she was a good cook and everything ticked over perfectly. Julia hated domesticity, and in any case she was always out at meetings and luncheons.

Still, he knew that it was hopeless to try to persuade her to keep Ivy on if she had made up her mind to sack her. She would stick to her decision as a matter of principle, whatever he might say. He went over to the record player and began his Mozart again.

N

'Suppose it breaks? It seems ever so thin.' Nicola fitted the condom over her left thumb and waggled it like a glove-puppet.

'They're pretty tough,' said Barry, lighting a cigarette.

21

'Are you worried?'

'No, not really.' She tried to grin but her lips were unsteady.

They were sitting in a dry grassy hollow in a lonely field. On the way to Hastings they had left the main road and driven along a succession of remote Sussex lanes, racing through leafy tunnels of overhanging branches then out again into the sweltering sunlight. At last they had found what they were looking for – a secret place so far from habitation that they could make love freely in the open air.

The little red sports car was parked on the grass nearby, its chromium fittings sparkling in the sun. Barry looked up at it, solemn with pride and pleasure. He had looked at it several times since they sat down in the hollow.

'It won't run away,' said Nicola. She was jealous of the car. She didn't want him to think about it, not now, of all times.

He smiled at her, blowing out smoke at the same time. 'I can't believe it's really mine,' he said. And he looked at it again.

His hair was thick and straight, touching his shoulders. It was the same coppery brown as his face and his eyes and his cotton shirt. His bony cheeks were faintly pitted with old acne scars but Nicola didn't mind. She liked the rough maleness of it, just as she liked the patches of dark sweat under his armpits and the glinting hairs on his thin brown arms. She looked at the bulge of his genitals in the thin old jeans and she desperately wished he would start making love to her.

She had half expected him to tear off her clothes the moment they sat down; it was the first real opportunity they had ever had. Yet she *was* afraid – afraid the rubber might break, afraid she might be no good at it and he would stop loving her. She took the condom off her thumb and put it on her nose, making a face at him.

He smiled at her indulgently, taking it away from her and putting it in the pocket of his jeans. She felt stupid and childish and began to talk, trying to cover her embarrassment.

'I haven't seen one before,' she said. 'My mother never told me a thing. She doesn't talk to me anyway – never has. I didn't even know about my periods till it happened – I thought I was *dying*.'

'Poor Nick. Freddie told me the whole caboodle when I was about five.' Freddie was his mother; her name was Freda.

'Yeah, well you're lucky. She's fantastic.' Nicola had learnt what she knew about sex from magazines and Sally Winters.

'What about your housekeeper woman?' said Barry. 'Can't you talk to her?'

'Ivy? No – not really. She hasn't a clue, poor darling. I tried it once but she's awfully prudish. "Cover yourself up" – you know? Her boy friend was killed in the war – he was a fighter pilot. Golly, I'm glad you're safe – I couldn't bear it if you had to go off and fight somewhere.'

'I wouldn't anyway,' said Barry. 'Not for bloody Capitalism with all the fascists on our side. I'd just go to prison – get bashed up by the fuzz, more than likely.'

'Barry, shut up. Let's be happy – please – ' She reached out and stroked his leg.

He flicked the stub of his cigarette away into the bushes and leaned forward, taking her face in his hands, kissing her deeply. His fingers smelt of tobacco and engine oil and she felt as if her love for him was the only thing in the world that mattered.

She had first met him in a sweetshop in Grassley the previous winter. She was buying chocolate and he was short of ten pence to pay for his cigarettes. She had given it to him, shy but insistent, and he had taken her home to collect the money to pay her back. His mother invited her to share their supper of spaghetti and red wine and she had fallen in love with Barry that first evening.

A bird chirped in the undergrowth close at hand, and far away a jet plane whined and whistled. Now he was unbuttoning her shirt and her heart began to thump. This was the start of it; she wouldn't be a virgin any more. She would be able to tell Sally . . .

Suddenly he held the open edges of her shirt together, covering her nakedness.

'What's up?' She felt anxious and bewildered.

'Oh, Nick – I'm worried.' His brown eyes were dark with concern.

She swallowed, and spoke in a husky croak. 'Don't you – *want* to?'

'Christ, of course I do. It's just that – '

'What?'

'I can't really tell you without upsetting you.'

'Upset me, then. I'm upset already.'

When he was troubled his face seemed bonier than usual and his long mouth turned down at the corners. 'O.K.,' he said. He picked up his cigarettes from the grass and began to take one out of the packet.

'Never mind your bloody fags,' she cried. '*Tell* me!'

He threw the packet down. 'Nick – are you absolutely sure you want to?'

'You *know* I am.' How could he be talking like this if he really loved her? The previous Wednesday evening they had walked round Grassley Park making their plans, and it had been Nicola's suggestion in the first place. Sally had said, 'For God's sake *tell* him if you want to do it.'

'We could wait till you're eighteen,' he said.

'You don't want me, do you? You *can't* do!'

'For Christ's sake – I want you like crazy. I'm only trying to be – '

'To be what?'

'Oh, hell – responsible or something. It sounds like shit but you know what I mean. You *are* bloody young.'

'But it's more than a year to wait. We might all be *dead* by then. Besides, if you don't have me, you'll have somebody else. Won't you?'

He picked a blade of grass and began to tear it down the middle.

'*Won't* you?' she repeated. She hated her voice; it was sharp and shrewish in the sunny air. It reminded her of her mother's.

'I don't know,' he replied carefully. 'But if I did it wouldn't mean anything.' He laid the two strips of bright grass along his thigh, smoothing them against the thin, faded denim of his jeans. 'Anyway,' he said. 'I don't think I would. Not now. You're the one I want.'

Her eyes filled with tears. 'Then *have* me,' she said. 'I want you terribly. I'm not a child, you know.'

He came forward, kneeling awkwardly in front of her, slipping her shirt from her shoulders. 'Oh, baby – forget what I said. Forget it. I just had to make quite sure that you really wanted to, that's all.'

'Well, I do – I do. I *love* you, that's why.'

N

The sun was hot on her breasts. Spikes of grass pricked her shoulders, her bare buttocks, the backs of her knees. Then his weight was upon her, his hair in her mouth. Over his shoulders she could see the car, bright against the dark trees. Whatever happened – even if he left her – he would always be the first. All her life she would remember today . . .

A strong pain made her gasp. And then again. 'Barry – it hurts –'

He was suddenly still. 'Oh, Christ – I'm sorry. Shall we stop?'

'No – no – go on –' It had to happen some time. But Sally never said it hurt; she only said how blissy it was, how you kept on wanting it over and over again.

The pain was deeper now but strangely exciting. He can't be *liking* it, she thought. He can't be. The sun was burning her eyelids, a fly crawled on her leg, another jet droned overhead. Now he was clutching her more tightly, moaning, pressing deeper. The pain was searingly strong but she knew she must be quiet, bear it, let him come . . . She bit her lip and at last, moving with his convulsions, her eyes filled with tears. Her arms and hands were greasy with his sweat.

He lay beside her, touching her wet cheek with his finger. 'I'm sorry, baby,' he said. 'I can't stand hurting you. I don't think it'll be so bad next time.'

'It doesn't matter – I don't mind – it was *wonderful*. I'm not crying because it hurt.'

'Why are you crying then?'

She didn't answer, only looked at him. His eyes were bright and his mouth was very grave. She couldn't have told him why she was crying because she hardly knew herself. At last she said, 'It's just because I'm happy – that's all.' She lifted his arm and kissed the underside of it. It was salt with sweat and as soft and white as a girl's.

He held her close, his head on her breast. 'Me too,' he said. 'Me too.'

N

'How often have you done it before?' said Nicola. She was sitting with Barry on the promenade at Hastings. Thunder clouds were gathering, great curdling masses of grey and silver, building up over the sea and bearing towards the town.

'Sex, you mean?'

'What else would I mean?' Nicola was feeling depressed. She couldn't sit down comfortably because she was so sore. And besides that, she hated thunder.

'Not very often.'

'How often? I mean ten times – or nearer a hundred?'

'Oh, Nick – for Christ's sake!'

'But I'm *interested*.'

He sighed and shook his head. 'Nearer ten.'

'With lots of girls, or just one?'

'Just the one. But she isn't a girl – she's forty.'

'*Forty*! Golly, that's only four years younger than my mother. Who is she?'

'A friend of Freddie's. She used to come and stay. Her husband went off and left her and she needed a bit of comfort, that's all. It didn't mean anything.'

'Oh, I'm not jealous, if that's what you're thinking.' But of course it was a lie. This woman would be practised, easy, perfectly geared to pleasure. How could Barry enjoy himself with a schoolgirl who squealed with pain? Still, it wouldn't always be like that. And she had better not upset him by asking any more questions.

He said, 'Helen looks a lot younger than she is. I thought she was about thirty till Freddie told me.'

'What's she like?'

'Oh, good fun. A bit brassy, but good fun.'

'Does your mother know you've been with her?'

'Christ, no – she'd have a fit.'

There was a distant growl of thunder and Barry stood up. 'Come on,' he said, taking her hand. 'It's going to piss down in a minute.' The sky had been cloudless when they arrived and they had left the M.G. in a car park some distance away, with the hood down.

'How did it happen?' persisted Nicola as they walked briskly along the quiet residential streets. 'I mean, did you go to her room in the middle of the night?' She let out a nervous giggle.

'No, she came to mine. I was scared stiff the first time, to be honest. Still, I wanted the experience and she was just the one. She's gone to Scotland now.'

'I wish *I* was experienced,' said Nicola wistfully. 'She must have been much more fun for you than I am.' She regretted the words as soon as they were out; she had betrayed her childishness, her jealousy.

'That's enough of that,' he said, putting his arm around her shoulder and tweaking her pony-tail. 'You shouldn't really have asked me, should you?'

She was silent. He was right, of course. She wanted to know what Helen looked like but she dreaded hearing him say that she was pretty. *I'm* not pretty, she thought. I'm skinny and stupid and funny-looking.

There was a clap of thunder and the rain began to spatter the pavement with big dark drops like twopenny pieces. Barry seized her hand and they began to run, as they had often run to the fish and chip shop when they were wild with hunger or to a secluded doorway when they were longing to kiss. But now it was no fun any more for Nicola. She had ruined their day with one stupid question.

ℝ

When he had taken a shower, Robert put on his favourite old grey trousers and a clean white sports shirt. Back in the drawing room he recoiled from the shimmering expanse of lawn beyond the terrace and returned to the comforting leathery creak of his chair. The sight of that sunlit grass reminded him of his first visit to Birch House nearly twenty years earlier. On that winter morning the lawn was white with snow and he had come to meet his future father-in-law. He remembered standing by those same French windows, waiting for Julia to bring her father down from his study. There had been nothing to break the blinding glare of the lawn but the criss-cross prints of the birds and the occasional smudge of a fallen leaf. On the terrace a wooden garden seat was thickly cushioned with snow.

There had been no headaches in those days, when he was thirty-four. He had no wife to hate, no daughter to love too much. His parents had been a little over-indulgent but by that time they were living in the West Country and Robert had his own flat in Sevenoaks, the first floor of an old house in a quiet side-street. It was a home that he loved, traditional, comfortable, with a cleaning lady who came in twice a week. He had begun to resign himself to a bachelor life until he met Julia at a country fête. She had made a play for him right from the start, and he had considered himself very fortunate that summer. Everything seemed to be in his favour: he enjoyed his work, he was in good health, and an intelligent woman nearly ten years his junior and the daughter of a well-known industrialist had agreed to marry him. She was by no means beautiful but she was slim and elegant and he found her sharp wit and air of cool aplomb extremely attractive. His own appearance, though pleasant, was undistinguished; a ravishing wife would have been an embarrassment. Julia, he felt, was the kind of woman to make him happy: a practical, self-confident, no-nonsense girl who would allow him to enjoy his own quiet life while she ran the house with calm efficiency. She was artistic, too, with an eye for colour. He could have wished for more communication, more personal warmth, but he himself was not a demonstrative man and he felt sure that things would improve once they were married. She was certainly pleased to be getting engaged to him, there was no doubt about that.

Nevertheless, his stomach had been knotted with apprehension as he waited in that now-familiar drawing room, with the cold light of the snow giving the furniture a strange unearthly lustre. He had seen Julia's father on television before he met her. Nigel B. Mason had occasionally been interviewed, making incisive comments which showed a political sympathy that matched Robert's own; there would be no problem there. But Robert had always felt a little uncertain of himself in social situations and now he wanted very much to make a good impression. Julia's mother had died when she was small and she had no close relatives apart from a married brother in Capetown and a grandfather she never saw and did not wish to see.

When the door opened and she came in, followed by her father, Robert was surprised to see a short, stocky man in a tweed suit. On television, seated with the interviewer, he

29

had appeared to be of average height. Robert, who was over six feet tall, found himself towering above him.

'How do you do, Robert?' The handshake was like a clamp of metal, and the broad pugnacious face was unsmiling. 'So you're the man who wants to marry Julia? I thank you, sir. I was beginning to think that no one would have her.'

Robert had no idea what to say. He tried to smile, looked at Julia who was staring stonily out of the window, turned back to the pale blue eyes of her father.

'You may call me Nigel B.,' he went on. 'That's what most people do. I do not wish you to call me Father because I am not your father. Now, what do you drink?' He approached the cocktail cabinet and opened the glass doors.

Robert had chosen whisky, although at the time he preferred beer.

'Ice?' said Nigel B.

'Er – yes, please.'

'Get it, Julia, would you?' Robert was appalled by the tone in which he spoke to her: no 'please' and an edge to his voice that was little short of vicious.

Lunch was served by a small elderly manservant, so thin and frail that he hardly seemed to have the strength to carry the soup tureen to the table. It was the most nerve-racking meal that Robert had ever endured. Julia, sitting opposite, ate in silence, speaking only to ask for the salt, and her face had hardened into a mask of hostility which not only shut out her father but Robert as well. He tried to make pleasant conversation but every attempt provoked a subtly denigrating remark from Nigel B., and Robert began to feel a peculiar congestion in his windpipe which made it quite impossible for him to enjoy the excellent *coq-au-vin*.

When he admired a picture on the wall, a competent water-colour of Kentish oast-houses, Nigel B. said, 'I don't think much of your artistic discrimination, Robert. It was painted by my late wife and I only keep it there for reasons of sentiment.'

Later, Robert remarked that the Stilton was very good.

'Haven't you tasted good Stilton before?' was the retort. And when, in desperation, Robert said how well Nigel B. had spoken in a recent television programme, the response was, 'I had no opportunity to explain my position in any depth. I should have thought that was obvious.'

There was one thing, however, that tempered Robert's dislike for Julia's father: there was an intermittent twitch at the left corner of his thin, sardonic mouth, a little rogue nerve over which he obviously had no control. Robert, who had always been of a nervous disposition himself, wondered what could possibly have made his future father-in-law so unhappy and so unpleasant. Julia was visibly suffering at his hands and he wondered why she continued to live with him at Birch House. He longed for their marriage the following June when he could take her away to the peace and comfort of his flat in Sevenoaks.

After coffee, Julia suggested a tour of the house, and when they were alone on the curving staircase, he said, 'My poor darling girl – I can see you've got a problem with *him*!'

She stared at him coldly. 'I shan't discuss my father,' she said, and continued up the stairs.

'I understand,' he said softly, close behind her. 'Don't worry – I do understand. You'll soon be out of here.'

'I said I shan't *discuss* it. Didn't you *hear* me?' She stopped, without turning, gripping the bannister, and he saw that her whole body was rigid with strain. Looking back on it, Robert knew that he should have been aware of the danger signs before he went through with the marriage. He should have seen the coldness in her eyes, the close set of her lips, known that she could offer no lasting contentment.

She led the way upstairs to the neat, formal guest rooms and to the large bedroom with the four-poster and the adjoining bathroom where, twenty years later, he had just taken a shower. The house was centrally heated, yet oddly chilled, on that first visit, by the aching blue light of the snow-filled sky. Down in the breakfast room, Julia had leaned against the oak-panelled wall, gazing out of the latticed window.

31

'One day all this will be mine,' she said. 'One day we shall live here.' And she had nodded to herself with satisfaction, looking not at Robert but at the lines of silver birches (saplings, then), at the apple trees under their load of snow, at the high brick wall encircling the grounds.

Robert had thought of his beloved flat and how he would hate to leave it. But of course Birch House was a splendid residence, finer by far than anything he could hope to provide for her. It had belonged to the Mason family since her great-grandfather's time and he understood how she felt. Or he thought he did.

R

If Robert had been softened a little by the nervous tic at the corner of Nigel B.'s mouth, his loathing was totally restored by a remark that was made in the hall before he left. At the front door, hinged and studded like the door of a church, farewells were said and Robert's hand was subjected to a painful grasp which Nigel B. would not relinquish.

Julia was hugging herself against the cold, and her father leaned towards Robert and said in a clearly audible undertone: 'Would you mind using a mouthwash before you come here again. I find your breath rather offensive.' Then he suddenly let go of Robert's hand and gave him a very slight push.

Robert recoiled, speechless with anger and distress. He would have liked to have cried out, 'It's only because you've churned up my stomach, you bastard!' but all he could say, with Julia there, staring at him without expression, was 'Sorry – of course.'

That was his last encounter with Nigel B. until the wedding. He refused to see him again and Julia did not argue. She always turned away with vacant eyes if his name was mentioned.

Robert and Julia were married at St Michael's church at Grassley on a windy day in June. It was a small church and a small wedding. Confetti swirled around their feet as they posed for the photographs, her veil blowing across his face, ruffling his hair which he had surreptitiously combed in the vestry. Julia would have liked a bigger wedding but her father would not foot the bill and Robert was secretly relieved; he disliked formal occasions.

The reception was held at a dreary Victorian hotel, since demolished, and Nigel B. hardly looked at his new son-in-law. He made a long and tedious speech, full of self-advertisement and barbed with innuendos. Robert had copied his own from a book on public speaking and read it badly from a quivering slip of paper. Julia, cool and immaculate in white silk, watched him with a pained little smile.

After the wedding, Robert never saw his father-in-law again. Two years later – and a year before Nicola was born – Nigel B. died of a heart attack in the middle of a Board Meeting. That was the day when Julia inherited Birch House, along with a handsome legacy and a large portfolio of investments.

R

Julia read her book on chairmanship all through lunch. She and Robert seldom spoke during meal times; sometimes he read the paper but today he was quite unable to concentrate although he had propped the *Sunday Telegraph* beside his plate. He was still in that room of twenty years ago, tormented by those old humiliations.

For years he had carried a packet of mints in his pocket to sweeten his breath; the fear of offending Julia had decreased the pleasure of love-making right from the start. Nigel B. had effectively undermined his confidence, as Julia herself was to do, progressively, as the years went by.

His own chair, at the head of the table, was the one that his father-in-law had occupied, and a ghostly malevolence seemed to pervade the room. It was all so much the same: the dining table, the leather-backed chairs, the Royal Doulton dinner service. The walls were now white instead of cream, and there were new velvet curtains, emerald green, but the oast-house painting still hung on the wall above the fireplace. Julia had been fond of her mother. There was a photograph on the sideboard – a frail woman with large frightened eyes and Julia's delicate bone-structure. Robert had thought at first that she was merely camera-shy, but the eyes betrayed much more than a passing apprehension and increasingly he understood that she must have been afraid of her husband. Especially in view of the horrifying story Julia had told him years ago about Nigel B.'s father and the Alsatian.

Julia's face was set into the old mask of discontent as she read her book and fiddled with her food. She's like she is because of *him*, thought Robert; I should be sorry for her really. Yet every word she uttered, every glance from her cold pale narrowed eyes (once wide and clear and inviting) drove away the possibility of sympathy. In middle age, he thought, when beauty is fading, the need for kindliness is the greatest need of all . . .

He carefully fitted his spoon under the cherry on top of his trifle, and glanced at Nicola's empty place, laid for her as usual. Most of the time she took her meals with Ivy but at weekends she was expected to join her parents. He thought of Barry, trying to imagine what he might be like, but no impression came into his mind. A boy like that, with wild unsavoury ideas, could distort her judgement and undermine the benefits of her sober Convent education: it was unthinkable. The cherry was moist and sweet and pleasantly flavoured with maraschino but for Robert it had no savour.

'Julia?'

She glanced up from her book with a frown of enquiry. It

occurred to him that she had not really smiled at him for years. She smiled at Emily Cartwright, a big aggressive woman with black protruding eyes who belonged to the Residents' Association. She smiled at her friends who came for coffee mornings and tea parties. She smiled at Bernard, the old gardener who had been there in her father's time. But she did not smile at Robert or Nicola or Ivy – except, of course, in company. Then there were smiles all round, her hand on his shoulder, affectionate and proprietary, laughing little quips at Nicola with barbs that did not show outside the family . . .

He said, 'What are we going to do to put a stop to this Barry business?'

Her lips twisted into an expression of cunning that he particularly hated. 'A few well-chosen words at the right moment can be very effective,' she said. 'Leave it to me – I know what I shall do.' And she returned to her book. Her trifle was untouched; she was careful about her weight and seldom ate a dessert.

He did not question her further. He knew from experience that she was an expert at scheming to destroy people; she revelled in it. Only that spring she had forced a Labour Councillor to resign by conducting, along with some cronies, an elaborate smear campaign against him. In some ways Robert felt quite sorry for Barry; the young were ill-equipped against Julia's kind.

The door opened slowly and Ivy came in with the coffee tray. She was smiling slightly, as she usually did on these occasions, a secret, wrinkled little smile, directed at the carpet. She looked much older than her sixty-seven years. Robert thought: She doesn't know yet; Julia hasn't told her. His headache had subsided, but now it came throbbing back again. The silver coffee pot was sending out splinters of sunlight, as it had done at the breakfast table, close to his face, bursting into his eyes.

He looked up at Ivy and did his best to smile at her. 'That trifle was delicious,' he said. 'Plenty of sherry – that's what I like.'

Her tired brown eyes came suddenly to life. 'Thank you, sir. Some folks make trifle as if they'd stood the sherry bottle beside it for five minutes – '

'With the cork in!' added Robert.

Ivy grinned and her top teeth came away from her gums a little. 'That's no good, is it, sir? Mind you, I couldn't do it if madam didn't give me the ingredients.'

Julia shut her book with a slam. 'That will do, Ivy,' she said. 'I'll see you in the kitchen – I want a word with you.'

'Yes, madam.' Ivy smoothed back a tendril of her thin white hair and hurried out.

When she had gone, Julia got up from the table. 'I don't want any coffee,' she said. 'I'll give her her notice now. I'm going out later – tea with Emily.'

'Julia – wait till we've discussed it. *Please!*'

'There's nothing to discuss. It's my decision – I pay her, don't I?' She threw her napkin onto the table and Robert closed his eyes as her sharp heels tapped across the parquet floor and the door slammed behind her.

She'll go to hell, he thought. She'll certainly go to hell. And the notion was a comfort.

R

After lunch Robert took a glass of brandy on to the terrace and sat in a deck-chair in the shade of a large buddleia tree. It was his favourite spot for an afternoon doze. Julia had driven off to see Emily Cartwright; it seemed there was nothing he could do about Ivy and he tried to put the matter out of his mind.

There was thunder in the air. He had already heard a distant grumble from the east, and an eerie stillness pervaded the garden. On the terrace, the potted geraniums and petunias glowed in every shade of scarlet, purple and pink, the colours more brilliant than he ever remembered them. Every sound was uncannily clear – a motor mower in a distant garden, the intermittent barking of a dog, the faint crack of a snail-shell on the path where a thrush was pecking and gobbling with all the force of its body. He thought of Nicola and Barry in Hastings – a jumble of images too painful to endure; when he had finished his drink he hoped to fall asleep and forget his jealous misery.

His eyes were beginning to close when he heard a footstep on the terrace beside him. The thrush flew away, leaving a mess of snail on the path.

'Could I have a word with you, sir?' Ivy always called Robert and Julia 'sir' and 'madam'. She had been brought up in the old school of domestic service and they had not discouraged the habit. Robert believed that everyone should know his place; he certainly knew his own.

She was standing beside him, hunched and shapeless in a limp blue dress. He smiled at her. 'Of course you may. Sit down.' He indicated the garden seat beside him, the same seat that had been rounded with snow on the day he came to lunch with Nigel B.

Ivy sat down slowly; her back gave her trouble. 'Thank you,' she said, smoothing her skirt over her thin legs. 'I'm sorry to disturb you, sir, but I thought I'd better get it over with before I start the ironing.' Her top lip, furrowed with fine lines, was quivering uncontrollably and there was a gleam of moisture on her cheek. 'I'm properly upset, sir. I expect you know madam has given me my notice?'

'Yes – I'm sorry – I really am. It's not a decision I agree with – I'd like you to know that.'

'I thought as much – and that makes it easier what I've got to ask you.'

'What's that? I'll try to help in any way I can.' Money, he thought. Poor old girl, he had already decided to give her a generous cheque.

'I'd never have stayed here,' she said, 'if it hadn't been for you and Miss Nicola. It's a beautiful house but I've been overworked and underpaid and I'd never have stayed here, never – I'm telling you straight.'

'I understand – but I'm very glad you *did* stay, Ivy. You've been marvellous and I hate the thought of you going. I don't know what Nicola will say – she'll be heartbroken.'

'I'll miss her,' said Ivy. 'More than you'll ever know. But she'll be all right – she's young. It's *you* I'm worried about.'

'But Mrs Slingsby is getting another housekeeper – didn't she tell you?'

'Oh, yes, indeed she did. But it's this I want to say, sir – and it isn't easy, without giving offence.'

'You won't offend me, Ivy. You can say what's on your mind.'

'If ever you should be on your own, sir – if you and madam should – come adrift, like – I want to be sure you'll let me know so I can cook and clean for you. You've been a real gentleman all these years and it hasn't been easy for you. I'm not blind, you know, though I have to make out I am sometimes. I want you to know that it doesn't matter where you are, or who you're with –'

'Ivy! What are you saying?' He picked up the empty glass and drained an imaginary drop of brandy.

'It could happen, sir. There's no love lost either way, I can see that. It's like a morgue, this lovely house, when madam is in it.'

'I expect you won't be sorry to go, then,' said Robert. He couldn't allow her to speak in that vein. 'Who wants to live in a morgue?'

'I'll send you my new address,' she said, ignoring the rebuke. 'And don't you fret about me – I'll be all right. There's plenty of go in me yet. You *won't* forget, will you, sir?'

'All right, Ivy. You're very sweet. And you can count on a cheque from me before you go.'

'It isn't money I want – you know that.' She stood up and her silver hair was bright against the dark slate grey of the sky. She gave him a trembling smile over her shoulder as she left him and he remembered her as she had been when she first came to Birch House, in her early fifties. Then her brown hair was hardly touched with grey and there had been a soft steady lustre in her eyes. Nicola was two, and Ivy was like a mother to her, endlessly gentle and patient. Julia had set her heart on a boy; the birth of a daughter had turned her against both Robert and the baby. She had promptly gone on the pill, refusing to contemplate another child. Robert's wishes were never considered, but in fact he was content. Nicola was endlessly beguiling, the natural recipient of all the warmth and fervour that Julia rebuffed.

'*If you and madam should come adrift . . .*' He realised, as he lay back in the deck-chair and watched the bees hovering among the pale mauve spikes of the buddleia, that he had never seriously considered the possibility. He and Julia were not the kind of people who 'came adrift'. They were the kind to carry on through all the miseries of a loveless marriage rather than expose themselves to the world as having failed.

A harsh crack of thunder tore at the sky and soon the rain began to fall, big dark splashes on the grey stone of the terrace. Hastily he folded the deck-chair, picked up his glass and carried them to the house.

N

'Well, at least he knows he's the first,' said Sally. 'Men love that. I often kid 'em along to think they are.'

Nicola was playing the fruit machines in a dingy amusement palace in Grassley, and Sally Winters was lounging beside her, her elbow on top of the machine, her auburn hair curling round her shoulders, glinting with sheens of orange and red under the harsh fluorescent lights. It was the evening following Nicola's trip to Hastings, warm and showery, with thunder still in the air. Sally had come in the hopes of seeing a lorry driver called Dominic. The place was half empty and strewn with litter but Nicola liked it. She was never short of money – her father gave her a generous allowance and she saved a regular amount – but the clatter of a jackpot win gave her enormous pleasure. Barry had taught her how to get the best out of a fruit machine.

'I don't know how you can have it off with lots of different guys,' she said, putting a ten-pence coin in the slot. 'I could never do it with anyone but Barry.' She pressed the Start button and frowned hopefully at the revolving symbols.

Sally shrugged. Her huge grey eyes kept swivelling towards the rainy open door. She was a big buxom girl of nineteen, and she always wore trousers to conceal her fat legs. She worked in a department store and had a collection of brightly coloured pants she had bought in a sale there. Today they were purple. She had no idea how to combine colours; her sleeveless blouse was tomato red and her plump neck was festooned with pink plastic beads.

She said, 'Does Barry feel the same as you do? I mean only having it off with you and nobody else?'

Nicola felt a sudden congestion in her throat. She swallowed painfully and before she could reply Sally cut in, 'He doesn't, does he? I can tell by your face.'

There was no way out; she would have to explain about Helen. 'He had another girl before me,' she said, trying to sound casual. 'Well, not a *girl* – it was a friend of his mother's. She's *forty*, for heaven's sake.'

'That's nothing,' said Sally. 'Lots of boys start off with an older woman – it gives them confidence. I shouldn't worry – it won't last.'

'She's gone to live in Scotland now, thank God. I hope she chokes on a haggis.' She put another coin in and pressed the button viciously.

'Just make sure you give him a good time,' said Sally. 'That's the safest bet if you want to keep him.'

Nicola felt a further pang of fright and uncertainty. Suppose she *couldn't* give him a good time? Suppose there was something wrong with her? Her vagina still felt sore. 'Maybe I should go on the pill, after all,' she said. 'I hate that rubber thing.'

'Don't you dare,' cried Sally. 'I'm serious, Nicky.

Remember my mother's blood clots – and that Nigerian girl with those awful depressions.'

'Just so long as he doesn't go off me.' There was a quiver in her voice. 'I couldn't bear it, Sal.'

Sally nodded, glancing at the door again and Nicola thought how sexy she looked with her round freckled shoulders and big proud breasts. She felt puny and childish in her skinny white T-shirt and jeans. 'I wish I could leave home,' she said, putting another coin in. 'My mother's just sacked our housekeeper – you know – Ivy. I've told you about her, haven't I? She's been with us since I was a baby. I heard her crying in her room last night, poor old thing. Daddy's in a terrible mood about it but mother says she needs somebody younger – Ivy's too slow.'

'That's life,' said Sally. 'Survival of the fittest.'

'Well, I think it's horrible. I *hate* my mother. I wish she was dead. She probably wishes I was, too. I won't be able to *stand* it at home without Ivy. Fancy having all my meals with my parents – I don't know how I'll bear it.' She kicked the fruit machine and hurt her toe. 'And I'm not spending any more money on *this* damned thing. I bet they've fixed it.' She suddenly felt close to tears.

'Why don't you move in with Barry,' said Sally. 'You like his mother, don't you?'

'Yeah, she's great.' The thought of living there had not occurred to Nicola before; now it exploded in her mind like a brilliant flowering firework. 'I could leave school and try to get a job,' she exclaimed. 'Hairdressing or something. Pay her a proper rent.' But even as she spoke she was picturing the scenes with her parents if she suggested such a thing.

'What's she like, Barry's mother?' said Sally.

'Oh, amazing. You can say *anything* and she understands. She writes children's books – and they're real horror stories. You'd never think she'd write like that. Barry says they're *gruesome* – isn't that a lovely word?'

'What about the house? Would there be room for you?'

'I think so – it's an old three-storey place near the station – tall and narrow. It's always in a terrible mess. You can hardly get into the living room for junk. I once spilt a whole mug of cocoa on the sofa and nobody ever knew. It just soaked away under a pile of newspapers.'

'I hope it was a *brown* sofa!'

'I can't remember – it's all faded anyway.' Nicola sighed. 'Oh, I'd *love* to live there. And not only to be with Barry. I'd feel so cosy.'

'Then *go*, you twit. Talk her into it. What are you waiting for?'

'I'm not like you, Sal. I'm too nervy. What about my parents? They'd never let me.'

'Christ, you're nearly seventeen – you should do what you *want* to do.'

Nicola nibbled thoughtfully at a bit of loose skin at the side of her thumb nail. 'It's Daddy that bothers me. He's terribly fussy and edgy but I'm really fond of him. And he's only got me, poor darling. He can't *stand* mother.'

'You can't stay at home for ever to keep your father company, can you? And it must be frightful being with your mother when you hate her like that.'

'Yeah – I'll have to get out. You're so good for me, Sal. I wouldn't do half the things I do if it wasn't for you.'

But Sally wasn't listening. She was smiling towards the doorway where two young men in working clothes were feeling in their pockets for coins. Nicola wondered which of them was Dominic but she didn't really care. 'I'm off now,' she said. 'Hope you get on all right.'

'See you,' said Sally. 'And don't forget what I said.'

'No – I'm going round to Barry's place now. Find out if there's any hope of moving in.'

R

Robert drove slowly home from work that Monday evening, down April Avenue, the tree-lined residential road that led

42

to the back entrance, and into the big double garage. He switched off the engine and leaned his forehead on the steering wheel, delaying the moment when he would have to go into the house. His longing to see Nicola and his dread of Julia were so strong that he resisted both, trying to think only of his day at the office. It had been a good day. He had got through much more work than he expected, chasing up some elusive estimates and finally preparing an account for a new department store two weeks ahead of schedule. But now that he was back at Birch House, his white company Rover parked beside Julia's dark green Datsun, the old pressures began to build up.

Where was Nicola? Somewhere in the house, lounging about with her magazines, lying on her bed listening to records or out with Barry again? He had thought she looked pale and tired on her return from Hastings the previous evening, but at least she had not been late. Presumably the thunderstorm had altered their plans.

The garage led into a utility room which was used for storage: garden chairs, a second freezer, a rickety table piled with discarded books, boxes of apples. Robert liked that room. He often paused on his way through to the kitchen, flicking through the stained and curling pages of a book. Now he caught sight of an old copy of Keats' poems, and as he opened it he remembered Nicola, at the age of eight, alone on the stage at a school concert. She was reciting *To Autumn*, her sweet almond eyes fixed on the rafters of the assembly hall as she pronounced those familiar lines in a clear sing-song voice. When she came to '*Thy hair soft lifted by the winnowing wind*' she ran her fingers through her long blonde tresses, raising her chin and shaking her head in a movement so obviously rehearsed and yet so beguilingly feminine that he winced at the thought of it.

She had remembered the first two stanzas faultlessly and then her memory failed her.

'*Where are the songs of spring? Ay, where are they*? . . . Ay, where are they? Where are . . . they . . . ?' Her lips quivered and suddenly her face crumpled into tears. 'I can't –' she mumbled. 'I can't –' and fled from the stage.

Robert opened the book with a sigh and looked at the fly-leaf. *Nicola Slingsby, Form 2B* was scrawled across the page in her round childish hand with the 'y' sweeping down and adorned with leaves like a tendril of vine. She had never been particularly clever at school but her imagination had always delighted him. He remembered the 'butterfly' of wrapping paper on the birch log in the hearth the previous morning. She could see beyond the obvious; she created her own world of magic . . .

He was just about to replace the book when he heard footsteps in the kitchen, followed by Julia's voice.

'This will be your domain, of course. Very well equipped, as you can see. Plenty of storage space and plenty of *surfaces*. One must have surfaces in a kitchen.'

'It's lovely. What beautiful tiles.' The voice that replied was just audible through the closed door, a low voice, firm and rather husky, as if its owner needed to clear her throat. The tiles she referred to were Italian ceramics with a floral pattern in turquoise blue. They ran above the long white formica counters to join the matching cupboards.

'I had the tiling done when I took the place over,' said Julia. 'I had the whole house modernised but I've kept the Georgian atmosphere, I think. That table is solid oak – it belonged to my mother.'

'It's a beautiful kitchen – a pleasure to work in, I'm sure.' Robert wondered what the woman was like. She didn't sound 'energetic and business-like' but Julia would know what she wanted; she certainly wouldn't hire anyone unless she measured up. Poor Ivy . . .

Julia was saying, 'You will have to take complete responsibility for running the house – cleaning, catering, cooking, telephone messages. As I said, I'm out a great deal. My daughter is sixteen – a rather difficult child – and my husband will expect a high standard of efficiency. He's a very fastidious man.'

Bitch, thought Robert. She had set the new housekeeper against both Nicola and him before she had even met them, making it appear that Julia herself was the only rational member of the family.

'I understand, and I shall take a pride in the work. It seems too good to be true – a job and a beautiful home. I can hardly believe it.'

'When can you start?'

'As soon as you need me.'

'Next Monday, then. A week today. My old housekeeper is keen to get away, so the sooner the better. I'll have your room prepared and later I'll have it redecorated to suit your taste. If you stay with us, of course.'

'That's very kind, but I don't really mind what . . .'

Robert heard the sound of receding footsteps and the woman's voice faded away as they left the kitchen. He shut the Keats and returned it to the pile. He decided to go through to the hall in the hope of seeing her before she left. He wanted to undo the bad impression Julia had given, show her that he was a kindly man and that as far as he was concerned her new post would be a happy one.

R

The front door slammed as Robert arrived in the hall, and Julia came towards him in a silky grey dress, looking very pleased with herself. So he was too late.

'I've engaged a new woman,' she said casually, walking past him on her way to the staircase. 'I think she will do quite well.'

'Good. What's her name?' It was useless to indulge in further recriminations about Ivy. They had wrangled for hours the previous night.

'Mrs Laurie – she's a widow. Her husband died six years ago – cancer. She's very grateful for the post. She was a teacher in London but she found it too demanding.'

'She's gone now, has she?' said Robert.

'Yes – I let her out the front way. Nice for her to see the

45

drive. And I told her about my wrought-iron hinges – she seems quite artistic.'

'Good.' He looked around vaguely. 'Where's Nicola?'

'How should I know? Out, I suppose. Probably with that boy.'

'Probably,' he said. Then, 'I had a very satisfactory day at the office. Got some difficult work done ahead of time.'

But Julia had gone.

He hurried through to the breakfast room and was in time to see the new housekeeper walking briskly down the drive. She was short and pear-shaped, wearing a pale yellow suit and flat-heeled shoes. She was hatless and her dark hair was done in a neat coil at the nape of her neck; it seemed that she was in fact the energetic and business-like woman that Julia had specified. Over her left arm she carried a large handbag and her right hand was thrust into the pocket of her loose jacket, pushing it out of shape.

When she was half way to the gate Robert saw her give a sudden little skip, as children do, hopping twice on her left foot and flicking her right one behind her. It was over in a moment, but Robert smiled to himself. He watched her until she vanished through the gate – pausing to look at Julia's iron-work – and then he made his way to the drawing room. A large whisky and Elgar's *Serenade for Strings* was what he fancied. The wallpaper had relinquished its screaming faces and presented a totally pleasing pattern of blues and greens. He wondered if Mrs Laurie was the kind of person you could talk to about screaming faces in the wallpaper. Judging by that lamb-like little skip, he felt sure that she was.

N

The summer shower was over by the time Nicola arrived at 27, Station Road. It was a poor street with grey old houses in need of repair. The tall nettles in Freddie's front garden were still gleaming and dripping, the dandelions bedraggled. Nicola knocked at the door. The brass knocker was a dull green, the blue paint blistered and peeling. She could hear the faint tapping of a typewriter as she stood on the doorstep and after a while she knocked again, more loudly.

The typing stopped and soon the door was opened wide and Freddie stood there smiling, her round cheeks flushed and blotchy, her frizzy brown hair sticking out in tiny corkscrews. She was wearing an old cotton kaftan which had once been patterned in yellow and green but now had the washed-out look of a faded water-colour.

'Hello, Honey-child,' she exclaimed, her brown eyes warm with welcome. (She always called Nicola Honey-child.) 'Barry isn't in, I'm afraid – he's got a darts match.'

'I know – it's *you* I wanted to see – if you aren't too busy?'

'Come on in – I could do with a break – I've been at it since lunch time. Phew, it's hot.' She led the way along the passage into the living room, and Nicola smelt the familiar odours of the house – oranges and garlic and cooking fat, mingled with various other indefinable and faintly sickly smells. Nicola didn't mind. Her own home reeked of furniture polish and her mother's perfume; this place smelt warm and alive.

Freddie was fat and quite tall. She walked with a regal air, erect and slow-moving, her kaftan billowing out behind her, her feet sliding along the lino in a pair of old mules. 'Sit down, honey,' she said, waving vaguely towards the sofa. 'Move those papers and make yourself at home. I'll get us some wine. Red or white?'

'White, please.' White would be cool and refreshing – provided, of course, that Freddie had a bottle in the fridge. Nicola wondered how she was going to broach the subject of moving in. The wine would help; she sometimes had a glass with her father when her mother was out and she dined alone with him. It always made her feel like talking about her troubles.

She moved a pile of tattered magazines on to the floor and

47

sat down warily; the sofa had broken springs. She could hear Freddie in the adjoining kitchen, clinking glasses and humming to herself. A grubby blue T-shirt of Barry's hung over the back of the sofa, and she leaned her cheek against it, sniffing the familiar smells of sweat and engine oil. She wished he didn't have to go off and play darts every Monday; she had specially wanted to see him after the traumas of the previous day. And tomorrow night was carpentry.

She looked around the room. The late sunshine glowed on the dusty bookcases, the big television set opposite the sofa, the stack of old picture frames in a corner. On the wall near the door hung a smiling photograph of Barry with his father. They both wore red polo-necked sweaters and had their arms round one another's shoulders. Barry had been thirteen; it was taken the Christmas before his father died. Next to the photograph was a painting of Barry's – a lively sketch in oils of a village street. Another wall was occupied by an enormous mahogany cupboard, its doors half open and the shelves crammed with oddments that looked like the leavings from a jumble sale. She saw an old toy fire-engine wedged on top of a broken vase, and thought how perfect it would be to live in the same house with Barry. It would be almost like being married. Making love would be easy to arrange and soon she would be able to 'give him a good time', as Sally had said. She knew it all in theory; surely it wouldn't be long before she could enjoy it as much as Sally apparently did.

Freddie called out from the kitchen, 'Can't open the bloody bottle – the cork's broken up.'

'Can I help?' Nicola didn't move. She knew Freddie would say no.

'No thanks. I'll have to push it in. Won't be a sec.'

Nicola looked round at Freddie's desk on the right of the window. A litter of papers lay on both sides of a big office typewriter, and on top of the papers were dirty cups and plates, an empty wine bottle and a packet of peanuts. Above the desk the faded green wallpaper was hanging off in strips, showing another paper underneath with bunches of red roses.

Since her husband's death, Freddie had written a series of children's story books about a wicked little girl called Cut-Throat Connie who wrought havoc with a carving knife wherever she went. Nicola had visited the children's section of the library and discovered that slashing train seats and demolishing the orchids at Kew Gardens were the least of Connie's atrocities. She was a demon girl, with the magical quality of changing into a tabby cat whenever she was about to be apprehended. The books sold in their thousands.

At last Freddie appeared with a bottle of wine and two glasses. 'Here we are – we don't mind a few bits of cork, do we? Just spit 'em out, honey.' She put the glasses on her desk and poured out the wine, spilling it on to a typed sheet of paper.

'I hear you had a good day at Hastings yesterday,' said Freddie, handing Nicola a brimming glass. 'Cheers!'

'Yeah – it was great.' Nicola took a sip of wine. It was ice cold and tasted like flowers. Did Freddie know that Barry had made love to her? And what a fiasco it had been? She had no idea how much he told her; it was very disturbing.

'Super little car, isn't it?' Freddie went on. 'I had a nice cheque from my publisher so I decided to splash out. Barry's been crazy on cars ever since he could push a Dinky toy about. He'd set his heart on an M.G. and I thought he might as well have it now and enjoy himself before we're all atomised.'

Freddie often talked about being atomised. She said it with a cheerful grin; her fears for the future were an excuse for making the present moment as delightful as possible for herself and everyone else.

Nicola didn't reply; it made her ill to think about it. Instead she decided to put her question. 'I want to ask you something – it doesn't matter if you can't – but I've *got* to ask you because it's –'

'Just a minute – let me come and listen properly.' Freddie sat on a stool at Nicola's feet, her glass cupped in her podgy pink hands, the kaftan falling around her like a tent. A hole

49

had been burnt in the front, so that a glimpse of her fat white midriff was visible between the charred edges. 'Now tell me,' she said, fixing Nicola with a warm encouraging gaze. Her eyes were very much like Barry's – a light coppery brown that seemed to be lit from behind with a soft inner glow.

'I wondered if I – if I could possibly – come and – and *live* here? I'd pay you, of course – leave school and look for a job – but if you had a room to spare I wouldn't be any bother.'

Freddie drained her glass and Nicola held her breath as she waited for a reply.

'What about your parents? Would they mind?'

'I don't care if they do – I'm old enough to live where I want. My mother's just sacked our old housekeeper – she was my Nanny when I was small – and I just couldn't *bear* it at home without her.'

'Barry's told me you don't get on with your mother.'

'I *hate* her, if you want to know.'

'Oh dear – then maybe you *would* be better away from home. Resentment is bad for a young person – bad at any age. It poisons the soul.' Freddie smiled and patted Nicola's knee. 'All right,' she said. 'It's all right with me – so long as you don't mind the muddle. You can have the little box room in the attic. There's a divan bed and a cupboard and a folding table – I'll find you some pretty curtains. Yes, of course you can come.'

Nicola felt the tears filling her eyes. She put her glass down in the hearth and knelt on the gritty old rug, flinging her arms round Freddie's neck and kissing her cheek. 'Oh, *thank* you – I'll never be able to thank you enough –'

'It'll be lovely to have you – and Barry'll be over the moon.' She touched the tip of Nicola's nose and pushed it gently upwards. 'Little rubber-nose! You can put your pictures up – paint the walls – make it your own.' She sighed. 'Barry's terribly fond of you – you don't need me to tell you that. He's a good kid – always has been. He'd give his last penny away if he thought someone needed it more than he did:'

'I know.' Nicola blinked away the tears. Her love for Barry was suddenly so strong she felt she would die for him.

'But he's young, honey – and so are you. I don't want the two of you to rush into anything you might regret. Think about it carefully and –'

'I have – I *have*. I love him – I really do –'

Freddie nodded gravely. 'I believe you. But stay on at school. You don't need to pay me any rent and I –'

'I *want* to leave,' interrupted Nicola. 'I hate exams and I'm hopeless at everything except art and English. I'd like to train as a hairdresser – have my own salon one day.'

'Well, that's up to you. If you do get a job you can pay me the same as Barry does. It won't break you but it'll help with the rates and things.' She got up and went to the desk. 'Let's have another glass to celebrate.'

She had just begun to pour it when the telephone rang in the hall. She put the bottle down and turned to Nicola. 'You do the wine – I won't be a minute.'

Nicola carefully poured two glasses and then she stood by the window, her legs unsteady with excitement and joy. Could it be true that this crazy, happy house was going to be her home? Beyond a rusty wire fence she could see down a steep embankment to Grassley station, the rails gleaming in the rain-washed sunshine. It was a small branch-line station, and the platform, with its canopied waiting room, green seats and neat little clock, reminded her of a Hornby model that Sally's young brother had shown her. She smiled to herself with love for it, with love for Freddie, for Barry, and with a sad tender love for Ivy who would soon be lost to her.

N

Freddie's voice was always rather loud and Nicola could hear her on the telephone. 'Come *tomorrow* if you like, you poor darling. Your room's always ready. Matter of fact I haven't changed the sheets since last time.'

There was a silence and Nicola's heart began to thump. *Could* it be? Could she have come back unexpectedly from Scotland?

Freddie went on again: 'O.K., then – Saturday. Come for lunch – you can tell me all about it over a schooner of sherry.'

Another silence. Nicola watched a porter wheel a trolley along the platform, saw him reflected in a pool of water as he passed. The roof of the station was drying out in the sun, some of the slates were dark and shiny, others a dry purply-grey. It was strange how you noticed details when you were stricken with distress.

Freddie was saying, 'Of course not, you fool. Stay as long as you like. I've got a friend of Barry's moving in but that doesn't matter. What? No – a *girl*. A darling child – you'll love her.'

Nicola turned from the window and saw the glasses of wine on the desk. She drank one down in two or three gulps and filled it up again. By the time Freddie came in she was sitting on the sofa, flicking through the pages of an old *Cosmopolitan*.

Freddie beamed at her from the doorway. 'That was a dear old friend of mine,' she said. 'She's coming on Saturday to stay for a while but that's no problem at all – the more the merrier. She's an actress and she was counting on a big part in Edinburgh but apparently somebody else has got it. Poor old Helen – she's a gorgeous creature but she can't act for toffee. Come on, Honey-child, let's knock this wine back and then I'll get us a bit of supper. How about that? You aren't in a hurry to leave me, are you?'

Nicola shook her head and drank the rest of the wine. She felt she couldn't have spoken if her life had depended upon it.

N

'Why didn't you bloody *tell* me she was a gorgeous actress, that's all?'

Nicola was sitting with Barry on a seat in Grassley Park the following evening, before he went to his carpentry class.

'Don't be silly – it would have ruined our day, wouldn't it? You were jealous enough as it was. You said you weren't but I knew damn well you were.'

Nicola was silent, biting her lip. She could see the children's recreation ground through a gap in the trees and she stared at the rhythmic movement of the swings and see-saws, heard the distant shrieks of laughter. She wished she could be one of them, a little child again.

Barry went on, 'I'm not blaming you – it's only natural – but you asked me why I didn't tell you.' He pulled a paint chart out of his pocket and handed it to her. 'Here you are – pick out a colour for your room.'

She took the chart without looking at it. 'It would have been so lovely – moving in with you –' Her voice broke and she couldn't go on.

'It *is* lovely. Don't *worry* – I've told you she doesn't mean a thing –'

'I bet *you* mean something to *her*, though. She'll be after you again when she comes back.' Now her voice was shrill and sharp. She could hear it echoing back in the clear evening air.

'No, she won't,' said Barry calmly. 'I'll tell her it's not on. But in any case, she'll have got herself another guy by now.'

'I expect she's so gorgeous she can have anyone she fancies.'

'Oh, Nick – *don't*! Don't spoil it all.' He took her hand, but the way he touched her felt somehow wrong and she couldn't respond. She let her hand lie limply under his; the

53

weight of it and the warmth of his skin were like a pain instead of the usual delight.

He went on, 'Let's choose a colour for your room – look at all those beautiful shades. Come on – how about that buttermilk yellow?'

Freddie had shown Nicola the box room the previous night after supper. It was bigger than she expected, with a tall narrow window looking down on to the toy railway station, but she had felt no excitement, no pleasure, only a sick fear at the thought of lying there in the night listening for Helen's footsteps on the landing below. One thing was certain: she must move in quickly, be firmly established as Barry's girl before Helen arrived. She stared at the swings, at a child in red who was flying there, carefree and happy. Or maybe not . . .

She remembered playing on those same swings many years ago, after a school concert when she had forgotten the words of a poem she was reciting. She couldn't remember what the poem was, but she knew that her mother had told her she was a disgrace to herself and to her parents. Her father had turned away at that, flushed and silent, and she had run out of the house and across the fields to Grassley Park. The recreation ground was deserted but she sat there on a swing, urging herself higher and higher, in such an anguish of humiliation that she wanted the chains to break and hurl her to her death. Her small disgrace had soon been forgotten, but now as she watched the child, a pitching blob of red against the trees, she felt herself engulfed by problems that could change her life. The overwhelming strength of her passion for Barry was something she had never bargained for. Loving him had seemed, until Sunday, a total blessing, but now she was tormented by her own inadequacy and by the threat of Helen. She remembered Sally's voice as she lolled against the fruit machine: *Give him a good time* . . . Sally had meant sex, but Nicola knew that a good time meant a great deal more than that. Good humour and fun were an essential part of it and she would have to overcome her jealousy and childishness if she were to make him happy.

She looked at the colour chart and then she glanced up at Barry with a shaky smile. 'I'd like that sludgy green,' she said. 'If it's all right with your mother.' Her room at home was yellow; she wanted something different.

'Anything will be all right with her.' He hugged her and nuzzled against her hair, gently biting her ear. 'Helen can take a running jump – you know that, don't you? When are you moving in?'

'She said as soon as I liked.'

'How about next Monday? I'll paint your room for you over the weekend.'

Over the weekend . . . Helen was arriving on Saturday morning and she imagined Freddie and Barry laughing with her over lunch, drinking wine, discussing books and plays that Nicola knew nothing about . . .

She had an urgent longing to see Ivy; Ivy who had always loved her unstintingly, bandaged her cuts, cooked her favourite dishes, wiped away her tears. It had never been possible to confide in her over personal relationships because she would never align herself with Nicola against her parents; the question of her friendship with Sally Winters had been taboo and the same would apply to Barry. Nevertheless, Nicola had always known that Ivy was on her side against her mother although she had never shown it by so much as the twitch of an eyebrow.

'Come to *The Star* for a shandy,' said Barry, getting up. 'I'm dying of thirst.'

Nicola shook her head. 'I'm going home – I want to see Ivy. I won't have her much longer.'

'I'll run you back.' The car was at the park gates.

'No thanks – I'll go across the fields.' She wanted to be on her own, free from the pain of trying to conceal her anxiety.

'When'll I see you, then?' He held out his hands and pulled her to her feet, kissing her gently. 'How about a drive tomorrow night after work? Find a little glade in a lonely wood.' He gave her a secret, intimate smile.

She nodded, hiding her face in his shoulder. She couldn't smile back because her mouth was out of control, quivering on the verge of tears. The thought of another failure was more than she could bear and she tore herself away from him and raced across the grass without looking back.

R

Robert was in the kitchen getting some ice out of the refrigerator when Nicola came in through the back door that Tuesday evening.

'Where's mother?' She looked pale and distraught.

'She's gone to her Council meeting – won't be back till late. Do you want her?' He shut the fridge door.

Nicola shook her head. 'Why should I want her?'

'I don't know. You asked where she was.'

She gave him a cool straight stare. 'Just so I could keep out of any room she was in, that's all.'

Robert looked down at his whisky glass. The ceiling light was reflected in the facets of the crystal and the familiar pain in his head began to throb. He never discussed Julia with Nicola, always ignored her outbursts, changed the subject. 'Did you have a good day at Hastings on Sunday?'

'Yeah, great.' She took a tumbler from a cupboard near the sink, filled it to overflowing with cold water and began to gulp it down. Nicola loved water; she was always drinking it – at mealtimes, in the bathroom, and here in the kitchen – gasping with satisfaction between the gulps, wiping her mouth with the back of her hand when she had finished. Secretly Robert found this gesture endearing but he always chided her for it: 'Nicola, where's your handkerchief?' He said it now.

She shrugged. 'Barry's got this super M.G.,' she told him. 'Spoked wheels and a stereo cassette player.'

'I hope he's a careful driver?'

'He's fast – we did ninety.'

'That's against the law – asking for trouble.'

56

'Don't be so stuffy, Daddy.' She slammed her glass down on the draining board. 'Anyway, Barry says it's the slow drivers who are really dangerous. Trilby hats and big ears. Ugh!'

Barry says this, Barry says that . . . He noticed that her nipples were large and pink through her thin white T-shirt, and he ached to touch them. 'You'd better not tell your mother he does ninety,' he said. 'She's got some friends in the police force.'

'Who cares? Barry isn't frightened of *them*. He isn't frightened of anyone, come to that.'

'You sound as if you're very fond of him?'

'I am. Is Ivy in her room, do you know?'

So she didn't want to talk about him. 'I think so – she said she was going to do some packing.'

'Mother's a shit to kick her out. I think it's –'

'Don't *use* that word – and certainly not about your mother.'

'Come on – be honest,' she said with her clear smile. 'You know damn well you really think the same yourself.' She didn't give him time to react; she swung away on the heels of her grubby canvas shoes and made for the door. She had an innate sense of kindness in letting people out of embarrassment, unlike Julia, who feasted on the disquiet of her victims. 'I'll go straight to bed when I've seen Ivy,' she said. 'Good night, Daddy.'

'Good night, darling.' I shouldn't call her darling, he thought. Not when she's just called Julia a shit. But of course she was right. He took his whisky glass into the drawing room, swirling the ice cubes around as he went, thinking about his daughter's nipples. My little darling, he muttered to himself, your mother has driven me to care for you too much and so wrongly. Oh, my little sweetheart, what will become of us all . . . ?

N

Ivy was sitting on the bed in a circle of mellow light from the bedside lamp. She was writing a letter and looked up with a sad smile when Nicola went in. The wardrobe was open, empty. A large suitcase was on the bed and another on the floor. Under the window was a pile of big cardboard boxes, tied up with string. Her eyes seemed older and more wrinkled than they had been before, and the upper lids drooped down like little fleshy canopies. Her cheeks no longer had that old-apple plumpness; they were flat and sallow. Nicola thought she had probably been crying a lot. They had already wept together the previous day.

She knelt on the Indian rug and put her head on Ivy's lap. The writing pad was sharp against her temple but she didn't move. Ivy stroked her hair with long slow movements and neither of them spoke. It was a scene that had been enacted many times over the years. When she was very small Nicola used to climb on Ivy's knee and rest her head against her warm flat chest. When she grew too old for that, she knelt on the floor as she was doing now, on that same old oriental rug with its worn and faded pattern of pink and red and grey. Her grandfather – Nigel B. as they called him – had brought it back from India after the war.

'Who are you writing to?' asked Nicola at last, getting up and sitting on the bed, squeezed between Ivy and the suitcase. She saw that the pictures were down, leaving dark oblongs of unfaded wallpaper, and the mantelpiece was bare except for a green vase that belonged to her mother.

'My sister. I'm going to stay with her in Yorkshire for a while – just a little while till I get fixed up. I wouldn't intrude on them – they're very happily married. Happy couples like to be alone together. I'm going up there on Saturday.'

'I'll never forgive my mother for sending you away.

Never! But I'll tell you something.' She looked at Ivy with a secret smile. 'Don't breathe a *word* – but I'm moving out of here myself next week. Moving in with my boy friend. No, don't look like that – he lives with his mother and she's sweet.'

'You mustn't leave, my cherub. Think of your poor dear father – he'd miss you terribly.'

'Maybe he will but I couldn't stick it here without you. Think of *eating* with them – *all the time*! They never stop sniping at each other and it makes me all nervy and sick. I'd *die*, honestly.'

Ivy sighed and shook her head. 'I wish you'd stay at home till you leave school – I really think you should.'

'I've left school already. Nobody knows yet, but I'm not going back. I'm getting a job at a hairdresser's and –'

'But what about your education? Your father won't want you to be a *hairdresser*.'

'Don't say it like *that* – you mustn't be so snooty, Ivy. Somebody's got to do people's hair. It's a very artistic profession. One day I'll have my own salon – beautiful colours, and everything going for young people. I'm going to fix it so they can have hamburgers and chips under the dryer if they want. You can get terribly hungry at the hairdresser's and there's only instant coffee or wishy-washy tea.'

'It's not a *café*, though, is it, dear? Not that I often go – I can't afford it.'

'I bet she paid you badly, didn't she? Mean bitch!'

'Shhh – you mustn't *say* such things.'

'What does it matter? We can say what we like now that you're not the housekeeper any more.'

'But I am until Saturday. The new lady starts on Monday, so your mother told me.'

'God – I wonder what she'll be like. I'm sure I shall hate her.' She groaned. 'Oh, dear – everything's changing. I must go to bed – I'm so *tired*.'

'You shouldn't be tired at your age, my cherub. Not when you're on holiday.'

'Everything's so *worrying*, Ivy. Barry says worry drains your energy. He's so lovely – I wish you could have met him.'

Ivy put her writing pad aside and turned to face Nicola, her lips trembling. 'One thing before you go – in case we don't get another chance to talk.' She looked down at the pale green candlewick bed cover, twisting a loose thread between her lumpy fingers. 'Be kind to your father – always look after him. He's a good man – a good, *good* man –' Her voice broke on a stifled sob and it occurred to Nicola that Ivy might be secretly in love with him.

'Yeah – all right,' she said uneasily. 'Course I'll be kind to him.'

'You're young now – but remember what I've said. He's having a bad time – and you're really all he's got.'

It was true, but she didn't want to think about it. There was something about her father that made her nervous and she didn't want the responsibility of being all he'd got.

She stood up and kissed the top of Ivy's head. 'Good night,' she said. 'I won't forget. And we'll write to each other, won't we? We'll always be friends.'

'Always,' whispered Ivy, reaching out for Nicola's hand and squeezing it so tightly that it hurt. 'Always.'

R

Nicola was standing beside Robert at the altar, a white veil covering her face. The church was full of people – Julia's friends, hard-faced, eyes glittering under flowered, feathery hats. Suddenly Robert was holding his daughter-bride in his arms, kissing her frantically through the veil. He could feel her lips warm and soft through the fine scratchy mesh. She was submissive, unresisting, and his heart was pounding, filling the church with its thunderous beat . . .

There was a knocking on the bedroom door, gentle, persistent.

'Come in.' He could hardly speak. He was gulping,

sweating.

The door opened and Ivy was there with the early morning tray. One cup of tea, a digestive biscuit on a plate, a glass of orange juice. She set it quietly on the table at Robert's side of the bed. 'Good morning, madam. Good morning, sir.'

'Good morning, Ivy,' said Robert. Julia never spoke during this ritual; she pretended to be asleep.

Ivy went to the window and drew back the rose-pink curtains. The daylight washed away his dream, giving him instead the sycamore branch against a cloudy sky, the flight of a bird, the carved oak pillars of the four-poster with its crimson hangings.

The door closed and he sat up in bed, running his fingers through his thin hair. He glanced with distaste at the back of Julia's head on the pillow, speared with pins and caged in its green hairnet.

'Julia?'

No answer. No movement.

'Julia – your orange juice is here.' He reached out and prodded her shoulder under the hump of the blanket.

'That *hurt*!' She turned on her back and glared at him angrily.

'Nonsense – I hardly touched you.'

'Yes, you did. You dug your finger right into my shoulder.'

Robert took a bite out of his digestive biscuit and a cascade of crumbs scattered down the front of his navy-blue pyjamas. He picked them up one by one and put them into his mouth. 'Perhaps I don't know my own strength,' he said drily.

Julia leaned on her elbow and inspected her shoulder as if there might be a bruise appearing. He passed her the glass of orange juice and she took it without thanking him, leaning back against the pillows, holding the glass in both hands and sipping it like a child.

'Tell me about the new housekeeper,' said Robert. 'Do you think she'll be permanent?' It was odd to think of a strange woman bringing in the tray.

'I don't see why not. She's only forty-five. But I suppose

you'll dislike her on principle because you wanted Ivy to stay.'

'That's not fair –'

'She used to be a Home Economics teacher – she's got excellent references. She says this is just the kind of work she wants. Time for reading – peace and quiet.' She frowned at Robert. 'There's one thing I shall *insist* upon,' she said. She paused but he refused to say what was expected of him, namely, 'What's that?' Instead he turned away from her and picked up his tea cup.

'You must be very strict with her,' Julia continued. 'It's no use me training her if you don't back me up. You were far too easy-going with Ivy and –'

'Ivy's well past retiring age and –'

'Exactly. That's why she's going. Mrs Laurie is comparatively young and there will be no excuse for any kind of slackness. If she doesn't measure up, she'll go too. And we won't use her Christian name. We'll be friendly, of course, but not too familiar. Don't you agree? And I shall tell her to stand no nonsense from Nicola.'

The sound of her name flashed through Robert's nerves like a pain. For an instant the dream came back, the feel of her lips through the veil. His tea tasted bitter.

'What sort of nonsense are you thinking of? She'll be busy with her A-levels soon.'

'All that rudeness and off-hand behaviour. We'll turn over a new leaf with her when Ivy's gone. I've been making some enquiries about that boy – Barry Mitchell, his name is. His mother writes the most appalling children's books – thoroughly unsavoury.'

'Have you read them?'

'No, but a friend of mine has. All about a girl with a knife – horrible. Anyway, I think I've seen a way to nip our daughter's little affair in the bud quite neatly.'

'What have you in mind?'

'John Cartwright has his car serviced at the garage where this Barry works. He knows the manager.' She put down her glass and began to take off her hairnet, feeling carefully to disentangle it from the pins. 'Barry could soon be out of a job. And worse.'

'I wish you wouldn't *meddle*, Julia. We haven't even *seen* the boy yet. He might not be so bad and –'

'All right – I'll invite him over.' Her pale eyes were as still as a snake's. 'That's a good idea, Robert, for once in your life – a very good idea. We'll have him here for coffee one evening. You'll see – he'll sign his own death warrant.'

'Death warrant?'

'In a manner of speaking. Be *clever*, Robert. You've never known how to be clever, have you? We'll soon see what his politics are – a few well chosen questions – I'll do the talking.'

Robert got out of bed and headed for the bathroom. 'Sounds like a bloody witch-hunt to me,' he said. 'But that always was your line of country, wasn't it? Like your dear father.' He shut the door and locked it, deadening the volley of abuse. If only he could get away from her for good, leave with Nicola, settle in another district. But of course it would be madness for him to live alone with Nicola. And in any case there was his work; he'd never get another job like that, not at fifty-four.

He watched his urine splashing into the indigo lavatory pan. Damn silly colour, he thought. If there was blood in your piss you'd never know about it. Another of Julia's stupid ideas. *Indigo*! He shut his mind against Barry's visit. The mouth that kissed Nicola's – what would it be like? And yet he felt uneasy for the boy, oddly in sympathy. Julia had a way of making him quite fond of anyone she disliked.

He took off his pyjamas, folded them neatly and laid them on the bathroom stool. Then he stepped into the shower. He was looking forward to another satisfying day at work. Things were going very well at the moment; he was in command. Which was more than he was at home. He could hear Julia in the bedroom, clattering her jars of cream on the dressing table. Hateful woman . . . He turned on the shower and held his face in the warm spray. Feeling the stream of water running down his body he thought of Nicola again, willing himself to remember the dream, praying that the next time there would be no veil, no dress, and that no one would awaken him too soon.

R

When Nicola was seven she had thrown a bowl of soup at Julia. Robert had thought it well deserved, but Julia had insisted that Robert punish her.

'Take down her knickers and thrash her,' she had demanded. 'Thrash her with a ruler on her bare buttocks. Humiliation is what she needs – that's the best medicine.'

Robert had protested and refused, but Julia's fury had mounted to such an extent that he had been forced to give in and make a pretence of doing as she wished.

Julia produced a ruler and Robert held the screaming child between his legs and pulled down her small pink briefs. He could still remember his excitement as Nicola writhed and twisted in her efforts to escape the blows – the gentle, token blows – of a ruler. It was possible, he knew, that the seeds of his obsession were sown on that day. It was certainly an occasion that persisted in his memory and even found its way into his dreams.

N

'Just relax, babe. It'll be all right. You're worrying – that's the trouble.' Barry was bearing down on her, squeezing into her, and the pain was little short of agony. Over his shoulder she could see the tall fronded larches, pale green against a thundery sky. The car rug was soft under her naked back, and the warm air was scented with pines. It could have been so perfect . . .

He was murmuring into her ear as he moved, reassuring her, kissing her neck, but the more she tried to relax, the tighter her muscles seemed to grow, knotting and closing against him when she longed to be soft and easy and welcoming.

'Barry – I can't,' she sobbed. 'You'll have to stop – I can't *bear* it –'

'My poor baby!' He withdrew and knelt on the rug beside her, pulling her into his arms, cradling her tenderly as if she were indeed a baby.

'I'm sorry – ' She clung to him, her cheek against his soft damp shoulder. 'What shall we do? What shall we *do*?'

'Don't worry – we'll just keep trying – take it very gently. It'll be all right. Won't it, darling?'

She heard the cadence of doubt in his voice and she cried out, 'Oh, Barry – I hope so. I'm so *frightened* –'

'Frightened?'

'Yeah – frightened you might go off me or something.'

'Of course I won't go off you. Teething troubles, that's all it is.'

'Some teeth!' said Nicola, and they laughed hysterically as they prepared to leave, pulling on their jeans, hopping about on the car rug, falling against each other. They were still laughing as they walked towards the car under the tall trees and the slate-grey sky. Nicola joked and giggled, holding her crotch and pretending she couldn't walk, but in her heart she was terribly afraid. She'd have to talk to Sally about it. Sally would tell her how to make things better.

N

'It shouldn't hurt like that – *I* never had any trouble.' Sally Winters was peering intently into the mirror at Grassley Public Conveniences, applying green frosted eye-shadow.

'Oh, Sal – what'll I do?'

'See a doctor. It's probably nothing much.' She smoothed the glittering powder with her finger-tip.

'But I *can't*! Our doctor's a friend of Daddy's – he'd be

sure to tell him. I couldn't *possibly*.'

'Oh, well, Family Planning might help.'

'Wouldn't they tell my parents?'

'Dunno, but you'd better do something pretty quick. He'll drop you like a hot potato if you don't give him a good time. Men are all the same.'

'Barry isn't,' cried Nicola. 'I *know* he isn't.'

'You're kidding yourself, Nicky. If you don't watch out he'll be having it off with somebody else. I can tell you that for sure.'

Nicola leaned against the wash-basin. She felt suddenly sick, and her knees began to tremble. 'Just got to spend a penny,' she lied, and went into one of the toilets. She slumped on the seat, taking deep breaths in an effort to calm herself. Oh, God, what was she going to do? She stared at the cream-painted door, reading the graffiti. '*Jack fucked me today.*' Lucky you, she thought. '*Jane loves Cliff;*' '*Karen Smith is a lousy shit.*' Near the top of the door someone had scrawled with a red felt pen: '*Suck your crusty drawers,*' and she felt an irrepressible bubble of laughter in her throat. Normally she would have exploded with delight and told Sally, but all she did was to pull the chain as if she had used the lavatory, and slam out.

'Come *on*, Sal, for God's sake,' she said. 'We'll be late for the film. Nobody's going to see you in the dark.' Sally smiled her wide unruffled smile and followed Nicola out into the street.

On the way to the cinema Nicola remembered the phrase again, and thought it so hilariously original that she had to tell Sally about it. They screamed with laughter till the tears rolled down their cheeks.

'These days I always seem to be either laughing or crying,' said Nicola at last.

Sally, serious again, was carefully dabbing at her eyes with a tissue. 'Well,' she said, 'that's life, isn't it? A bit of this and a bit of that. Don't worry, it'll all come out in the wash.'

'Like the crusty drawers,' said Nicola, and they burst out once again into shrieks of laughter.

N

'This boy friend of yours,' said Julia. 'Barry Mitchell. I'd like to meet him.'

Nicola said nothing. She was sewing up a torn seam in her pink shirt, sitting topless on her bed. She couldn't ask Ivy to do her mending now, with only another day to go.

'Bring him round for coffee after dinner on Wednesday night.' Julia was leaning in the doorway.

'Can't,' said Nicola, without looking up. 'Going out.' The walls of her room were so bright so that even on dull days it seemed sunny. She wished her mother would go.

'Thursday, then.'

This was unusually accommodating and Nicola raised her eyes suspiciously. 'Why do you want to see him?' she said.

'Just interested. His mother's a writer, I believe. Have you read any of her books?'

'No – they're for kids.' She had read two of them from beginning to end and found them rivetting.

'Well, bring him round next Thursday, then.'

'I'll see what he says.' Nicola bit off a length of thread, turning her back on her mother, dismissing her. 'I don't suppose he'll want to come.'

By that time, she thought, I'll be out of here, thank God. But her fear of Helen was increasing and she was terrified of jumping out of the frying pan into the fire.

R

'Goodbye, Ivy. I – I hope everything turns out well for you.' The taxi was waiting at the rear entrance, beside the garage. Ivy, in a grey coat and a blue, stiff-brimmed hat, looked at

Robert with swimming eyes and he felt an enormous sorrow welling up inside him.

'Well – I'd better be getting in,' she said. Her luggage had gone in advance. This was the taxi which would take her to Tonbridge; there she would catch the London train. Robert thought: I should have run her to the station in the car. What had come over him to let her go in the taxi Julia had ordered.

'I've got your address,' he said lamely. 'I'll send you a Christmas card.' As soon as the words were out he regretted them. A Christmas card! After fourteen years of devoted service, fourteen years of cooking and cleaning and never complaining, of finding things that were lost, of being a mother to Nicola . . .

'Don't forget that cheese and bacon flan for your lunch,' she said. 'It's in the pantry. And thank you again for the cheque – it was much too much –'

'No – no – it was nothing. Money can't say what I want to say – it's just too – too difficult, Ivy. I can't –'

Suddenly his voice was unsteady and regardless of the taxi man who was watching them, he embraced her clumsily, holding her light, frail shoulders, catching a whiff of lavender, bumping his forehead against her hat.

'You won't forget what I said,' she choked. 'If ever you need me – *please* –'

'I won't forget.'

He watched the taxi drive away, saw her white face through the rear window as she waved to him.

He waved back and just before she vanished, he blew her a kiss, smiled, and blew another. He saw her hand fly to her lips and then she was gone.

The house was empty. Julia had gone to a luncheon and Nicola was out with Sally for the day; she said she couldn't bear to say goodbye to Ivy. It's the end of an era, he thought, as he went into the pantry to have a look at his flan. Nothing will ever be the same again . . .

N

At five-thirty on Monday afternoon, Nicola carried the last item of her luggage – an old school satchel full of gramophone records – from her bedroom into the utility room, where the rest of her things were hidden under a dust sheet. She had left her winter clothes behind, and her books, and a chest of drawers full of oddments; she could collect those later. It was time now for Barry to arrive with the car.

Crossing the hall on her way back to the bedroom she could hear her mother talking to the new housekeeper in the breakfast room. ' – a special furniture cream for the panelling,' she was saying. 'I'll show you the one when you've noted all this down. It preserves the wood as well as giving it a sheen. My husband always says . . .'

My husband always says I'm a pain in the arse, thought Nicola with an inward chuckle, as she raced up the blue stairs. She was breathless with the effort of carrying down all her belongings, and with the excitement of her secret departure. For the moment, her dread of meeting Helen and her tormented imaginings of what might have happened since her arrival on Saturday, were overlaid with the joy of leaving home. She had told her parents she was going out that evening with a friend from the Convent, but she didn't really care what their ultimate reaction would be. Nothing her mother said would upset her; her hatred had become a shield against the cruel or sarcastic words which had bombarded her for as long as she could remember. She loved her father and didn't want to make him unhappy, but he had never understood her problems and she found it difficult to talk to him. Sometimes there was humour in his comments, but it seemed he couldn't allow himself to laugh and joke with her. As far as she was concerned, he was dreary and fussy, aquiver with nerves, and resolutely opposed to new ideas. She pitied the new housekeeper, landing unsuspecting into *that* little set-up. Nicola had seen her earlier that afternoon, going into Ivy's old room. She had only caught a brief smile, the gleam of large luminous eyes on the shadowy landing, and the vague impression that there was something wrong with her face. Then she had vanished, closing the door very quietly behind her. Nicola had not smiled back; she couldn't bear the thought of a stranger in Ivy's room. But she had liked the warmth of the woman's smile and later regretted that she had not responded.

Now from her bedroom window she could see the red glint of the M.G. through the trees in April Avenue near the back entrance, and Barry's watchful brown face as he sat at the wheel of the open car, waiting for her signal. She had arranged to beckon from the window when the coast was clear. Then he would reverse up to the garage, load the luggage into the back, and drive away with Nicola beside him. Her father never got home before six-thirty and by the time he found her note in his whisky glass she would be safely installed at Station Road.

She ran downstairs to make a final check that her mother was still in the breakfast room at the front of the house and heard another snatch of monologue: 'I always like a mid-day meal on Sundays with something light about eight. Are you a church-goer, Mrs Laurie?'

Nicola heard the new housekeeper's voice for the first time, a soft, throaty kind of voice which made her mother's strident tone seem all the more unpleasant. 'No – I'm a believer but not a church-goer.'

Like me, thought Nicola. She raced upstairs again, beckoned from the window, received an answering salute from Barry, and tore down to the utility room. She dragged out her possessions as he reversed through the back gate, and in two or three minutes they had loaded everything into the back of the car. They worked in silence but Nicola was breathless with fright in case her mother should appear.

'Drive *quietly*,' she gasped as she flopped into the

70

passenger's seat. 'Don't rev up or anything.'

He nodded, started the engine and drove slowly through the gate and down April Avenue towards Grassley.

'I can't believe it!' cried Nicola. '*Now* you can step on it.'

She laughed with relief as they sped past the tall trees and set-back frontages, her hair blowing wildly across her eyes and lips. She had done away with her pony-tail, wanting to look older for her meeting with Helen.

'No regrets, have you?' he said. 'You won't be homesick?'

'You must be kidding.'

By the time they had slowed down through Grassley, stopped at traffic lights and zebra crossings, and pulled in for petrol, her relief at the easy get-away had been replaced by a growing dread of the ordeal in front of her. She sat with icy hands and thudding heart as he swung the car round the corner into Station Road, and then they were there, bumping up the kerb to park half on the pavement as he always did, to make more room for the traffic.

'We'll bring your stuff in later,' he said as they climbed out. 'I'm dying to show you your room – I think you're going to love it.' She knew that he had worked all the weekend to get the painting finished.

'Yeah,' she said, trying to sound enthusiastic – which she would have been, without Helen. 'I know I am.'

Outside the front door he stopped with a cry of surprise. 'Hey, there's a note. They must be out.'

A scrap of paper was tucked under the door-knocker and he unfolded it and read it out to her. '*Gone to Sevenoaks. Please light oven at 7.30. Number 6.*' He threw the note into the privet hedge with a groan of irritation. 'Hell,' he exclaimed. '*You'd* better do it – I'm sure to forget.'

Nicola retrieved the note and put it in the pocket of her jeans. So that was that. Another spell of sickening apprehension. And the awful suspicion that Barry was disappointed to discover that Helen was out.

R

When he got back to Birch House on Monday evening, Robert had forgotten that the new housekeeper was moving in that day. There had been complications at work: the air conditioning had broken down and his office was much too warm, his best audio-typist was off sick, and he had been tormented by one of his nervous headaches.

Now he looked forward to a drink on the terrace in the calm evening sunshine. He decided not to go into the drawing room to collect his whisky; he would open a new bottle in the pantry. He couldn't risk seeing Julia.

It was when he entered the kitchen that he remembered about Mrs Laurie. There was an unfamiliar ferny scent in the air, quite unlike anything that Julia used. When he took off his jacket and hung it behind the kitchen door, he had another surprise: a strange new apron was hanging there, patterned with brown and yellow daisies.

He opened the whisky bottle, praying not to be disturbed, poured himself a drink, and hastily added some ice. There was no sign of Nicola, no music upstairs, no voices. And then he remembered her saying she was going out with a friend. Where was Mrs Laurie? In her room, unpacking? Talking to Julia in some other part of the house? He took his glass and the *Financial Times* onto the terrace, blinked at the glaring, glowing colours of the flowers, and settled himself in the deck-chair under the buddleia tree. As he sipped his drink, he began to think about Mrs Laurie. He had liked that little skip of pleasure as she went off down the drive a week ago, and now he liked the scent and the apron; there was a kind of lightness and freshness about them. He had a vague preconception of her face, based on her pear-shaped figure and sensible shoes and the fact that she was forty-five. Heavy features, he thought, no make-up,

72

spectacles perhaps . . . He took a sip of his drink and then another, put his glass on the little garden table, leaned back in the deck-chair and opened the paper.

He had hardly read a paragraph before he heard footsteps on the path behind him. He swivelled his head and saw that Julia was approaching, followed by a woman in a pink-flowered dress who was partially hidden. He hastily folded the paper, put it on the table, and struggled to his feet. Deck-chairs were hard to get out of in a hurry.

'Robert – this is Mrs Laurie. My husband.'

'How do you do – welcome to Birch House.' He held out his hand. He had always been shy with strangers, but her grip was warm and firm and he thought he had never seen a pair of eyes so lively and arresting. They were a deep sea-green, very widely set, and as she stood there in the stippled light under the buddleia tree, he knew he was going to like her. 'I hope you'll be very happy here,' he added.

'I'm sure I shall.' He remembered the husky voice he had heard through the door of the utility room when she came for her interview, then suddenly she turned her head into a dapple of sunlight and he was stunned by what he saw. Across her left cheek, from nose to ear, ran a deep scar, as if a piece of jagged metal had at one time ripped her face to the bone. The flesh had been so obscenely mangled that the indentation cast a heavy black shadow, and Robert was compelled to speak in order to cover his disquiet. 'If there's anything you need,' he said, 'anything for your room – to make you more comfortable – you have only to ask.'

'That's awfully kind of you, Mr Slingsby. I'm sure I've got all I could wish for. It's a *lovely* room.' Her nose and mouth were small and undistinguished; her face was dominated by those amazingly lively and beautiful eyes – and by the scar. How on earth did it happen? A motor accident perhaps? Why hadn't Julia mentioned it? He supposed she had wanted to enjoy his shock and discomfort. He hoped he had concealed his inner reaction well enough. Such a disfigurement must be a perpetual cause for despair, yet her face, despite the scar, was a contented face, and her smile was humorous and unreserved.

Julia, lipsticked and coiffured and dressed in pale blue silk, laid an elegant hand on Robert's sleeve. 'Dinner will be early tonight, dear,' she said. 'I've just had a call from Emily. She wants me to go round at nine to advise her about some carpet patterns.'

Dear! thought Robert, with disgust. She never called him that except in company, and every time she did so he wanted to slap her face. She turned to Mrs Laurie. 'I'm rather good at décor,' she explained with her thin smile. 'I used to study art.'

'I can see by your house. The colours are beautiful. And I love the design of your gate.'

Robert sighed, wanting now to be alone with his drink and his paper. 'Fine,' he said. 'Dinner at seven-thirty.'

'It's *Boeuf Stroganoff*,' said Mrs Laurie. 'With fresh broccoli and sauté potatoes. Will that be all right? And lemon soufflé to follow?'

'Splendid.' This sounded promising; she talked about food as if it was a pleasure and not just a need. 'I like the sound of that, don't you, Julia?'

'I think we need another vegetable,' she said. 'Creamed carrots, perhaps? I don't eat potatoes.'

'Whatever you say, Mrs Slingsby.'

No 'sir' or 'madam', thought Robert. The end of an era, indeed . . .

When the two women returned to the house, he leaned back in the deck-chair and closed his eyes. He had forgotten his whisky and the *Financial Times*; he was thinking of Mrs Laurie's face, those eyes, that scar.

R

The dinner was excellent. Mrs Laurie served it with quiet efficiency and Robert found it hard to keep his eyes off her. He was fascinated by the way her daisied apron clung to the wide curve of her hips and flicked out with a swirl that was almost jaunty as she moved briskly around the table with plates and dishes. He was fascinated by her hair, thick and dark and wiry, knotted at the nape of her neck with a silver skewer affair. And by her large soft breasts, lifted and restrained, he guessed, under the flowered dress. But most of all, he was fascinated by the scar, less prominent indoors than it had been on the terrace, but nevertheless extremely disturbing.

Julia refused the lemon soufflé and went off to visit Emily Cartwright who lived in a village south of Grassley. Robert heard the Datsun drive away and sighed with relief. Julia was a good driver, that was one consolation; he didn't have to worry about her knocking the gatepost down or backing into his beautiful Rover.

'I'll have my coffee in the drawing room, please, Mrs Laurie,' he said as she took away his dessert dish. She smiled and nodded without comment, and as she went out of the room he noticed that she was wearing attractive brown shoes with fairly high heels. Perhaps the sensible shoes had been a diplomatic choice for the interview. Her calves were sturdy but her ankles very slim. An *interesting* woman, he thought.

In the drawing room he went to the cocktail cabinet for the usual drink, and was surprised to see a folded blue envelope in his crystal whisky glass. His heart seemed to stop: 'Daddy' was written across it in Nicola's childish scrawl. He took it to his armchair and stared at it in dismay. She hadn't written to him for years, except for Christmas and birthday cards. What was the matter? It must be something she felt unable to talk about. He hardly dared to open it and decided to wait until Mrs Laurie had brought in the coffee.

What an indictment, he thought, that his daughter should leave him a note in a whisky glass. He must be drinking too much. He stared at the envelope, following the characters and the long tail on the 'y'. Her writing had matured, of course, but it still had that same careful roundness.

Suddenly he could wait no longer, and with trembling hands he tore the envelope and withdrew the single sheet of blue writing paper.

Monday

Darling Daddy,

I have gone to live with Barry and his mother at 27, Station Road. It's a lovely happy house and I've got a super little room in the attic. Barry's mother is terribly kind and you've no need to worry about me. I'm leaving school and getting a job at a hairdresser's. Please don't be upset – I know what's right for me. I'll bring Barry over on Thursday night like Mother said if it's still O.K. Let me know if it isn't. In any case I will come and see you sometimes on a Tuesday when she's out.

Lots of love from Nicola.
P.S. Barry's name is Mitchell in case you didn't know.

Robert sat staring at the piece of paper which was shivering in his hand. He felt as if all the energy had drained from his body. She had gone already, without a word, without a 'by your leave'. But of course she could hardly have asked permission when she knew it would never be granted. '*A lovely happy house . . . Barry's mother is terribly kind.*' It was only to be expected that she would leave as soon as she had the chance. Julia had not been kind to her and the house had never been a happy one in any sense of the word. He hoped that he had not been unkind but he couldn't be sure of it; he knew that he had never understood her. That wasp, the things she had told him about Barry, her socialist ideas, her untidiness – he couldn't understand them at all. The one thing he *could* understand was her hatred of her mother. And her love for Ivy.

It struck him with blinding force that it was Ivy's departure that had decided her to go. It was Julia's fault for sacking Ivy . . . He clenched his teeth, glaring round the room in an anguish of rage and despair. The faces in the wallpaper were screaming, screaming, and suddenly he heaved himself out of the chair and stumbled across to the cocktail cabinet, the letter falling to the floor. With shaking hands he splashed the whisky into the glass and drank it neat, coughing and gulping in a hopeless effort to deaden his misery.

He was standing by the cabinet, the empty glass in his hand, when there was a light knock on the door. Instinctively he said 'Come in', and stood with his back to Mrs Laurie as she put the tray on the coffee table. Out of the corner of his eye he saw her stoop to pick up Nicola's letter from the carpet.

The moment her fingers reached it, he cried out, 'Put that *down*! Don't *touch* it!'

Mrs Laurie stood up and looked at him in consternation. 'I'm so sorry –'

He covered his face with his hands. 'No – it's me to apologise – I'm sorry – I'm *sorry* –' His voice broke into a sob and he dropped his hands and stared at her with the tears welling into his eyes. 'It's my daughter,' he told her. 'She's just left home – quite unexpectedly – that's the letter.' He drew a deep shuddering breath. 'I should never have spoken to you like that –' He looked down at the glass in his hand. 'I've been drowning my sorrows, I'm afraid – please forgive me – I'm not myself.'

Mrs Laurie had been listening in silence, gazing at him with such a steady look of sympathy that he was amazed and comforted.

'I understand,' she said gently. 'You mustn't blame yourself – not for a moment. Shall I leave you? Or would you rather not be alone just now?'

'Don't go – please. Sit down – have some coffee – get another cup.'

Mrs Laurie hesitated. 'I'm a little hungry,' she explained with a faint smile. 'My dinner's on the hot-tray – would you mind if I brought it in here?'

'Of course not – oh, God, I'm so thoughtless – whatever must you think of me?'

77

'You've had a nasty shock, Mr Slingsby, and you mustn't apologise – I'll go and get my supper and you might like to tell me a little about her. I hope it isn't my arrival that's driven her away? It seems as if it might be.'

'She loved your predecessor – very dearly. Ivy had been her nanny since she was two. You can understand.'

'Of course. People one has loved can never be replaced. Never. But others may stand where they stood and help to ease the loss. I hope you can persuade your daughter to come home.' She spoke in a quiet measured way that was calming and reassuring. Robert hardly noticed the scar when he was talking to her; her eyes and her serenity were the things he was most aware of.

'Go and bring your supper,' he said, 'and I'll tell you about her. I've never understood her and you might be able to advise me.'

'I'll do my best,' she replied from the doorway, 'but what a pity your wife isn't here. I'm sure you'll be able to sort things out between you.'

Then she was gone, and he wondered about the honesty of her last remark. Had she not sensed already that he and Julia could never sort out *anything* between them?

R

'Tell me about your daughter,' said Mrs Laurie. 'I'll carry on with my supper if you don't mind, but I'll be listening very carefully.' She was sitting in a small swivel chair beside Robert, with her plate on her lap.

While she was out of the room, Robert had picked up Nicola's letter and put it in the pocket of his grey velvet smoking jacket. Now he tried to take a sip of coffee but the cup rattled against his teeth and he put it down again.

'She's not academic,' he said, trying to keep the quiver out of his voice. 'She's only got three O-levels. But she's

78

intelligent and I think she has great potential if she'll use it. Now she talks about leaving school and working at a hairdresser's. It's quite preposterous.' He watched Mrs Laurie spear a piece of steak with her fork and raise it to her mouth. Her hands were sunburnt and rather large, with strongly-curved unvarnished nails and no adornment apart from a narrow platinum wedding ring.

'I saw her on the landing upstairs this afternoon,' she said. 'Just for a moment – not to talk to. She's a sweet-looking girl – such sad brown eyes.' She smiled, glancing up at him from her plate. 'Like yours,' she said. 'She's like you, isn't she?'

'Do you think so?' He had heard this said before. Of course she was nothing like Julia; Nicola's face was round and blunt and gentle . . . 'She's always been a good, well-meaning child but she's got a will of her own – and she's very outspoken – rude, in fact, sometimes. And rather quick-tempered.'

'Has she gone to live with the housekeeper who left?'

'Oh, no – it's her boy friend, I'm afraid. He lives with his mother, so it's not so serious perhaps, but it seems a most unconventional household – she's a writer. Children's books of a most unsavoury kind, according to my wife.'

'And how about the boy friend? Don't you approve of him?'

'I – we haven't met him yet. He sounds like a militant type. Unstable. Works in a garage – no real prospects –'

'Has she known him long?' Mrs Laurie was eating her dinner very slowly, looking up from time to time.

'She's been talking about him for weeks – months. As a matter of fact he's supposed to be coming for coffee on Thursday night but I'm sure that won't happen now, the way things have turned out.'

'Why's that? Mightn't it be a good idea – a chance to talk things out between the four of you?'

Robert let out a short bitter laugh. 'You'll understand as time goes on, Mrs Laurie. It isn't quite like that, I'm afraid. And that's why Nicola's left us – there's nothing for her to stay for now that Ivy's gone. I can't seem to get through to her – God knows I've tried. And she's never got on with her mother. No wonder she's gone away – ' His voice trembled and Mrs Laurie looked down at her empty plate, putting her knife and fork more neatly together.

'I shouldn't have said all that,' he burst out. 'It's in confidence – talking here like this. You understand, don't you? I feel you do.'

'Of course,' she said. 'Of course I understand.' Her shining blue-green eyes held his for several seconds and he felt a thrill of pleasure even in the midst of his distress. He noticed for the first time that there was a gleam of blue make-up on her eyelids. She wore no lipstick but her small mouth was soft and red and the cheek without the scar had a warm russet glow.

She said quietly, 'I expect you're afraid for your daughter – afraid she might get pregnant? Is that what's worrying you?'

'She's only sixteen,' he managed to say. 'I want her here at home, where I can keep an eye on her.'

Mrs Laurie nodded and there was a faint rueful smile on her lips. 'It's not so easy, is it – keeping an eye on them?'

'Have you any children?' he asked, unable to bear any further talk of Nicola.

She shook her head. 'I had a son who died when he was eight months old. Pneumonia. He'd have been about Nicola's age. I don't feel maudlin about it – not now. What's the use? Life is for living, not regretting. But I love kids.' She sighed. 'Anyway I hope I can make friends with Nicola.' She put her plate on the tray and stood up. Robert got to his feet, stumbling a little. What an odd relationship with a housekeeper, he thought. And on her first day, too. 'You're a wonderful cook,' he told her. 'We're very lucky to have found you.'

'I'm lucky to *be* here, Mr Slingsby. I know that very well. And I'm sorry you've got this problem with your daughter. Maybe she'll be happy with her boy friend – it's good for the young to find their own feet and break away from their parents.'

'Thank you, Mrs Laurie. Thank you for listening so patiently.' He heard the sharp note of dismissal in his voice and dreaded that she might guess the quality of his attachment to Nicola, recognise his abnormal possessiveness. 'You've been so kind,' he went on. 'I do appreciate it. It's just that I'm very tired and upset.'

'Of course.' She bent to pick up the tray and he caught a drift of her perfume and saw the scar more closely than before. She doesn't try to hide it, he thought. She wears her hair swept back from her face, makes no effort to train it over her cheek, as most women would have done.

'Is there anything I can do for you?' she asked. 'Make some fresh coffee – pour you another drink?'

He shook his head. 'I'll have another Scotch but I mustn't allow you to pour it for me – that would be an unspeakable indulgence on my part.'

'Just as you say.' Her tone was warm and humorous, with a hint of mockery. 'I'll see to the dinner things and then I think I'll go to bed and read, if you're sure there's nothing else I can do?'

'Nothing at all, thank you. Good night.'

'Good night, Mr Slingsby.'

He watched her carry the tray to the door, balance it on one hand while she turned the knob, and gracefully make her exit like an actress who has performed the same ritual a hundred times. When she had quietly shut the door behind her he leaned back in his chair and closed his eyes. A fantastic woman, he said to himself. Totally different from anyone he had ever known. Thinking of her, he was free for a while from his anguish over Nicola's letter. He marvelled at the way she had adjusted herself to wear that scar with such calm acceptance. And what was her Christian name? It was a nonsense to call her Mrs Laurie. He was still thinking about her when he heard the slam of a car door and knew that Julia was back.

R

Julia was not inclined to comment on her comings and goings; she often drove away without telling Robert her destination or when she expected to return. Coming home, she would go straight upstairs or busy herself in the kitchen, making no contact with him. Not that he cared where she was, only that it would sometimes have been convenient to know.

On this particular evening he heard the closing of the garage door, followed by the doors of the utility room and the kitchen. Then there was nothing to indicate her whereabouts until, several minutes later, he heard the far-away flushing of the lavatory upstairs.

He decided to stay up until she was asleep, save the inevitable row until the next morning; he would be able to escape at five to eight, when he invariably set out for the office. There was certainly nothing they could do until the following day. He had considered phoning Nicola, pleading with her to come straight home, but he knew it would be useless. And in any case he would have to discuss the matter with Julia. After all, Nicola was *her* daughter, too, something he always tried to forget.

He put on a Haydn record and prayed that Julia would not come down and begin to regale him with the details of Emily Cartwright and her carpet patterns. If she did, he would have to tell her about Nicola, and then they would both be up until the early hours, wrangling, blaming one another. What was it Mrs Laurie had said? *Life is for living, not regretting* . . . What a wise woman! Yes, that was it – a *wise* woman. Ivy had been far too docile, too uncertain. Mrs Laurie, he felt, was strong and happy in her own identity, and this in spite of the scar, the lost child and early widowhood. She had an air of quiet confidence which radiated comfort as well as a peculiar excitement. He must make certain, absolutely certain, that she didn't leave.

In her newly painted bedroom, Nicola stood by the window and stared down at Grassley Station. A pigeon was ambling jerkily about on the platform roof, its sunlit plumage exactly the colour of the slates. An appetising smell came faintly up from the kitchen; at any moment Helen and Freddie would be back.

She turned to look at her room. The bed and the floor were piled with her belongings which Barry had brought up from the car – cases and haversacks, cardboard boxes and bulging plastic carriers. She loved the grey-green walls, the white gloss paint, the red curtains that Freddie had found for her, but half the pleasure was gone because of Helen. She could hear Barry hammering in his room below, making her a bookcase, and she told herself that she was stupid to worry.

She set off down the attic stairs to the bathroom. Outside her bedroom door on the narrow landing was the astronomical telescope that had belonged to Barry's father. Now it was pointed blindly at the dirty sloping ceiling. The hefty white tube was furred with dust, the framework interwoven with cobwebs, a sad reminder of the days when Barry and his father used to look at the stars in the back garden.

The bathroom was large and untidy. It was very warm because of the hot-water tank, and it smelt of toothpaste and damp towels. Her parents would have been horrified to see the string of washing over the bath, the cream-painted walls stained with rust and mildew, the basin, grimy round the taps and littered with old face flannels, worn-out nail brushes and slivers of soap. She gazed at her wan face in the mirror. By this time her father would have found the note; she knew that he always had a whisky when he got home. As she washed her sticky hands she wondered anxiously what he would do about it. She wasn't going back, that was certain. Nothing would induce her to live in the same house with her mother again . . .

Suddenly the door flew open behind her and a voice said, 'Oh, I'm sorry – can I come in? I'm bursting for a pee. Don't go away – I shan't be a sec.'

Nicola swung round, trembling, to see a tall sturdy blonde in a flouncy apple-green dress, already pulling down her briefs and settling her large white bottom on the lavatory seat.

'I'm Helen,' she was saying cheerfully as the urine tinkled down. 'Sorry to barge in on you like this but I just couldn't wait.'

'It's all right.' Nicola turned back to the mirror but not before she had seen that Helen's hair was straight and shoulder-length, turned under at the ends and had the metallic look of tarnished brass. It was obviously dyed. Her eyes were small and rather puffy and her wide mouth had been painted with a brownish lipstick which had now worn off except at the edges. She was so much less attractive than Nicola had feared, that she faced her reflection with new pleasure. She recognised the flawless purity of her own young face compared with Helen's, and her heart was flooded with such relief that the corners of her mouth lifted involuntarily into a happy smile.

'I've been dying to meet you,' she said. 'I've never met a real actress.'

'I'm out of a job at the moment,' said Helen, pulling up her briefs. 'That's why I'm down here – hoping for something in Brighton. Got an audition for the lead in *A Doll's House*.'

Nicola knew nothing about the play but she made a little crooning sound which was meant to imply that Helen would be ideal for the part.

'God, I'm hungry,' said Helen, washing her hands with so much gusto that she splashed Nicola's shirt. 'What a super smell. Freddie's jolly good at throwing a casserole together, isn't she?' She dried her hands and tossed the towel over the edge of the bath. 'Super house, this. I always feel so much at home here. I gather you've just moved in.'

'Yeah – Barry's painted my room for me.'

'You can say that again. I hardly saw him over the weekend

'– he was covered in it. Where is he now, for God's sake?'

'In his room – he's making me a bookcase.'

'Christ! He can turn his hand to anything, can't he?' She was stretching her lips to receive a new coating of lipstick. 'Freddie tells me you're sixteen,' she said at last, dabbing her face with powder. 'You look more like twelve.'

Nicola felt her cheeks flare. 'I'll be seventeen in October.'

'And you left home with parent trouble, I hear? It's a common complaint. Only cured by death. Theirs, I mean.' She led the way downstairs.

'My father's not so bad,' said Nicola, noting that Helen's legs were bare and perfect, and that she was wearing exotic sandals with gold thongs round the ankles. 'It's my mother I hate. She can drop dead tomorrow for all I care.'

Helen looked back at Nicola over her shoulder, her eyes bright with interest. 'At least you're honest about it. If there's one thing I can't stand it's hypocrisy.'

'That's what Barry always says.'

They were passing his door and he came out, grinning. 'What does Barry always say?' he asked, putting an arm round each of them and propelling them along the landing.

'Never you mind,' said Helen, freeing herself and walking ahead with a slight sway of her hips.

'It was something nice,' said Nicola, taking Barry's hand and smiling up at him.

But he wasn't looking at her; he was watching Helen as she ran down the stairs, her hair bouncing gently like the hairspray ads on television, her green dress swirling round her legs.

R

Robert hardly slept that night. He lay in the great bed, as far away from Julia as he could get, hardly daring to move in case he woke her and had to talk. By dawn the muscles of his neck and shoulders were knotted with tension and the familiar headache had tightened round his scalp; it even seemed to throb in his jaw-bones. The time was approaching when he must tell Julia that Nicola had gone. He turned his head very slowly and saw that she was lying on her back with one arm across her eyes. The bend of her bare elbow was slim and white (she never sunbathed) and could have belonged to a much younger woman, but her mouth was hard and relentless, even in sleep. He knew that he would never want to kiss her again as long as he lived.

The curtains were not drawn and the grey oblong of the window revealed the dark movement of the sycamore leaves as they shivered and twisted in a strong breeze. Where was Nicola now? Lying in bed with that boy, her legs parted beneath him, his lips on her childish breast? Or was she alone and frightened in a strange room, wishing she had never left home? There was time for her to see her mistake, come back to Birch House and return to school next month as if none of this had happened. He certainly wouldn't notify the Convent; he would leave her free to change her mind, even at the last moment. Tomorrow he would phone her and arrange to take her out to lunch, buy her wine and a mountainous sundae, talk to her kindly, make her see how misguided she had been.

Mrs Laurie had asked if he were afraid of Nicola getting pregnant. Of course he was, but if only that were all! In his case the torment was a thousand times more crucial because he could not bear the thought that any boy should touch her, even to hold her hand or kiss her lightly on the lips. His love for her was a shameful obsession and he knew that he must never allow her to guess the faintest part of it. No word or glance or gesture must ever betray him; the knowledge could damage her for life.

He lay there watching the sky grow brighter and as the velvet drapes changed imperceptibly from black to red, he considered the following Thursday night. Surely that coffee arrangement would have to be cancelled? Then at least he would be spared the torture of meeting Barry, of seeing them together. The thought of it was so painful that he let out an involuntary little moan of despair, and Julia started, stretched out her arms above her head and turned to look at him.

'What's the matter?' she said irritably. 'What time is it?'

He looked at his watch. 'Ten to seven.' At seven o'clock, no doubt, Mrs Laurie would bring their tea and orange juice, as Ivy used to do.

Julia grunted and settled herself more comfortably. 'I've a very busy day ahead,' she told him. 'A Townswomen's lunch at Croydon. And the Council tonight. Sounds like a gale blowing up – I *hate* wind. It always –'

'Julia – I – I've got something to tell you – something very important –.'

'It can wait, can't it? Tell me when the tray comes. I want to close my eyes.'

'No – I must tell you now. It *won't* wait.' She was silent, staring at him, and he saw that she had understood his urgency.

'Nicola has gone.' The words came out on a quiver of breath so that they were hardly audible.

'Nicola *what*?'

'She's gone. Moved in with that boy and his mother. I found a note last night – after you'd left.'

'Why didn't you ring me at Emily's?'

'I didn't want to worry you.' In fact the idea had never occurred to him.

'Why didn't you tell me when I got in?'

'There was nothing we could have done last night. She's taken her things.' He had gone into her room on the way to bed, seen the desolation, the broken necklace left on the bedside table, the scraps of Sellotape on the walls where her posters had been.

'Where's the letter? Let me see it.'

'It's downstairs somewhere – it was only a little scribble.' He had locked it away in his briefcase. Julia would be incensed if she saw it: *Darling Daddy* with no mention of her mother; *I'll come and see you on Tuesday evenings when she's out . . .*

Julia sat up in bed and began to remove her hairnet. 'I suppose you're heartbroken,' she said, looking at him sideways with her arms raised, taking out the hairpins.

'Losing your little darling. But not to worry – she'll come crawling back. I've found out where they live – down by the station. There are blacks in that area and God knows what. Muggings, too, I shouldn't wonder. And she'll soon get fed up with her precious Barry when he finds himself out of a job with no references – he won't know what's hit him.'

'What do you mean?'

'We'll have them here on Thursday – the two of them, just as we planned. Pretend we accept the situation – and let the boy condemn himself. It won't be difficult. The Cartwrights are behind me, of course –'

'We mustn't be *too* drastic, must we? She's at a very difficult age and –'

Julia fixed him with a wide sardonic stare. 'Angel child! Daddy's little sweetheart. No wonder she's gone – I don't suppose she could stand the way you moon and drool over her. It's *nauseating*. If only you could *see* yourself.'

His heart began to thump. Could it be true? Could he have driven her away with his secret lusting? Could she have felt the tremor in his body when she casually kissed him goodnight, caught the look of longing in his eyes?

'You've never cared about her,' he burst out, hardly able to speak. 'I've had to love her enough for both of us. No wonder I've got too fond of her.'

'So you admit it? You *admit* you're too fond of her? That's *very* interesting.'

He got out of bed, unable to endure her watchful stare, the flinty eyes that seemed to wither and destroy him. 'You *bitch*,' he cried, stumbling over the bedside rug. 'You thrive on people's misery, don't you? You never want to understand or help or take some blame upon yourself. It's *your* fault she's gone – all *your* fault. It was sacking Ivy that did it – the last straw on top of all the other things –'

'*Rubbish*! It was you and your –'

'Don't say "Rubbish" to me. You're a bitch and you've always been a bitch, I ought to have seen it before I married you. You've ruined everything and I wish to God you were *dead*!' His voice was out of control, a shriek of hatred echoing back from the elegant wallpaper, the crystal chandelier. It was followed by a moment of silence, and into that silence came a small persistent sound, a knocking at the door, a rhythmic tap-tap-tap of knuckles on wood. Robert rushed into the bathroom and shut the door behind him. A moment later he heard Julia's voice, drowsy, contented, as if she had just awakened from a pleasant dream. 'Come in,' she called. 'Come in, Mrs Laurie.'

R

One autumn evening before Nicola was born, Julia had given Robert one of her rare confidences. Nigel B. was still alive, and they were living in Robert's flat in Sevenoaks. They had drunk a bottle of wine with their dinner and were sitting by the fire with the curtains drawn. Julia had since given up alcohol almost completely, and Robert thought it was because she was afraid of speaking the truth too freely.

They had been much closer in those days and that evening she told him a macabre story about an occasion when her grandfather – Nigel B.'s father – had deliberately terrorised his wife.

Apparently a friend of his had called at Birch House with a large and vicious Alsatian dog. Julia's grandmother was very much afraid of dogs, particularly Alsatians, and her sadistic husband had locked her in the kitchen with this animal while he and the owner went out in the car. She managed to climb on top of a tall cupboard and escape any physical injury but she never recovered from the experience and ended her life in a mental home.

'But why did he *do* such a thing?' Robert had asked, sick with horror.

'How should I know? I hardly remember either of them – I was only small. She seemed a nice little woman – she used to make chocolate fudge with bits of chopped walnut in it.'

Robert had been surprised to see that Julia had tears in her eyes; she seldom registered emotion.

'How old was your father when it happened?'

'About twelve, I think. He told me years ago – he was very upset.' And she had refused to discuss the matter further.

Robert was increasingly disturbed by the story. Seemingly this calculated cruelty went back to her grandfather. And who could tell how long before that? Family trees were all very well, with their heraldic notions of grandeur, but it might be more useful to trace the tyrannies of men over their wives, women over their husbands, parents over children.

He himself had little cause for complaint. His grandparents had left vague but pleasant memories of ball games in summer gardens and smiling old faces under paper hats at Christmas. His mother and father had been kind in every way – too kind perhaps. They had deprived themselves of holidays to buy him expensive toys, good clothes and a public school education (which nevertheless he had not enjoyed). His mother had certainly fussed and worried a great deal but only out of love. His father, a conscientious schoolmaster, had been rather lacking in humour and often cloistered away with a book, but Robert had grateful and loving recollections of both his parents. He often pictured the two of them on their garden seat in the sun, in old age very much alike with their wispy hair and faded old jerseys, smiling at one another and holding hands.

He knew he had been lucky. Until he met Julia . . .

She'd had the tall cupboard removed from the kitchen at Birch House but he could not rid himself of the image of that poor woman, crouching close to the ceiling, palpitating with terror. She had been driven out of her mind by the man she had married, the man who had fathered her only son. And the son, of course, was Nigel B.

R

'I shan't come back,' said Nicola, 'so please don't go on at me.'

They were sitting at lunch in *The Five Gables*, a country hotel near Tonbridge. Robert had reserved a table in an alcove, insisting on its position as if he had been planning a meal with a mistress.

The window beside them looked out on to a putting green where two elderly women in white cardigans were prodding and jabbing at the ball, sending it yards past the hole, then back the other way. The green was in the shelter of the building but their skirts were flapping in the wind and wisps of grey hair blew across their faces. Nicola had giggled about them all through her prawn cocktail, refusing to talk seriously. Then, before the second course arrived, he had asked her why she left home. 'Was it because of Ivy going – or because you wanted to be with Barry? Tell me honestly, darling.'

She took a gulp of wine and shrugged her shoulders. 'I just decided to go. Don't want to talk about it.'

Robert had a sudden recollection of Julia on the curve of the stairs at Birch House twenty years ago. '*I shan't discuss my father* . . . ' Now he could see in Nicola's pale stubborn little face a touch of her mother, not in features (heaven forbid!) but in the set of her mouth.

When the roast duckling had been served, with its four delicious vegetables, he said, 'The new housekeeper's extremely nice. I'm sure you'd like her – a really warm-hearted person. She has a terrible scar on her cheek, poor soul, but she –'

'I saw her going into Ivy's room,' said Nicola. 'I *hate* her.'

'That's ridiculous! She said she thought you looked very sweet – she wants to make friends with you.'

'Shit that,' said Nicola, and a middle-aged couple at a

nearby table looked up from their plates, clutching their knives and forks in horrified amazement. The dining room was almost empty; you could have heard a rose petal fall.

'Nicola – *please*!' he muttered.

'Oh, for God's sake, Daddy. Why did we have to come to a place like this? I can't stand whispering.'

'The food's good, for one thing. You like good food, don't you?' Why did she have to be so *rude*? It was on account of her misery, of course – losing Ivy, hating her mother. He must try to be understanding. 'Couldn't you just come home until your birthday?' he pleaded, hoping that the request for a small concession might give her a loophole, make her change her mind. 'Just till you're seventeen – it isn't asking much.'

'What difference does my *birthday* make? It's only a bloody *date*.' The wine had made her garrulous, her cheeks were pink, her eyes unnaturally bright. 'I won't like my mother any better, will I, just because I'm seventeen?'

'No, I suppose not.' He took a deep breath, thinking how exquisite she looked with her shiny cheeks and her hair falling loosely round her shoulders. She was wearing scarlet nail varnish (a new departure) and through her silky white dress he could see a lacy brassière which lifted her small breasts into greater prominence.

She had finished her second course and was gazing out of the window at the putting green again. 'Just *look* at those women,' she exclaimed. 'They've lost the ball now – miles away in those bushes. I'm sure I could do better than that. Shall we have a game after lunch?'

'My darling, I can't. I've got to be back at the office by half past two.' He groaned inwardly; he would have loved to show off his prowess, give her advice.

Now she had started on a maple walnut sundae and her eyes were wide with pleasure. 'I must see if Freddie can make something like this,' she said.

'Who's Freddie?'

'Barry's mother.'

'His *mother*?'

'Yeah – her name's Freda. Oh, she's fantastic. You'll really have to meet her. She types all day, writing her books.' There was cream on her top lip and she was waving her spoon about, dropping maple syrup on the white tablecloth. 'She's nothing like mother – you can really *talk* to her. Say *anything*.'

'Your mother's very busy, Nicola. She always has been. She's doing excellent work for the community and she's greatly respected, you know. She doesn't have much time to spare for talking. I only wish she had – that's a problem for me as well.' This was a confession of great importance, a break-through in communication, but Nicola seemed hardly to hear him. She scraped the bottom of the sundae dish and put down her spoon with a clatter. 'Could I have some more wine, please, Daddy. And some of that triangular cheese on the trolley over there?'

'Yes, of course.' He filled her glass and signalled to the waiter, a Spanish-looking young man with a sullen, handsome face. 'Now what about Thursday? You're bringing Barry over for coffee, aren't you? About eight-thirty?'

'Might as well. He wants to meet you and we can pick up my books. He's made me a super bookcase.'

So he had really lost her; it was no use pleading any more. 'Don't be rude to your mother, darling,' he said in a low voice. 'It won't help anyone and it'll make me very unhappy.'

'It depends how *she* behaves, doesn't it? If she's rude to Barry I'll go *mad*.'

The waiter was now placing a large slice of Brie on a plate in front of her and she looked up at him with a smile of approval. Robert saw their eyes meet, saw the young man glance down the front of her dress as he served her, and was stricken by a helpless agony of longing. She was totally beyond his reach. Nothing could ever make her his; never in all his life would he be able to caress her, even for a second, in the way he wanted to . . .

The waiter had gone and Robert said, 'You're not *really* going to work at a hairdresser's, are you?'

'Why not?' She was talking with her mouth full. 'I'm going to work my way up – have a salon of my own. We'll sell snacks and things – that'll pull 'em in. Girls, I mean – not the old biddies.' She buttered another biscuit. 'But I expect I'll be married to Barry by then. Hope so.'

Robert drank the last of his wine. The duckling had disagreed with him and he had declined a dessert. Now he felt sick.

'I'm looking forward to meeting him,' he said, holding the stiff white napkin in front of his mouth, hoping he sounded casual and sincere. 'He must be nice if you're so fond of him.'

'*You* won't like him,' she said. 'He never wears a tie and he doesn't say much. Besides, he hates the Tories. Better keep off all that.'

'Of course,' said Robert. 'Unless your mother opens the subject.'

'If she *does*,' said Nicola, 'there'll be a battle, I can tell you *that*.'

And of course, thought Robert, she will. That's what the visit was all about.

He signalled for coffee.

N

'I'm so glad you were in, Sal. Barry's at his carpentry and I'm dying for a talk.' Sally was sitting at her untidy little dressing table, sorting out lipsticks. There must have been about twenty of them, lined up on end like a squad of soldiers. The flat was above her father's pet shop in Grassley High Street, and Nicola, lounging on the bed, could hear the squeal of puppies down below. She had seen them in the window as she came in.

'Glad you came,' said Sally. 'Mum's at Bingo and Dad's at the pub – just like all the millions. Makes me ashamed, really. Can't see beyond their spectacles, I told them once.'

'What did they say?'

'Mum said I couldn't see beyond my fanny. Right enough, I suppose. How's *your* sex life, Nicky? Getting better?'

94

'No – I've got the curse. Came early – I expect it's all the worry I've had. Helen isn't a bit what I expected. She isn't pretty – she's all sort of *greasy* – all around her nostrils is greasy. But she's dead sexy and I know damn well she's after Barry again.'

'Is she nice to you, or what?'

'Not so bad, I suppose. She gave me this nail varnish.' Nicola waved her fingers. 'But she keeps putting me down – says I look about twelve – talks about plays and books I've never heard of. Then she says, "Oh, I'm surprised you haven't heard of so-and-so – it's terribly well-known." Makes me feel so stupid.'

'Is she having it off with Barry, do you think?' Sally turned round on her stool. She was wearing no make-up and her eyes looked strangely tender without their usual load of eye-shadow.

'I don't think so. He's terribly sweet to me – but of course it could be a cover-up. I just can't seem to be *easy* with him any more.' Her eyes were suddenly swimming with tears. 'Oh, Sal – I'm so unhappy – there's no fun like I thought there'd be. I get so *nervy* with Helen around. If only she'd go!'

The tears ran down her cheeks and Sally rushed over to the bed and hugged her tightly. 'You poor love – don't worry – I'm sure Barry loves you. Just give it time – it'll all come out in the wash, like those crusty drawers!'

Nicola's sobs turned into hysterical giggles and the girls clung together, rocking and screaming with laughter. Oh, Sal, thought Nicola, my friend – my best, best friend!

'What's his mother turning out like?' said Sally at last.

'Oh, she's great. She's lovely to all of us – I don't think she knows what's going on. In any case, she's always thinking about her books.'

'She probably knows jolly well,' said Sally, toying with a big blue cloth elephant she had won at a fair. 'But there's nothing she can do so she isn't interfering.'

Nicola said, 'How's your lorry driver?'

'Driving fucking lorries. He's lovely but he's never *there*. Always on the road – Carlisle, Penzance, Liverpool – it's *hopeless*. That's why you found me in – playing with my bloody lipsticks.'

'Daddy took me out to lunch today,' Nicola said. 'He phoned me at Barry's and I got the bus to Tonbridge. He met me in the car and we went to this snooty hotel. He kept nagging at me to go back home, but I can't see why it matters to him anyway – he was always on at me about leaving my things about and banging doors and not combing my hair. I'd have thought he'd be better off without me.'

'P'raps he fancies you,' said Sally with a grin.

'*Fancies* me?' Such a notion had never occurred to Nicola. 'I should think he's sexless. I can't imagine him *ever* doing it with my mother.' She had sometimes tried to picture her parents in the four-poster, gasping and sweating in a frenzy of passion, but she found the idea both ludicrous and disgusting.

'Well,' said Sally, holding up the elephant by its blue suede ears and dandling it on her knee like a baby, 'he must have done, mustn't he? At least once!'

The fact that she owed her existence to such a coupling was something Nicola did not want to think about; she hated the idea of her mother's blood in her veins. And she wished that Sally had not joked about her father having designs on her. The possibility was growing in her mind, making her uneasy. 'What happens if a man fancies his daughter?' she said. 'Does he actually want to *sleep* with her?'

'What else? There's a lot of it about, you know. It all gets hushed up. I knew a girl at school whose father raped her on the bathroom floor while her mother was making jam in the kitchen.'

'*Honestly*?'

'Course. Oh, Nicky, you're so *innocent*. It must be that frightful Convent.'

Nicola felt a shiver of disquiet, remembering occasions when her father had flushed and trembled when she put her arms round his neck and kissed him goodnight. She had thought it was just his natural nerviness but now she began to wonder . . .

'Daddy's never tried anything on with me,' she said firmly.

'He'd be horrified if he could hear you – he's terribly prudish.'

'Maybe he isn't the type. But your mother's a bit of a cold fish, from what you said, and that's when a guy can get funny ideas.'

'Oh, Sal – *do* shut up. You're getting me worried.'

Sally laughed. 'Forget it. What does it matter, anyway?'

'No, I suppose it doesn't.' She sighed. 'It's just that I wish I'd never *thought* of it, that's all.'

'So that's *my* fault, isn't it?' Sally hurled the elephant across the room. 'Am I supposed to apologise, or what?'

'No, of course not – don't be silly.'

Sally got up and went to the window. 'You'd better go now – I'm going to wash my hair.'

Nicola retrieved the elephant and sat it on the bed. 'Sorry, Sal. Don't be cross.'

'*I'm* not bloody cross – it's *you*!'

'I'm not. It's just that I'd never have *thought* of it if you hadn't said –'

'Oh, get *lost*!'

Nicola picked up her bag and went out, slamming the door. It was the first time she had quarrelled with Sally, and she felt shaky. Outside on the landing a tabby cat was waiting patiently with its front paws neatly together, blinking mournfully at the closed door. She bent to stroke it but it gave a little cry and flashed away down the stairs. Nicola followed it slowly, kicking at the wall and noting with satisfaction that her rubber sole had left a black streak on the pale blue wallpaper.

N

'I wish Freddie'd get rid of all this junk,' said Helen. 'There's never a square inch in here to put your arse down.' The two armchairs and the sofa were piled with all the yellowing *Guardians*, *Tribunes* and *Listeners* she never had time to read.

'You'd need more than a square inch,' said Nicola.

Freddie was out and she was typing patterns with o's and x's and asterisks.

'No need to be rude – just because you've got a skinny backside. Did she *say* you could play with her typewriter?'

'She doesn't mind what I do.' Nicola swung round in the swivel chair. 'Why do you stay here if you don't like it? You're always complaining.'

'Why indeed?' said Helen, throwing a pile of papers on to the floor and flopping down on the squeaky sofa. 'Several reasons. A, Freddie's my best friend – we were at college together and she likes having me. B, I can't afford an hotel at the moment because I'm out of work. And C, I'm very fond of Barry. We've known each other a long time.' She stretched out her legs, smoothing her skirt. It was an Indian cotton with a rich pattern of reds and pinks.

'Yes, he's told me.' Nicola began to type a new line of patterns, trying to swallow the pain that was swelling in her throat.

Helen said, 'Where is he now? He was polishing the car when I came in. Is this the night you're taking him home to meet your parents?'

'Yeah. He wants to make a good impression.'

'What's your mother going to think of him?'

'I don't give a shit,' said Nicola. 'I wish to God we weren't going.'

Helen picked up an old *Listener* and began to flick through the pages. 'I've got this audition on Monday,' she said. 'I wonder what sort of competition I'll have.'

Nicola's only interest in Helen's success was to get her away from Grassley to Brighton as soon as possible. She said, 'Well, I hope you get on all right. Is it a big part?'

'I thought I told you – it's Nora in *A Doll's House*. Don't you know the play? I thought *everybody* knew it.'

Nicola ripped the paper out of the typewriter and crushed it into a ball. 'I haven't had time to read plays,' she snapped. 'I've been too busy with homework. When I'm as old as you are, I expect I'll have read it.' Helen brought out the worst in her, as her mother did.

'Keep your hair on,' said Helen mildly. 'I expect you're feeling groggy with your period. Is that it?'

'How do *you* know I've got my period?' She felt a pang of anxiety in case her white skirt was stained.

Helen looked up. 'Barry told me.'

'What did he tell you *that* for?' The pain in her throat was there again.

'Better not mention it to him,' said Helen. 'It might be embarrassing.'

'I'll mention whatever I like. Why did he tell you?'

Helen tossed back her hair and frowned. 'Listen to me,' she said. 'I know you think you own him, but you don't, you know. He's a free person, and so am I. If you want the truth, I asked him if you were good in bed, and –'

'You *what*?'

'You heard me. He said not yet, you hadn't got it going properly and things were held up because of your period. There, does that satisfy you?'

'No, it doesn't.' Nicola stood up but her legs were shaking so much that she sat down again. 'You should never have asked him – it's nothing to do with *you*.'

'Oh, yes it is. He told me you knew about us sleeping together so you needn't pretend. It's –'

'And have you been with him again?' She could hardly breathe.

'That's *our* affair, isn't it? But you don't have to worry – he isn't the only man in my life – not by any means. Don't be so old-fashioned, Nicola – you're behaving like a jealous wife.' She got up and turned on a bright false smile. 'And now I must go and look through my lines for tomorrow. You really should read more, you know – give you a bit of perspective.' She went out, closing the door, and Nicola was alone, the ball of screwed-up paper clenched in her hand. Barry and his father were smiling at her from the wall, and in a sudden agony of rage she stuffed the paper against her mouth, biting and gnawing it, bruising her lips. It was the kind of hysteria that her mother had sometimes provoked, but this was an adult passion, totally different, stronger, more frightening.

At last she tore the damp crumple of paper from her mouth and dropped it into the waste paper basket, where it lay among the latest discarded sheets of Freddie's book. She wanted with all her heart to run to Barry, out into the sunny street where he would still be polishing the car. She wanted to tell him what Helen had said, to ask for his reassurance, but she knew he would be impatient with her jealousy as he had been before. She would just have to stifle her fears and try to behave as if nothing had happened.

R

Robert stared down into his coffee, trying to focus all his thoughts on the small gold-rimmed cup in its small gold-rimmed saucer, the tiny row of bubbles at the rim of the dark liquid. Beyond the cup he could see Nicola's feet poking below her frayed dirty jeans. The toes of her white shoes were streaked with tar and grass stains. She was sitting on the drawing room settee with Barry, and his feet were close to hers on the blue carpet. He was wearing sneakers, white with red stripes. Julia was sitting slightly behind Robert on an upright chair, but he was aware of her bright green dress. Mrs Laurie had just served the coffee and gone out; the four of them were alone together for the first time. Julia was using her 'company' voice, pleasant, well-modulated, treacherous.

'So what are your plans, Barry?' she was saying. 'You won't encourage Nicola to leave school, will you? Not till she's taken her A-levels?'

'I'll do what *I* want to do,' said Nicola. 'Don't try to get at him, mother.'

'Let Barry answer for himself,' said Robert. The headache he had been expecting gave its first tentative throb. He had, as far as possible, avoided looking at Barry. His handshake had been warm and firm and the general impression was of a thin, sunburnt youth with bad skin and brown hair neatly combed but a great deal too long. Nicola looked incredibly untidy and her skimpy red blouse hung open at the front, revealing the gentle cleft between her round little breasts.

Barry said, 'If she doesn't want to stay at school it seems a waste of time. She's got these ideas for a hair salon. Start at the bottom and work up to having her own place. Sounds great.'

'And you don't need A-levels for hairdressing,' said Nicola. 'Thank God!'

'We had higher ambitions for you,' said Julia. 'Why do you think we paid for you to go to the Convent.'

'I didn't ask for it, did I? I'd rather have gone to Grassley High, like Barry.'

'That's very ungrateful. Don't you think so, Barry?'

'I don't see why, to be truthful. I liked it there.'

'But you've only got a job in a garage, haven't you?' said Julia. 'Don't you feel the need for something better?'

He shook his head. 'I like working with cars. I don't want to get into the rat race anyway.'

Robert forced himself to look at Barry more closely. Wide brown eyes – gentle and luminous, small nose, long, curving mouth. It was a peaceful face and he couldn't dislike the boy as he had imagined he would; he could only envy him.

Julia said, 'But don't you find it *stultifying* – lying on your back under cars all day?'

'I'm not on my back – I'm under the bonnet half the time – but I really enjoy it. A car comes in with something wrong and I suss out the problem and fit a new part. Make it go again. It's a good feeling. And I like working with my hands.'

Robert looked at Barry's hands holding the delicate coffee cup. They were brown and slender, with garage grime under the finger-nails. He thought of them slipping into Nicola's open shirt . . . He drained the last of his coffee and put his cup and saucer down on the table with a clatter.

'More coffee, dear?' asked Julia behind him.

The false lilt in her voice, wifely and solicitous, made him wince. 'No – no, thanks.'

'What did your father do, Barry?' Now her tone was cool and patronising.

'He was a milkman. My mother says he'd be alive today if he hadn't been out on deliveries that last freezing winter. He died of pleurisy.' He sighed and took a sip of coffee. 'He never complained – he was great.'

'I'm *sure* he was,' said Julia. 'I have a great respect for the milkmen –'

'Then why don't you have a respect for garage mechanics?' said Nicola accusingly.

'I *do* respect them, darling. It's just that some of us are equipped for better things, that's all.'

'Better things!' scoffed Nicola. 'You really look down on working people, don't you? They're a kind of *enemy*, to your way of thinking.'

Robert didn't want to get involved but he felt he must make his position clear. 'You've got it wrong, Nicola – we don't think that at all. The British working man is the salt of the earth and –'

'Yeah,' cried Nicola. 'So long as he doesn't make any trouble! But as soon as he stands up for his rights and goes on strike you say he's irresponsible or militant or something.'

Barry said, 'Cool it, Nick. It won't do any good.'

Nicola stood up. 'I'm thirsty – can I have some wine, Daddy. I don't like this coffee.'

Robert thought the coffee delicious – better than Ivy ever made. 'Just one glass, then,' he said. 'There's a bottle opened in the fridge. Barry, would you like some wine?'

He shook his head, smiling first at Robert and then at Nicola. 'I think the coffee's great.'

'You think *all* coffee's great,' said Nicola, making a face at him over her shoulder as she went out.

Julia said to Barry, 'I imagine you're some kind of a Socialist?'

'That's right.'

'Which end of the spectrum?'

'Oh, the red end. I'm into Marxism at the moment.'

'Is that so?' Robert heard the ring of triumph in her voice. 'And what does your mother think about it?'

'She's sympathetic. A bit woolly, but she feels the same

102

basically.'

Julia drew in her breath, a prelude, Robert knew, to some kind of pronouncement. 'You can imagine we're not in favour of Nicola leaving home,' she said. 'And especially so after what you've just told me.'

'She'll soon be seventeen,' said Barry. 'And anyway she's got the same ideas as I have.'

The door opened and Nicola was back, carrying a glass brimful of white wine, spilling it on to her jeans as she slumped beside Barry on the settee. She looked pale and tired and there was a fiery little pimple on her chin, but Robert's love for her, his wild impossible desire, was stronger than ever before.

'Are you giving them the works, babe?' she said, taking a gulp of wine.

'Not really,' said Barry. 'Just answering your mother's questions.' He looked intently at Julia as he spoke. His eyes were dark and glittering, his mouth taut with strain. Robert could sense the approaching storm.

'What's up?' said Nicola, glaring at Julia over her glass. 'What have you been saying?'

'I've been saying that I want you home. I want you back in this house by Saturday evening, with all your belongings –'

'That's *rubbish*!' exploded Nicola. 'I've moved in to Barry's place for good – we're taking my books with us now. He's made me a super bookcase, haven't you, Barry?'

'You are *not* taking your books.' Julia got up and stood near the settee. The vivid green dress gave her face an unnatural pallor.

Robert's headache was hammering unbearably. He longed to escape into the garden or out in the car, but he knew he would have to see it through. 'Just a minute, Julia,' he said. 'Let's work this out in a friendly manner, can't we? There's no need to –'

Nicola had put down her glass on the table and was clinging to Barry's hand. 'Come *on*,' she was saying. 'Let's get the books and *go*!'

'You will *not* get your books,' went on Julia. 'The door of your bedroom is locked and I have the key. If you aren't back here on Saturday by six o'clock you'll be very sorry. *Both* of you.'

'You *bitch*!' Nicola picked up the wine glass and hurled it across the room. It missed her mother's shoulder by inches and splintered against the wall. She covered her face with her hands and broke into a torrent of weeping.

Barry got up and put his arms around her, pulling her against him. She buried her face in his shoulder, crying helplessly. Robert felt ill. He didn't know what to do or say; then the telephone rang, a merciful intrusion.

Julia marched across the room to answer it. 'Hello, Emily. Hang on a minute and I'll take the call in the bedroom. There's a bit of a problem at the moment.'

She put the receiver down on the table and glared at Robert. 'Tell Mrs Laurie to get rid of that broken glass. And put the receiver back when I've got there.' She hurried out of the room, slamming the door behind her.

Barry was stroking Nicola's hair. 'I think we'd better go,' he said. 'I'm really sorry it had to turn out like this.'

'I'm sorry, too,' said Robert. 'It's not the way I wanted it – you know that, don't you? I want Nicola home of course – but only if she's happy here. I want you both to be happy –'

He meant it, and she must have known that he did, because she pulled away from Barry and flung her arms round Robert's neck, pressing her soft lips on his cheek. He caught the scent of her hair, a special fragrance he had always noticed, always loved, and her nearness was such ecstasy that he held her closely for an instant, clutching her against him as if he would never let her go. Suddenly she pushed him away and twisted out of his arms. He could not speak, terrified that she had felt the trembling of his limbs, the stirring of his erection.

Barry was shaking him by the hand, bidding a friendly goodbye. Nicola was already out of the room. Alone in the drawing room, he saw the screaming faces in the wallpaper, a silent multiple outcry of pain and dread. The light was fading and as he switched on the standard lamp, the faces disbanded. Slowly he went to the telephone. He could hear Emily

Cartwright's grating monotone droning from the table top and he picked up the receiver and listened for a moment as she explained to Julia about some leaflets she was having printed. Then he replaced it and stared at the carpet, defeated by his own helpless misery. Fragments of glass glinted on the thick blue pile and he saw the severed base of the wine glass, gleaming like a silver medal in the light from the lamp.

He couldn't tell Mrs Laurie about the broken glass. Not yet. Later, when he had downed a whisky or two. But one day, he felt sure, he would tell her everything.

R

After two large whiskies and a Beethoven Quartet, Robert lifted the receiver to see if Julia was still on the telephone in the bedroom. The voice of Emily Cartwright came yapping out at him. '*John and I will fix it up between us,*' she was saying. I bet you will, thought Robert, replacing the receiver. Half an hour on the phone! How true it was that you could assess people by their friends. He disliked all Julia's; there wasn't one he would have chosen as a friend for himself.

He found Mrs Laurie in the kitchen, ironing one of his white shirts. The smell of the hot iron and steaming cotton reminded him of the days when his mother used to iron his school cricket shirts, the happy summer days of his childhood, before he even knew that Julia existed. She looked up with a smile, flushed with the ironing. He was drawn to look at the scar, but avoided it, concentrating on her eyes and her small, tender mouth. She carried on pressing the shirt, and as he watched her deftly weaving around the buttons he thought how competent she was at all her tasks; she had already proved her skill at cooking, sewing, arranging flowers and mending the vacuum cleaner. Perhaps Julia had been right to send Ivy away . . .

'I'm afraid there's been a small calamity in the drawing

room,' he told her. 'A wine glass was broken. I wonder if you'd mind sweeping up the bits?'

'Right away, Mr Slingsby.' She switched off the iron and folded his shirt, putting it on top of the pile and giving it a gentle little pat as she did so, a pat that seemed almost affectionate. She went to the broom cupboard, bending down to reach for the dustpan, and as she did so he saw a frill of pink lace appear below the hem of her brown skirt. Watching the lace as it frothed around her legs, he felt a surge of sexual excitement and turned away. Lusting after his daughter one minute and his housekeeper the next! What in God's name was the matter with him?

Mrs Laurie straightened, nursing the red plastic dustpan. 'I saw Nicola drive off with her boy friend,' she said. 'What a lovely-looking pair. So *young* – it breaks your heart.'

'Yes, well, I'm afraid there was a bit of trouble.' He hadn't meant to speak of it, knew that he shouldn't, but he desperately needed to talk to her.

'I'm so sorry.'

'Yes – Nicola threw the wine glass – lost her temper with her mother –'

Mrs Laurie paused on her way to the door and looked at him with a sad little smile. 'Try not to worry. It's the same in every family – youngsters asserting their independence. We wouldn't respect them if they didn't, would we?'

He gazed at her helplessly, shaking his head. 'My wife has no respect for anybody,' he said in a low voice. 'That's the problem.'

She met his eyes, a look which told him that she understood and sympathised but knew that she was not allowed to say so. She turned to go but he laid a restraining hand on her arm. 'We don't need to pretend, not between ourselves,' he said. 'You know the situation – you could hardly miss it. It can't be pleasant for you, but don't leave us, will you? Nicola might come back – she might be forced to – and she'll need you very much.'

'I shan't leave,' said Mrs Laurie. 'Not yet awhile. I'm happy here, in spite of the problems.' She glanced down at his hand,

106

still resting on her sleeve, and he was suddenly aware of the warmth of her arm through the thin white blouse. He gave it the ghost of a squeeze before he withdrew his hand and turned away, pretending to study the calendar on the wall above the refrigerator. Pretence, he thought, as she went out. All the time, *pretence* . . . It struck him that all his relationships were undermined by hypocrisy. Hatred for Julia, desire for Nicola, boredom with old Dick Benson, a forced and difficult patter of jokes with the men and girls at Granger Coe, and now a deepening attraction for Mrs Laurie. In none of these relationships was he permitted to be honest. But of course there was nothing strange about that; it was everybody's problem. *I hate you, I want you, you bore me, you frighten me, be quiet, die, go away, talk to me, don't leave me* . . . All for the most part unspoken, boiling under the surface of our daily lives while we compose a face that will never betray the truth. No wonder we are sick, he thought. No wonder I suffer with these appalling headaches . . .

He was on his way to the door (back to the drawing room, to another whisky, another record – and perhaps to Mrs Laurie) when he saw a typed envelope on the counter near the pile of ironing. He looked at it closely as he passed, wondering if it might be a letter for him that had come by a later post, but it had already been opened. *Mrs Alison Laurie*, it said. Alison. Oh, yes – the perfect name! Suddenly she became for him a woman in her own right: not a housekeeper, not a widow, not an ex-school-teacher, but *Alison*. He remembered Julia saying that they would not call her by her Christian name as they had done with Ivy. Keep her in her place, she had said. Julia could do what she liked, but he would call her Alison.

N

'She can't *make* me go back, can she?' said Nicola.

'Shouldn't think so.' Barry steered the car with one hand while he lit a cigarette. 'I think she could get a court order or something till you're eighteen, but she'd hate the publicity. She'd never do it, would she?'

'So I'll stay put. Is that O.K.?'

'Course it's O.K. You like it with us, don't you? No problems?'

'No,' she lied. 'It's marvellous.'

It was a cloudless dusk, the dark sky fading to a silvery green at the horizon, and Barry had suggested a country spin to cool off after the row at Birch House. She sat in the low bucket seat beside him, huddled in her anorak, her hair whipped across her face as they tore along a quiet road. She couldn't tell him how she felt about Helen. It was terrible, really, the way you couldn't be honest with people. It was partly because of hurting them, but mostly because you were ashamed of your feelings and afraid they wouldn't like you.

She glanced at Barry now, his cigarette glowing against the dark hedgerow. She wanted to tell him about her father, too, her fear that Sally could be right, that the way he had clung to her that evening was more than just a normal fatherly hug. But Barry would never believe her. He'd think she was imagining things – or trying to dramatise herself.

He said, 'I know what you mean about your mother. Phew, what a woman!' He increased their speed, ripping the quiet road with the long glare of the headlights and the roar of the exhaust.

'Thank God you agree with me about her,' she shouted. 'People sometimes think she's charming – can't see how phoney she is.'

'It's in her face – hard as nails.' He looked at Nicola and

smiled. 'You're like your father, aren't you? I think he's great. A bit nervy, but really nice.'

'He's all right.'

'I'd like to see him on his own some time,' Barry went on, slowing down for a bend. 'Meet him in a pub for a beer or something.'

'Why not?'

'Yeah – maybe I'll phone him up and fix it.'

They drove in silence for a while and she leaned her head back, watching the sky with its first pricking of stars.

'I'm not going back,' she said. 'My mother can do her worst. You aren't bothered, are you? I mean all that crap about "you'll both be sorry"?'

'Course not. What can she do? Stop you getting your books back, maybe? Stop your pocket money?'

'She never gives me any – never has. It's Daddy. He gives me masses.' They were driving under an arch of trees, the winking lights of an aircraft mingling with the stars among the branches. She sat up and hugged her anorak around her. The night wind was cold as they raced along the lanes. 'I *hate* my mother,' she said. 'I hate her sodding guts!'

'Don't be vindictive, Nick. I wish to God you hadn't thrown that wine glass. So *childish*.'

'It wasn't childish – you don't understand.'

'Yes it was.'

'It *wasn't*. Stop the car – I want to *talk* to you –' The tears rushed to her eyes.

He slammed on the brakes and pulled in to the side of the road, bumping onto a grassy verge. 'Now tell me – what's all this about?' He switched off the engine and the lights, plunging her into an anguish of darkness and silence.

'You just don't *understand*,' she sobbed. 'You'd be the same if Freddie was like *her*.' How could he know of the madness that can strike when you are goaded and tormented, year after year?

He put his arm round her shoulders. 'I know it isn't easy, babe. But you only upset yourself. It was lucky you missed her with that glass. Suppose you'd cut her eye or something.'

'I wish I had!'

'Don't *talk* like that! I must say I don't fancy having things thrown at *me*.'

'I wasn't throwing it *at* her – I was just *throwing* it. I want you to *sympathise* – not be *against* me.'

'I *do* sympathise, for Christ's sake – but I hate tantrums.'

'If you call that a tantrum you *don't* sympathise.'

He took his arm away from her shoulder. 'Females!' he groaned. 'They're all the same – I thought you were different.' He started the car and they roared away.

She wanted to scream at him about Helen, taunt him for telling her about their private problems, but her tongue felt swollen and she couldn't make a sound. Her blowing hair was sticking to the tears on her cheeks and she wiped her face on the sleeve of her anorak. At last she managed to speak. 'I want to go back,' she sobbed. 'Take me *back*.'

'What? To your parents?'

'*No – no* – to Freddie –'

'O.K. I'll turn round when I can. But *she* doesn't like tantrums either, you know. Cut-throat-Connie goes berserk with that knife but she won't have *me* blowing up – never has. I think that's why I smoke so much, to tell you the truth. She wants me to be too bloody perfect – like my father.'

Nicola glanced at him as he slowed down to reverse into a country track. She hadn't realised that he had trouble with Freddie.

On the way home she closed her eyes. The movement of the car, the roar of the exhaust and the wind in her face were suddenly all she wanted to think about. There were too many problems . . .

N

Nicola was awakened the next morning by a gentle knock on the door. She began to tremble, sure that it would be Barry; she had told him that her period would be over on Friday.

'Come in,' she said, pushing the hair out of her eyes.

The door opened slowly and Freddie appeared, carrying a mug of tea. She was wearing a blue housecoat with frayed cuffs and her frizzy hair was tied up in a yellow chiffon scarf.

'Oh, hello.' Nicola rubbed her eyes and sat up, disappointed yet relieved. She dreaded making love again; she was frightened of the pain but much more frightened of failing to please him.

'You've overslept, Honey-child, so I thought I'd bring you a cuppa and have a little chat. We've hardly had a chance, have we?'

Nicola took the heavy mug in her hands and sipped the hot sweet brew. 'That's gorgeous,' she said. 'Fancy you carrying it up all those stairs.'

Freddie smiled and went to the window. 'Another lovely day. Helen went off early – I hope she gets that part, poor love.'

Nicola thought, You don't hope it as much as I do. Without Helen she was sure she could be happy at Station Road. Get the sex thing right, find herself a job – and everything would be great.

'She went to bed early last night,' Freddie went on. 'Getting her beauty sleep for the big day. I sat up late with Barry – he was telling me about the row with your mother.'

'Yeah – it was ghastly.' Nicola sipped her tea. She hoped he hadn't mentioned the wine glass. The previous evening was like a bad dream; here in her cosy room with Freddie and the comforting tea and a patch of sunlight on the freshly-painted wall, she was suddenly happy. Next week she would have another try for a job. She had enquired at every hairdresser in Grassley without success; she would have to go to Tonbridge.

Freddie sat down on the end of her bed. 'I've been worrying about you, love,' she said slowly. 'Lying awake for hours. I wonder if perhaps you ought to go back home – just for a while?'

'*No – never*! Oh, *please* don't ask me – you don't know what my mother's like.'

111

'I know she's a very difficult lady but she doesn't ill-treat you, does she, and –'

'She *does* ill-treat me. She doesn't *hit* me or anything but she makes me miserable – *that's* ill-treating!'

'Tell me about it,' said Freddie. Her eyes, so much like Barry's, were sad and attentive. 'What does she do that upsets you so much?'

'She never listens to anything I say – she never has – it's hopeless. We hardly ever speak to each other now. She's always making me feel horrible – I think she really hates me. She tried to split me up from my girl friend – she wouldn't let me have a cat – she burnt my favourite poster, just because it was modern and sexy. Oh, there are millions of things. And she's beastly to Daddy – you should hear the way she speaks to him. Then all smiles and lovey-dovey crap when visitors come. Makes me *sick*!' She paused for breath, trembling.

'Tell me something nice about her – there must be *something*.'

Nicola was silent. She didn't want to remember, but one incident flashed into her mind – the day when she had fallen out of an apple tree in the orchard and broken her wrist. Her mother had driven her to the hospital for an X-ray, waited with her for hours and read her stories from a magazine.

'She's quick at doing things,' said Nicola grudgingly. 'She always does what she says she'll do – but it's mostly something nasty. She's very clever – always at meetings and lectures. Barry says she's a fascist.'

Freddie smiled. 'Don't take too much notice of Barry – he's a bit of an extremist at the moment. He's always on about fascism.'

'Well, I agree with him,' said Nicola hotly. 'He really cares about *people*. My mother doesn't – you should hear the things she says. And she's terribly mean with money – she won't even buy a cancer flag. Serve her right if she got it.'

'Nick – you mustn't talk like that. Really you mustn't.' She scratched at a milk stain on the front of her housecoat. 'I wonder *why* she's so difficult. Have you ever asked yourself that question?'

'She just *is*, that's all. Always has been.'

'Maybe she had trouble with her own parents?'

'Dunno – she never mentions them. Anyway, I'm not going back – I'd rather sleep in a bus shelter.'

Freddie shook her head. 'Poor lamb – I just want to do the right thing, that's all.'

'Staying here with you – that's the right thing. For *me*, anyway.'

'I hope so, I really do.' Freddie got up and took the empty mug. 'I must get on,' she said. 'I've got a chapter to type before lunch or I'm behind schedule.'

'And I *can* stay, can't I?'

'I think you'll have to, honey. Bus shelters are so draughty!'

R

'Well, that's another week gone by,' said Dick Benson. 'The older you get, the faster they seem to go.'

'True enough,' said Robert. He found it tiring to respond to this kind of remark but one had to make an effort. Dick was a good friend, always pleasant, always interested in his welfare. They were in the office block washroom at Granger Coe. Dick was standing at the urinal and Robert was trying to dry his hands in the feeble draught of the hot-air machine.

'Working at your garden again this weekend, Dick?'

Dick smiled and nodded, zipping up his fly and joining Robert at the washbasins. His round pink face was alight with enthusiasm. 'I'm going to fix up a new arrangement I've got for the greenhouse,' he explained. 'Marvellous gadget for watering and ventilation – does the lot while you're away on holiday. Bloody ingenious.' He fondled the bulge of flesh which hung over the top of his trousers; he didn't seem to mind being fat. 'You aren't a gardening man, are you, Bob?'

'No, we've got an old chap comes in – really takes a pride

in it. I just like to see the flowers.' This kind of chit-chat was infectious – and rather soothing. He took out his handkerchief and finished drying his hands.

'How are things at home?' said Dick. 'You were having a spot of bother with your daughter going off.'

'Still am. Julia and I don't see eye to eye about it, I'm afraid.' He had argued for hours with her the previous night – if you could call it arguing; Julia kept turning her head away, yawning, examining her nails, letting him state his views then totally ignoring them and telling him dogmatically what she had decided to do.

'It's the same with us over Caroline,' said Dick. 'Hettie always takes her side. They're like a couple of schoolgirls – giggling together – no discipline at all. Makes me look like the heavy-handed father.'

'I can't imagine that,' said Robert. 'With us it's the other way round. Julia is much too strict – always has been. That's why Nicola's pushed off – I'm sure of it.'

'Ah well – takes all sorts, I suppose. See you on Monday.' He made for the door. 'Have a good weekend.'

'And you.'

Have a good weekend . . . What a hope! If Nicola came back it would be even more traumatic than if she didn't. He couldn't forget the way she had torn herself from his embrace the previous evening and his stomach turned cold whenever he thought of it.

It wasn't until he was in the Rover fastening his seat belt that he began to think of Alison. How did she get that scar? And what had her husband been like? They weren't things you could ask, exactly, but maybe she would tell him of her own accord. He thought of her bending down at the broom cupboard, the pink lace, the wide, firm hips, and his desire returned, disturbingly strong. He gripped the steering wheel and drove home a great deal faster than he usually did.

R

Julia was in the utility room when Robert went through from the garage. She stood beside the dusty window, the low sun gleaming on her blue silk blouse and the formal scrolls of her bleached hair.

'Hello,' he said. 'Had a good day?' He always tried to start the evening on a friendly note but she hardly ever responded and soon came out with some abrasive comment.

'Tiring,' she said. 'Mrs Laurie and I have been defrosting the freezers this afternoon. Ivy should have done it weeks ago – thank heaven we've got someone reliable at last. Tomorrow she's going to clean things up in here – it's an absolute pig-sty.' She waved a glittering hand. 'All those books can go for a start,' she said. 'I might get a pound or two for them at that shop in the High Street.'

'There's a poetry book there that belongs to Nicola,' said Robert. 'Hadn't you better make sure there are no more of hers – or mine?'

'You can look through them if you like – it's a moth-eaten collection.'

You can look through them if you like . . . you can look through them if you like . . . 'I shall certainly look through them,' he said bitterly, 'with or without your permission.' He saw the Keats on top of the pile, its gilt-lettered spine catching a gleam of sunlight.

Julia said, 'If she doesn't come back tomorrow she'll never see any of her books again – I shall take them all along with these and get rid of them.'

'You'll do no such thing!' he cried. 'What about those teenage novels – and that set of encyclopaedias my father gave her?'

'I can't help that. I said she'd be sorry, didn't I? Punishments are useless unless they really hurt.' She picked up a broken china vase from the window ledge. 'She needs to be taught a lesson. She's an evil-tempered child. She broke this vase, if you remember – threw a book across the room and knocked it off the mantelpiece. You were going to mend it, but you never did.'

Robert had not repaired the vase because there were fragments missing and the join would have been too obvious. 'It was that kitten – she wanted it so desperately.' He heard a catch in his voice. 'It would have been good for her to have a cat to care for – an only child needs a pet, and –'

'What nonsense!' She dismissed the subject, turning away to inspect an old transistor radio which stood beside the vase on the window ledge. Robert made for the kitchen, stopping on his way to pick up the Keats and slip it into his pocket. He could hardly stop Julia disposing of the books – she had the key to Nicola's room and could easily do it while he was at work – but if she did, he would buy some new ones to replace them. At least he wasn't short of money, thank God.

In the kitchen he came face to face with Mrs Laurie, who was hurrying in from the hall. 'Oh, Mr Slingsby,' she said. 'You're wanted on the telephone. I thought I heard the car.' Her eyes were brimming with light and friendliness.

'Who is it?' he said.

'I didn't ask – I'm sorry.'

'Always ask, would you, when you take a call?' He smiled at her.

'Of course.'

He went into the drawing room and shut the door. Could it be Nicola? He sat down at the telephone table before he lifted the receiver. Surprisingly, it was anxiety he felt, rather than the usual excitement – anxiety and a hint of irritation. Mrs Laurie's eyes – Alison's eyes – had been so bright and untroubled, so incredibly soft and sympathetic. It was Alison he wanted to talk to, not Nicola. And that was a most amazing and liberating thought . . .

R

'Slingsby, here.'

'Oh, hello. This is Barry – Barry Mitchell.'

'Hello, Barry. Anything wrong?'

'No – I was wondering if we could meet for a bit of a chat? Just half an hour or so.'

'Of course. I'd like that very much.'

'How about Tuesday? My carpentry class finishes at nine. I could meet you about ten past in *The Star*.'

Julia's Council Meeting. 'That would be splendid, Barry. I'll see you there. In the Lounge Bar?'

'Great.'

'Will Nicola be coming home tomorrow?'

'Not a chance. Sorry.'

'I thought not. Goodbye for now.'

'Cheers.'

Why had Barry made this contact? His own father was dead; was this the reason? The need for a father figure? But maybe he liked me, thought Robert. Maybe he actually liked me.

Apprehension was mingled with pleasure as he considered Tuesday's meeting. He knew no other teenagers, apart from two or three of Nicola's friends from the Convent who used to come for tea in the kitchen with Ivy. There were typists and filing clerks at Granger Coe, of course: girls with painted eyes who were polite to him and giggled behind his back; boys with spots and B.O. who seemed to talk about nothing but sex and football.

Nicola had called him a 'fuddy-duddy' and a 'silly old square' and he knew it was true. He envied men who could wear old jeans and T-shirts and mix quite happily with people half their age. Perhaps when he got to know Barry it would help him to adjust. He guessed that Nicola and Barry would be sleeping together, but there must be no possible question of her becoming pregnant. It was Barry's responsibility and Robert knew he must raise the matter, however difficult it might be.

N

'I'll have to go to the doctor, that's all,' she said. 'We can't go on like this.'

They had been to the same wood as before and now they were sitting in the open M.G. with Coke and hamburgers from a transport café. The car was parked in a lay-by and they were blown and buffeted by the heavy traffic, but Nicola hardly noticed. She could think of nothing but the pain and misery of yet another failure.

'It's rotten luck,' said Barry. 'Why did it have to happen to *us*?'

'To *me*, you mean,' she said, eating slowly without appetite. 'There's nothing wrong with *you*.' She would have to ask for advice at a clinic or something. 'Trouble is,' she went on, 'I haven't a clue where to go without it getting back to my parents. Mother knows so many people with all her committees and things.' It was Saturday, the deadline day for going home, a sultry afternoon, overcast and windless. The trees were motionless and dusty; it hadn't rained for nearly a fortnight.

Barry ate the last of his hamburger. 'Why don't you ask Helen?' he said. 'She's been married – she knows all about these things and – '

'Helen? I'm not asking *her* – I'd rather *die*!'

'What's wrong? She's great – I thought you got on O.K. with her.'

'Well, I can't *stick* her, if you want to know. She's always putting me down. She'd like to get me out – I know she would.'

'That's rubbish, Nick. You're jealous because I've had it off with her, that's all it is. You're not to talk like that.'

Nicola wanted to ask if he'd had it off with her again, but she daren't, in case he had. 'And *you're* not to talk to her about me behind my back,' she cried. 'Telling her I'd got the curse and everything.'

Barry looked hurt and bewildered, an expression she had seen before when he was cornered. 'I don't know what you're on about,' he said, picking crumbs off the front of his blue T-shirt.

'Yes you do – she told me – so you needn't put on that innocent act. I think it was horrible of you to tell her about our private things like that –'

'She asked me,' he said. 'I just told her the truth, that's all.'

'You should have told her to mind her own damn business.' Nicola threw her empty Coke tin out into the road where it clattered away in the slipstream of a passing lorry.

Barry looked at her, raising his eyebrows. 'Throwing things again?' he said.

'Oh, shit – it's only because I'm so *miserable*!'

'Baby, I'm sorry.' He put his hand on her thigh, and the touch of his fingers through her thin dress made her tremble. 'You've got it all out of proportion,' he said. 'You asked me about Helen, didn't you? That day at Hastings? I told you the truth, like I told her. What's the difference?'

'We're in love with each other – that's the difference.'

He took his hand away. 'Oh, *I* don't know. You always seem to *complicate* everything.'

'But don't you understand that I couldn't possibly ask her about – about us?'

'Sure I can. Yeah, I was a fool to suggest it.' He smiled at her but it wasn't his usual easy smile. 'Go to the Family Planning, Nick. They'll help. Maybe you need a little op. or something?'

'An *operation*? I'm bloody well not having myself cut about – not up *there*!' A wave of horror ran through her body, making her legs tingle.

'It wouldn't be anything serious. You'll have to do *something*, won't you, so we can enjoy ourselves properly.'

'I'll *never* enjoy it,' she burst out. 'I'm sure I won't. All this has put me right off.'

'Oh, Christ! Don't say that – *please*!'

A coach went by, belching fumes. 'Let's go,' she cried. 'I'm sick enough as it is without these beastly traffic smells. I don't know why you had to park on the main road, anyway.'

'It was near the caff, that's why. We wanted our hamburgers, didn't we?'

'*I* didn't. I didn't want *anything*.'

He started the car and drove off with a scream of skidding tyres. Then she let herself cry.

N

'What's up with the two of you?' said Freddie, as Nicola and Barry slumped down at the kitchen table for supper. 'You look all in. Trouble?'

Nicola said nothing, leaving Barry to answer.

Two candles, in old Chianti bottles, flickered over the red and white checked tablecloth, giving the scene a Bohemian glamour although Nicola knew that the cloth was stained with tea and wine and bacon fat. The sink and the fridge and the untidy dresser glinted vaguely in the background. No place was laid at the table for Helen; that was a consolation. Nicola was deeply upset by the failure of the day. After the row in the car they had mooched around Grassley until dark, ending up in an amusement arcade. Barry had been moody, betraying his distress by the set of his lips, the flat tone of his voice and the angry way he kicked at the fruit machines when no winnings appeared.

'No trouble,' he said now, tilting back his chair. 'Tired, that's all.'

'You shouldn't be tired at your age.' Freddie spooned out macaroni cheese from an oven-blackened dish. Nicola remembered Ivy saying the same thing to her. Older people expected too much; they thought that because you were young you should always be bursting with energy.

'Well, I *am* tired,' said Barry. 'Bloody tired.'

'It's hard work on those fruit machines,' said Nicola.

'Funny,' said Barry, unsmiling.

'You smoke too much,' said Freddie. 'Nick, can't you talk some sense into him?'

'He'll do what he likes, won't he.' It was a statement, not a question; she'd probably start smoking herself before long; it would make her feel closer to him, stronger, not so childish . . .

Barry put a large forkful of macaroni into his mouth and they all ate in silence for a while. This kind of atmosphere was unusual at Station Road, and Nicola could hardly eat. She poured herself a tumbler of water from the big glass jug but when she tried to drink it she found she couldn't swallow without making a loud gulping sound and she gave up.

At last Barry put down his fork and looked at his mother. 'Any news of Helen?' he said.

Nicola's heart began to thump.

Freddie nodded. 'I forgot to tell you – she phoned at teatime. She hasn't got the lead – too old – but she's got a smaller part in the same play. She'll be coming back tomorrow to collect her things – they start rehearsals next week.' She reached out and took an apple from the fruit bowl. 'She's pleased but miserable, if you know what I mean. She'd really set her heart on playing Nora.' She took a large juicy bite from the apple and munched it thoughtfully.

So Helen would soon be gone for good. Nicola took a deep breath and approached her half-eaten macaroni cheese with new interest. It was a special recipe of Freddie's, mixed with crispy fried bacon and onions and flavoured with nutmeg.

Barry pushed away his empty plate. 'Oh, well,' he said. 'I suppose she couldn't have stayed here forever.'

'She certainly couldn't,' cried Freddie. 'Eating like a horse and not paying me anything.'

'I'm going to Tonbridge next week to look for a job,' said Nicola quickly, feeling her cheeks go hot.

'I didn't mean *that*, honey! You're welcome – you've got special problems.'

'So has Helen,' said Barry.

'Yes,' replied Freddie, 'but she's old enough to look after herself.' She pushed the bowl of fruit towards them. 'I haven't made a sweet,' she said. 'I didn't have time. I've finished that frightful Chapter Fifteen – hope to goodness it's all right.'

Barry took a banana and got up. 'I'll see what's on the telly,' he said.

'I'll wash up,' said Nicola. 'I don't want any fruit.'

'Bless you, Honey-child. I'll have another look at that chapter, then. I'll take it up to my room.'

Alone in the kitchen, Nicola cleared the onion skins and bacon rind from the draining board and washed up the dishes, putting the macaroni dish to soak. Freddie could do that tomorrow. She would have loved to tell her everything, ask for advice, confess her jealousy of Helen. But of course it was impossible; it wouldn't be fair to Barry. It's terrible, she thought, when you can't say what you want to say. It's as if your mind is shut away behind bars, cold and helpless, while your body moves about the ordinary world. She had to talk to *someone*. Maybe she'd try to get things going with Sally again . . .

From the living room she could hear the shouts and gunfire of a television film, and she decided to go and watch with Barry. She didn't enjoy that sort of film – she preferred the sad and sentimental kind – but she had to do everything she could to make him like her, make up for the sex thing.

She reminded herself that Helen was leaving, but the thought of it didn't really comfort her; in some peculiar way it made her even more uneasy. She hung up the wet tea-cloth, took a deep breath and went into the living room.

N

The curtains were drawn and there was no light but the flicker from the television screen. The gangster film was still in progress; a boy in jeans was tied to a chair, sweating with fright and faced by a brutal-looking man who was smoking a big cigar, his thick lips smiling round it.

Barry was lying back on the sofa, his legs outstretched, a cigarette glowing between his fingers, the smoke curling gently in the half light. As Nicola slumped beside him, it flurried for a while then settled again into softly floating wisps of blue. Like little chiffon scarves, she thought, pleased with the simile, happy to be close to Barry and alone with him.

The man with the cigar approached his victim, waving the lighted butt close to his face. Nicola shuddered and turned away. She hated sadistic scenes like this and tried to forget the film, concentrating on Barry's profile, the sheen on his hair, the glint of the gold crucifix on a chain at his throat. I'll never want anyone but him, she thought; no one else in the world could ever be right. She longed for him to make love to her, not properly – she dreaded that – but to kiss and caress her as he used to do when they first went out together. She put out her hand and gently began to stroke his thigh, hoping to lure him away from the film.

For a while he did not respond, frowning a little as he gazed at the screen. Then suddenly he stubbed out his cigarette in the ashtray beside him and turned to face her. 'Oh, Christ,' he muttered, and his arms were around her, his lips on hers, kissing her so fiercely and so long that she was breathless and even a little frightened. When he released her, he knelt on the floor at her feet and began to caress her in a new and unexpected way so that soon she was aroused more strongly than ever before.

'Switch off the telly,' she whispered, trembling, but he seemed not to hear her, and over his shoulder she watched the screen through half-closed eyes, witnessing a scene of appalling violence as he touched her again and again with exquisite tenderness. She wanted to turn away or close her eyes, shutting out the agony of the boy in the chair, but she found it impossible to do so, for in some disturbing way it increased the intensity of her pleasure. Horror and ecstasy were fused into such a bewilderment of warring emotions, that as she reached her climax, she hardly knew which was which.

After a while she heard the slam of a door upstairs and she hastily pushed Barry away, pulling down her shirt and skirt; when she heard the flap of slippers on the lino in the hall, she was sitting sedately beside him, staring at the screen.

Freddie put her head round the door. 'Why are you gawping at all that American rubbish?' she said. 'You must be out of your minds.'

'We are,' said Barry, lighting a cigarette. 'Aren't we, Nick?'

She nodded, leaning her head on his shoulder and smiling with happiness. There was no need to see a doctor; she could be satisfied for a long time by that kind of pleasure and she hoped she would be able to satisfy Barry as well. Everything was going to be all right. He could never have made love to her like that if he'd cared about Helen. Surely he couldn't.

R

'I thought we could let her have it here,' said Julia. 'That should be big enough – from here to the kitchen window.'

Alison had asked if she might have a plot of ground to call her own – to grow a few flowers and perhaps to start a herb garden. It would give her a great deal of pleasure, she said; she used to enjoy gardening in the old days.

Robert stared at the rough plot, once a strawberry bed, now overgrown with long grass and buttercups. 'I should think that would be fine,' he said. 'Bernard could dig it over for her – put some fertiliser down.' He was oddly embarrassed to be standing there, discussing the matter with Julia. It reminded him of occasions when they had talked about their plans for Nicola – a swing in the orchard, a bicycle for her birthday – dutifully discussed with no sense of fun or excitement.

'There's no need for fertiliser,' said Julia. 'The buttercups are doing well enough.'

Robert said nothing. He would get some liquid manure and put it there himself. Anything to avoid more friction, more headaches. Alison was being discussed as if she were a child, in some subtle way demeaned, and Robert would have no part in it.

'The lunch was excellent, I thought,' he said.

'Yes – we're much better off with Mrs Laurie. Don't you agree?'

He nodded. 'She's very good – you were quite right.'

Julia gave him a thin smug smile. 'I told you, didn't I?'

It was Sunday afternoon and Nicola, of course, had not returned. Neither he nor Julia had mentioned their daughter. A taboo subject; guilt was keeping both of them quiet. There was nothing like guilt, he thought, to keep people quiet – or to make them speak too loudly . . . It was an unthinkable situation. He had the feeling that Julia neither expected nor wanted Nicola to come back, that she relished the thought of plotting a punishment and carrying it out with her usual efficiency.

He could see the gardener beyond the shrubbery, tending a bonfire. He was slow-moving, hump-backed, withdrawn, but good at his job and devoted to Julia; he had worked for her father and known her as a child. He always wore the same old deer-stalker hat, winter and summer, and often had an unlit pipe drooping from the corner of his mouth. It was there now as he prodded the bonfire with a stick, provoking a fresh cloud of blue smoke. The scent hung on the air, and the Sunday sounds of a motor-mower and shouting children echoed faintly from a distant garden.

'I'll tell Bernard to dig it over for her, then,' said Robert.

'*I'll* tell him. I've got to speak to him about the drive – the edges need cutting again.' She began to pick her way across the rough grass to the shrubbery, unsteady in her elegant shoes.

Robert went slowly into the house, childishly disappointed. He had wanted to tell Bernard himself.

R

He found Alison in the drawing room, arranging roses in a bowl on the telephone table by the window.

'It's all fixed up about your garden,' he told her. 'There's a nice little patch under the kitchen window. It's full of weeds at the moment but Bernard will dig it over for you. Mrs Slingsby has just gone to tell him.'

'Oh, thank you – I shall love it. I'll get some seeds for a herb garden – rosemary, marjoram, basil, thyme – aren't they beautiful names?'

'I'm sure they are, but it's double dutch to me – I'm no kind of cook. But why are you working on a Sunday afternoon?'

'The gardener's here – *he's* working.'

'Oh, he likes pottering about with his bonfire. He's on his own and it's something to do. He's worked here all his life.'

'I'm on my own too,' she said, smiling at him. 'And flowers aren't work. Anyway, I enjoy it – the cooking and cleaning and everything. I feel at home, you know. I can hardly believe I've only been here a week.'

'A week tomorrow, isn't it? When Nicola went off. I shan't forget how helpful you were that awful night.'

'It was a terrible cheek, I thought afterwards – inviting myself to bring my supper in here to eat with you. A *terrible* cheek, on my first evening.' She gave him a mischievous, unrepentant smile. 'But I couldn't leave you on your own – and you'd never have suggested it yourself.'

'You did absolutely right. A woman of character, I thought. A courageous sense of what is necessary, regardless of protocol. I liked it.'

'Thank you.' She adjusted a rose, pricked herself, squeaked like a schoolgirl, then laughed. He smiled at her, happy and excited to be with her like this, talking so easily.

She sucked her finger, inspected it off-handedly, and said, 'Will Nicola be coming back? I thought it would be nice to make her bed up – clean sheets – just in case. Put some flowers in her room. But the door's locked and –'

'I'm afraid she won't be coming back. Last night was the deadline.'

'Deadline?'

'Yes.' He decided not to explain. 'I'll give you her address and perhaps you'd forward any mail that comes for her.' He wrote it on a blank page in his diary, tore it out and handed it to her.

She nodded, putting it in her apron pocket. 'I'll do that,' she said. And then, very softly, 'I'm sorry.'

'Yes. It's a great sadness for me.' They stood looking out of the window, watching a blackbird running, listening, tipping up its tail. The smell of wood-smoke, a scent he had always loved, was suddenly so poignant that sorrow and happiness were fused into one strange indefinable emotion, swelling in his throat, bringing him close to tears.

'That lawn,' said Alison. 'Isn't it a picture? So smooth and flat. You could have a putting green. Have you ever thought of it?'

'Never.' He looked at her. Her scarred left cheek was turned away from him, and standing by the roses in the glow of the summer afternoon she seemed to him not only beautiful but intensely exciting. 'It's a nice idea,' he said and heard the waver in his voice. His nerves were throbbing and it seemed she must surely be aware of his feelings.

'I used to play a bit of golf with my husband,' she said. 'We were great pals and he liked me around but I was no golfer – except for the putting. I was good at that.' She looked up at him and grinned. 'You won't believe it – but once I did two holes in one on a putting green – both on the same day!'

'I believe it,' said Robert. He wanted to touch her, if only her arm or her shoulder, to say he would believe any lovely thing of her. But of course it was impossible. 'I like the idea,' he said. 'Maybe I'll fix it up.'

Nicola would like to play, he thought, remembering the

hotel lunch. It might be a way of luring her back for a visit at least, even if she brought Barry. And yet, he wondered, did he really *want* her back? It seemed that his passion for her, like a diverted mountain torrent, had suddenly transferred its force into a new channel. Faced with a totally impossible course, he had unwittingly – but following natural laws – taken a path of lesser resistance. He knew without doubt that he was falling in love with Alison, and he exulted in it.

'What about Mrs Slingsby?' she was saying. 'Would she like a putting green?'

'No. No she wouldn't.' He turned from the window, afraid that Julia might see them from the garden. 'It won't be easy,' he said. 'I know you understand.'

'Nothing in life is easy.' She gave him a clear, steady look. 'But friends can help, can't they?'

He smiled at her. 'Yes,' he said. 'Friends can make all the difference in the world.'

N

It was Sunday evening, calm and sunny. The M.G. was parked outside 27, Station Road, half on the pavement as usual and Barry sat with his bare brown arms folded over the steering wheel, waiting to take Helen to the station with all her luggage. The two enormous suitcases, strapped and bulging, were in the back of the car and Freddie and Nicola stood at the gate while Helen went upstairs to 'spend a last penny' as she put it. Nicola was happy. Not only was Helen going, but there had been no word from home; she had dreaded a phone call – or even a visit – from one of her parents. They must have accepted her departure, realised at last that she was old enough to live her own life. She was free from her mother, free for evermore. She would see her father, of course – she wanted to see him – but she would keep her distance in case there was any truth in what Sally had suggested. Not that she really believed it – he was nervy, that was all. Barry was meeting him in *The Star* on Tuesday night and she was glad about that; she wanted them to know one another.

Now Helen came bounding out of the house in a white blazer and red pleated skirt. Her hair was smoothly combed and her mouth bright with lipstick. 'I don't want to *go*,' she cried mock-tearfully, and threw her arms round Freddie's neck.

'Have fun,' said Freddie. 'And come again whenever you like.'

'You'd better change the sheets before next time,' said Helen, laughing, 'or they'll be walking out to meet me.'

'Did you take them off and fold them up?' asked Freddie, obviously nettled.

'You must be joking. I didn't have a second – getting packed and all.'

'Then don't blame me if they're still on the bed next time you come. I don't have a second either – writing books and all.' Her round blotchy face was a deeper pink, her mouth tight with annoyance.

'Come *on*,' called Barry from the car. He tapped his watch significantly.

Helen turned to Nicola. 'Bye, Nick. Don't do anything I wouldn't do – and that gives you all the scope you want!'

'Goodbye,' said Nicola. The implications of the remark were so clear and so biting that her happiness was gone in a flash. 'I hope you get on all right in the play,' she said, trying to be polite for Freddie's sake, but she heard the coldness in her voice and felt so hopelessly distraught that she turned and went into the house. She knew she would never be able to stand there and wave a cheerful farewell.

In her room she stared out of the window, pressing her forehead against the cool glass. The little station that she loved was awash with evening sunshine. Waiting on the strip of platform visible between the booking office and the signal box were two men in dark suits, heads thrown back in laughter, faces pink in the mellow light. The sun was low in a clear sky, the shadows of the men elongated on the golden platform. An old woman in a long black coat hobbled into view, pulling a suitcase on wheels. Two pigeons waddled and pecked beside her feet as she waited for the train.

And then, at last, as Nicola knew they would, came Barry and Helen. He was carrying her cases, bent with the weight of them, and she sauntered beside him in her dazzling white blazer. The scene was like a stage set, amazingly clear although it was some distance away. Barry put down the cases and stood facing Helen in the spotlight of sunshine, his gold crucifix flashing. The train was approaching, slowing down. Its rattle and bump and hiss had become familiar to Nicola in the past week and now she rejoiced in it; this was the train that would carry Helen away, leave Barry free to think of no one but herself, free to make love again and again in her room as he had done last night on the sofa . . .

The train appeared, sliding slowly to a standstill, and in an instant Barry was holding Helen closely against him, his thin arms dark against her blazer. Then she was clinging round his neck and they were kissing as if they would devour one another. He pushed and pressed against her lips in a strange circular motion, moving his hands behind her head as if he were fighting to force her mouth more deeply into his.

The two men were already on the train, the old woman heaving her suitcase into a compartment. A door slammed, yet still Barry and Helen clung together, until a porter alerted them and she drew away and leapt aboard. Barry handed up her cases, the back of his brown shirt dark with sweat, and the door was shut between them. Helen leaned out of the window, reaching out her hand to him as the whistle blew. Their fingers clung until the last moment as the train pulled out, and he stood alone, waving after the train. Then Nicola saw him turn and walk away behind the booking office, his shadow following him slowly out of sight.

Trembling uncontrollably, she sat down on the bed. She couldn't even cry, the pain of her jealousy was so immense. He must have known she would be watching; he was hurting her deliberately, flaunting his power, wanting her to be unhappy. Faintly from the living room she could hear the rhythmic thump of the typewriter. *She* didn't care if Barry was carrying on with Helen. All she cared about was that stupid Cut-throat-Connie or whatever her rotten name was.

Nicola picked up her shoulder bag and ran downstairs. Out in the street she had no idea where she would go. All she knew was that she had to get out of the house before Barry returned. And then she thought of Sally. Still trembling, she headed for the pet shop.

N

Nicola was disappointed to find no pets in the window; she had hoped to see a kitten or a cockatoo or a snuggle of hamsters to ease her spirits. Animals always made her feel better.

On her way up to the Winters' flat she saw the mark of her shoe on the wallpaper. There was no way to remove it except by repapering, and remorse was added to her jealousy and resentment, deepening the sickness of misery that overwhelmed her. She knew that Sally might well be out with a boyfriend but she prayed for her to be at home and to listen with patience and sympathy as she had done so often before.

At first there was no reply to the bell, but eventually the door was cautiously opened to reveal a frowning Mrs Winters. She wore a gaudy overall and her nose seemed longer and redder than usual, like a false nose at a party. From somewhere in the background came the chatter of a television programme.

'Oh, hello, Nicky,' she said. 'Sally isn't here.'

'When will she be back?'

'She won't. She's gone up north to be with Dominic. Packed up her job and gone up there for good by the sound of it.'

'Oh, Lord.' Nicola stared helplessly at Sally's mother who obviously wanted to get rid of her.

'We're watching the telly,' she said. 'You'll have to excuse me. Sally phoned you before she left – she wanted to say goodbye – but your mother answered and she wouldn't even take a message. If you want to know, she was very rude. She told Sal not to ring again. Think of that, after all the teas you've had here. Sally was furious – told her where to get off.'

Nicola was pleased about that but all she wanted was Sally, here and now, her big grey eyes, soft and attentive, her strength and honesty and warm-heartedness.

'Give me Sal's address and I'll write to her,' she said coldly.

'That's a laugh. She didn't leave one – didn't know where she'd be.' Mrs Winters began to close the door. 'We're watching a serial,' she said. 'I'll never catch up if I miss it.'

Nicola turned away and as she went downstairs she kicked at the wallpaper again, rucking it up and leaving a torn triangle hanging off the wall.

Out in the street she felt suddenly more alone than she had ever felt in her life. It seemed there was no one to turn to for comfort. Only Ivy – darling Ivy – far away in Yorkshire. But in any case, Ivy would only tell her to go back home again, go back to school, look after her father . . .

She realised that there was nothing to do but return to Station Road. Luckily Barry was going out with his mates that evening. If she missed out on supper she could avoid seeing him; she wasn't hungry anyway. She set off for the park, kicking a stone along the gutter, feeling perversely satisfied by her misery, her isolation and the picture of herself as a wayward and untidy teenager.

N

The old telescope that stood on the landing outside Nicola's room had one of its feet on a loose floorboard, so that the whole thing rattled when anybody passed. Nicola hardly noticed it herself, rushing to and fro, but late that night, sleepless with misery, she heard the rattle and knew that someone was approaching her door.

Of course it would be Barry – who else, at that time of night? She had just heard a distant clock strike two. The scene she had witnessed on the station platform had not diminished her love and longing for him – rather the reverse – but now were added jealousy and bitter resentment. How *could* he have paraded his passion for Helen in view of her window? And how could he now, after that, be visiting her room? She turned her face into the pillow, feigning sleep, determined to reject him, although her heart was pounding.

The door handle clicked and then came the whisper of his voice in the darkness: 'Baby? It's only me – can I come in with you?'

She breathed more heavily, as if she were deeply asleep, but her legs began to quiver and she knew it was useless. She made a pretence of waking with a start. 'What's up?' she mumbled.

'I want to come in with you – move over.'

She could smell his sweat, his toothpaste, the special scent of his hair, like almonds, and it was impossible to refuse. Her shoulder was pressed against the wall as she made room for him in the narrow bed. Then his arms were around her, his rough cheek nuzzling into her neck. 'That's better,' he said. 'I couldn't sleep – I wanted you so much.'

'Well, I didn't want you, did I? I was dreaming.'

'Sorry, babe – but you don't mind, do you? Not really?' His hand was on her breast and she knew he must feel the thudding of her heart.

'Yes, I do – after what I saw at the station.'

'What d'you mean?' She felt a quiver of tension in his arm.

'You know damn well – kissing her like that. And you *knew* I could see from my window –'

'Christ – I never thought of it. Never crossed my mind.'

'It must have done!'

'It didn't. *Honestly*. But we were only saying goodbye – it didn't mean anything.'

'Of course it bloody meant something!' She wriggled away from him. 'I'm not a *fool*. You're in love with her, aren't you?'

'Oh, Nick – for God's sake – here we go again. I love *you*, don't I?'

'*I* don't know. *Do* you?' She was helpless with confusion and her eyes filled with tears.

'You worry too much,' he said gently. 'Can't we just enjoy ourselves?'

'I want to, but –'

'Come on, then. Forget it. Helen's in Brighton and you're here with me. Right?' Slowly he pulled up her nightgown until it was no more than a ruffle of nylon round her neck. 'Just relax,' he murmured. 'Think about nothing but us – O.K.?'

She let out a long anxious breath but it was closely followed by a sigh of pleasure and soon the memory of Helen had ceased to trouble her.

R

Robert opened the boot of his car when he arrived home on Monday evening and smiled with satisfaction as he saw again the collection of brown-paper parcels. There were several packages containing the various components of the putting set – balls, numbers, little red flags with their sticks, and plastic cups to line the holes. He had bought only two putters because that was the way he wanted to play. With Alison.

He decided to leave the parcels in the boot until he had a chance to fix up the green when Julia was out. She was out now – her car wasn't there – but she might return at any time. He thought he might do it the following evening before he went to meet Barry; it would take his mind off the ordeal ahead, and it would be very pleasant digging out the holes with a knife and a trowel, fitting the plastic cups, putting in the flags. He would have to plan the positions carefully before he began – on paper perhaps – and he thought how delightful it would be if Alison would help him. After all, it had been her idea.

He found her in the kitchen, as he had hoped, and his heart quickened as he looked at her. She was standing at the worktop, preparing a salad.

'Good evening, Mr Slingsby.' She looked up with her warm smile and continued to slice a fat juicy cucumber.

'Good evening, Mrs Laurie.' He paused and sat on a high stool beside her. 'Look,' he said. 'I know your name is Alison and I'd like to call you that – it's a beautiful name. Will you allow me to call you Alison?'

'Of course. I should like you to.'

'Thank you.' He took a deep breath and watched her strong steady hands working with the knife on the cutting board. Now she was slicing a green pepper, pausing to pick out a seed. 'Mrs Slingsby wouldn't approve,' he said, 'so I'd better call you Mrs Laurie when she's around.'

She nodded without looking up. 'I understand.'

'And you must call me Robert,' he said. 'That's only fair.'

She went on chopping rhythmically. 'I couldn't do that,' she said quietly. 'That would be out of order.' And then she raised her head and gave him a clear unwavering look, her sea-green eyes so large and bright that he could hardly return her gaze without flinching. 'But I can *think* of you as Robert – I shall certainly do that.'

The conversation was exciting him beyond belief. This

short exchange had roused him as deeply as physical contact. From his waist to his knees was one great ache of pleasure and longing. It was the way he had felt about Nicola but now he was ashamed and appalled to remember it.

'Come with me,' he said, getting up. 'I've got something to show you. It's in the boot of the car.'

She put down the knife, wiped her hands on a towel and followed him to the garage. Looking round to make sure she was still there, he saw that her head was quaintly dipped, like a nun, but that she was smiling the secret, mischievous smile of a naughty schoolgirl.

R

Julia returned an hour later, bringing Emily Cartwright with her. Robert was sitting in his leather chair, a writing pad on his knee and a glass of whisky beside him, working out a plan for his putting green, and when he heard Emily's voice in the hall he hastily tore off the page and stuffed it into the pocket of his smoking jacket. Julia must have brought her home for dinner, must have arranged it with Alison. He couldn't help resenting the fact that there were things which Alison and Julia discussed between them, unknown to him. It was quite illogical, he knew, but love was always illogical and his love for Alison was growing stronger hour by hour. He had unwrapped the parcels in the garage and together, with childlike excitement, they had examined the components of the set. She had tested out one of the putters, swinging at a leaf on the garage floor, and he knew by the way she held the club and by the stance of her strong yet graceful legs, that there would be no ineffectual jabs, no shrieks of mirth or dismay as the ball missed the hole by yards. The following weeks would be warmed and cheered by well-balanced competitions on that wide and secret lawn. There would be intimate conversations, quiet laughter, immense delight.

But now, of course, the pleasure of the occasion was marred by the arrival, not only of Julia, but of Emily as well.

The door opened to admit the two of them, and he stood up, summoning a polite and hypocritical smile. Emily Cartwright was tall and stout, with a bosom that was hoisted in front of her like a cushion on a tray. The lower half of her torso gave the impression of being strapped and laced into a foundation-garment that was much too small, so that her thighs bulged out like balloons under the blue silk dress. Behind her, Julia was almost obscured.

'Good evening, Robert.' Emily's eyes were like black marbles as she looked him up and down. He always felt that she was trying to find fault with his appearance.

'Good evening. What would you like to drink?' He went to the cocktail cabinet and opened the doors.

'A dry sherry, please, if you have it.'

'Oh, I think we can just about manage that. Julia – how about you?'

She shook her head, grimacing irritably, as if he had insulted her. Emily was her closest friend and no doubt they complained to each other about their husbands (John was a blustering, red-faced man, full of his own importance); there was no need for Julia to keep up the appearance of a happy marriage as far as Emily was concerned. Robert shrugged, poured the sherry and refilled his whisky glass.

Emily lowered her huge elasticised bottom onto the settee and took the glass he handed her without a word of thanks.

Julia was sitting on a hard upright chair, as usual. She never lounged or relaxed, always kept her back straight and her chin raised. 'Emily and I have been doing some good work this afternoon,' she said. 'John's left the car for servicing at the garage where Barry Mitchell works. The manager is an old friend of theirs.'

'Oh, yes?' Robert sat down again with his drink. 'Tell me about it.'

'Oh, it's all arranged,' said Emily. 'There's nothing to tell.' She sipped her drink and leaned back. Her gigantic legs would never stay together and he averted his eyes. 'John pointed out that the Mitchell boy is an undesirable and he'll get his notice. No references, of course. He'll go because of inefficiency – John will report on the way the car's been serviced.'

'But I got the impression that Barry was conscientious – takes a real pride in the work.' Robert tossed back his whisky so angrily that it made him cough.

'But we know all about him, don't we?' cut in Julia. 'He told us quite plainly.' Her eyes glittered.

'That's nothing to do with inefficiency. I hate all this meddling with people's lives – you can do more damage than you realise.' He was thinking of Nicola, picturing her distress, wondering what Barry would do, with jobs so hard to come by.

'I don't understand you,' said Emily. 'I thought you were one of us.'

'I don't like dirty tricks – they can easily rebound against you. And in any case it's quite unethical. Lies and frame-ups – I thought you were a church-goer, Emily?'

She threw back her head and laughed. He saw her grey tongue, the black fillings in her teeth. 'Oh, Robert – you're so naive,' she cried. 'Isn't he *naive*, Julia? Not of this world, at all.'

'I wouldn't call it naive,' said Julia. 'I'd call it stupid. And extremely irritating.'

Robert looked at the two women, their faces smug and hostile, and his head began to throb. 'If you'll excuse me,' he said. 'I have work to do in the garage.'

Emily nodded, smiling sideways at Julia, and as he went out of the room he heard her say, 'You never can tell which way the cat will jump, can you? And men say *women* are unpredictable!'

Out in the garage he sat in the warm plushy gloom of the Rover and took the crumpled sheet of writing paper out of his pocket. The first hole, he decided, must be a short one, to build up confidence; somewhere near the eucalyptus tree. He rested the paper on a road atlas, took out his pen and drew a little triangular flag with a figure '1' inside it. The second hole could be a shade more difficult – over by the peonies, perhaps . . .

But as he doodled he was thinking anxiously of Barry, the unsuspecting victim of the kind of chicanery one associated with power politics. He was determined to stand against it, not only for Barry's sake and for Nicola's, but in some odd way for Alison's. He felt certain that her concepts of right and wrong would be the same as his.

R

Robert had few friends in Grassley and he hadn't been inside *The Star* for years. It was smaller than he remembered, and much noisier. The only pubs he visited were in Tonbridge where he sometimes had a drink with Dick Benson and a few other colleagues from Granger Coe. In any case, Robert wasn't the kind of man to enjoy 'a drink with the boys'.

Barry was late. He was wearing a grubby yellow shirt and seemed much older than Robert remembered. His face had a look of fatigue and his smile was shaky. Perhaps he's as nervous as I am, thought Robert as they found a corner table and sat down with their pints of bitter. He felt reassured.

'Nice to see you, Barry. How was the carpentry?' He had prepared this opening.

'I didn't go tonight. Didn't feel like it.'

'Oh, why was that?'

'I lost my job today. Feeling a bit rough.'

'I'm sorry.' Robert's cheeks began to burn. He hadn't expected Julia's plot to mature so quickly. 'What happened? Redundant?'

'No. Apparently I didn't tighten up the wheel nuts on a client's car. I can't believe it but I suppose it must be true. I don't know what came over me – I'm so *careful*. I've always been careful.' He lit a cigarette and Robert saw that his hands were trembling.

'Who was the client?' He had to make sure.

'Bloke called Cartwright. I've serviced his car before – no trouble. But this is serious – somebody might have been *killed*.' He drank some beer and looked at Robert despairingly. 'Sorry – it's really upset me.'

'Can't you claim unfair dismissal?'

'Maybe it isn't unfair – I just don't know. Anyway, it's his word against mine – I wouldn't stand a chance. The boss is furious.'

Robert felt sick. Damn Julia! It was criminal. 'Any ideas for another job?'

'No, but I expect I'll find something. Can't see myself in a dole queue. I just – ' His words were lost in the clatter of coins from a fruit machine.

'Your mother must be upset?'

'She doesn't know – I haven't been home. I hate the thought of telling her – I've never done anything like this before.' He drew on his cigarette. 'Nick as well – oh, Christ!'

'How is she?' said Robert. 'Settling down all right?' He wanted news, details, a letter.

'Yeah – she was off to Tonbridge today to look for a job at a hairdresser's.'

'She's set her heart on that, then?'

'Seems like it.' His mouth was sad, his eyes bleary and tired-looking. No message. Not even 'She sent her love to you.'

Robert drank some more beer. 'What's your relationship, Barry? I think I've a right to know. She's very young.'

Barry was silent, toying with a beer mat. At the next table an old woman with black ringlets screeched with laughter. Then he said, 'Nothing to worry you – nothing at all. You really don't have to worry.'

'Things are different these days,' said Robert. 'Anything goes – I know that. But it would be a tragedy if she – if she became pregnant.'

'She won't, that's certain. Not by me, anyway.' He looked at Robert, then down at his beer which was almost gone. 'Look, I think she's great – a marvellous kid – but like you say, she's terribly young – really only a child. It's a pity she left home.'

'I know – I know. But you understand the reason –'

'Sure I do. And it's tough for you as well.'

Robert felt a glow of gratitude that tempered his dislike for the sweat-stained shirt, the acrid smoke, the long untidy hair. 'But Nicola's happy with your mother, isn't she?' he said. 'Everything's all right?'

'Mother's always writing her books – thinks of nothing else – and the place is a bit of a madhouse, to be honest. There's plenty of food and all that – and mother's fond of her – but I think maybe Nick needs more security. She really needs a solid kind of *base*, if you know what I mean.'

'She's got you, hasn't she? You seem a steady sort of chap.'

Barry laughed and shook his head. 'Steady? Me? And just been fired? You must be joking!' He shook his head and was suddenly grave. 'I'm not steady, Mr Slingsby – I'm in a hell of a mess, to be honest. And I don't mean losing my job.' He looked round the bar as if he were afraid of being overheard. 'I shouldn't tell you this – but I think I will – I think it's right to tell you.' He stubbed out his cigarette in the big ashtray.

'Go on.' What on earth was coming? Trouble with the police? Drugs? The woman at the next table was shrieking with laughter again.

'I'm in love,' said Barry in a low voice. 'And she's twice my age – a friend of my mother's.' He drained the last of his beer and slammed the glass on the table. 'She feels the same as I do – and I don't know what the hell to do about it.'

Robert was silent. Another delivery of coins came pumping out of the fruit machine. Then he said, 'Does Nicola know?'

Barry shook his head vehemently, frowning. 'You won't tell her, will you? I'll have to break it gently.'

'Of course. I understand. I'll get you another pint.' He

141

stood up and turned quickly to conceal his expression. It wouldn't do to betray his overwhelming relief.

R

'Good morning! Another sparkling day.' It was Alison's husky voice and when Robert opened his eyes she was setting the tray on his bedside table, leaning so close that he could feel the warmth of her rounded capable arms, pink with sunburn and slightly freckled. She was wearing a cotton dress printed with a pattern of yellow irises and the bodice was shaped and gathered to contain her soft full breasts.

'Good morning, Mrs Laurie. I'm glad it's a nice day again – you'll be able to get on with your herb garden.'

'Yes, I'm really thrilled with it – I'm planning a kind of wheel shape.'

'I know – I saw it last night.' After returning from *The Star* he had wandered round the garden in the dusk, stopping to look at her plot, neatly divided into sections with little stones.

Julia grunted in obvious disapproval of the disturbance, and Alison bit her lip, giving Robert a quick smile, bright and mock-abashed, as she turned away. She isn't afraid of Julia, not in the slightest, he thought as the door closed softly behind her. She had left behind a faint whiff of her scent and an aura of sweetness and excitement that made him curl his toes in the cool depths of the bed. He could hardly speculate about the future – though his fantasies sometimes took his breath away – but one thing was certain: his incestuous passion for Nicola was now extinguished. It had died with remarkable speed and finality, as infatuations often do when a steadier love takes hold. Now he was able to think of her with a normal fatherly concern, and the sense of release was enormous.

He sat up and reached out for his cup of tea. Alison's tea

was more refreshing than Ivy's had been. There was a flowery fragrance to it – a dash of Earl Grey, perhaps? He sipped it with pleasure. Barry's revelation about an older woman had given him the hope that Nicola might now come home and return to school. Her studies would stop her from brooding, and Alison would soon win her over and provide the security that Barry had talked about. He was an honest lad. Quite unsuitable for Nicola, of course, but an honest lad all the same. And he would surely find another job; there must be a demand for good motor mechanics. Robert felt certain that Barry *was* a good mechanic, and his hatred for Julia suddenly soured the taste of his tea. He wondered what he could do to expose her treachery and get Barry reinstated. Julia and the Cartwrights and Barry's boss were all a party to the plot; it was like a Mafia in miniature. For the first time Robert felt he understood a little of the despair of the political dissident, whether he was under the tyranny of the left or the right.

He looked at Julia with disgust, and as if she sensed his thoughts, she yawned and stretched her arms above her head. 'Emily phoned last night,' she said. 'It seems the boy has played right into our hands.'

'What do you mean?' He put down his cup.

'He didn't tighten up the wheel nuts on John's car – the wheels could have dropped off for all *he* cared. You can't trust his type at any level. Not at *any* level.'

Robert sipped his tea in silence. Did she really expect him to take her seriously? He was almost tempted to tell her about his meeting with Barry but he couldn't face the inevitable fireworks.

'Well?' she said irritably. 'Aren't you going to *say* something?'

'What is there to say? You know my views on the subject.'

'But surely you're pleased he's lost his job? It could have been *my* car, couldn't it? Or yours. Anybody's.'

'You don't believe he was to blame, any more than I do, so for God's sake keep quiet about it.' He switched on the transistor radio which stood on his bedside table, tuning to

Radio 3, which Julia disliked.

Someone was playing a Chopin *Nocturne*, and he leaned back and closed his eyes.

'Switch that off,' cried Julia. 'There's something I want to say to you.'

'Say it later. I'm listening to this music.'

'I said *switch it off*!'

A rage of anger blew up in Robert's head like an explosion. He stared at her for a moment and then he leaned over and turned up the volume to its maximum strength so that every note was distorted into a ringing, pounding cacophony that made Julia's shouts of protest almost inaudible.

Instantly she was out of bed, bizarre in her green hairnet and lacy black nightdress, plunging round the bottom of the four-poster and appearing for a moment between the red drapes like a demented figure in a play. Her face was twisted with fury as she seized the radio, fumbling with the switches, trying in vain to turn it off. Every deafening note seemed to taunt her as she grappled hopelessly to silence it.

Then Robert made a grave mistake: he laughed. He threw back his head and laughed with a brutal harshness that surprised him.

With a cry of rage, Julia flung the transistor across the room. It struck the wall, still playing, then crashed to the floor, silent at last, its aerial gently vibrating. Outside the window a blackbird sang, a liquid warble of intense beauty.

Julia leaned against the carved oak pillar of the bed, and he saw that she was shaking uncontrollably. Neither of them spoke for a while and then he said, without irony, 'What was it you wanted to say? It must have been very important.'

She shook her head, staring wildly at the ceiling. 'No, I've forgotten – I've completely forgotten.' She sat down on the bed and began to take off her hairnet, as if nothing had happened. 'Oh, I know what it was,' she said suddenly. 'I'll be out all day, that was it. I won't be back till late. Lunch in Croydon and a meeting in London tonight.'

'I should have thought a thing like that could have waited

until my Chopin was finished? Why the panic?'

She said nothing. She was taking out her hairpins and placing them neatly side by side on the bed-cover.

He glanced at the tray beside him. 'You haven't had your orange juice,' he reminded her.

'I don't want it.' She gathered up the pins and went slowly towards the bathroom, her flimsy nightdress floating from her drooping shoulders. She normally held herself so straight that he felt a pang of pity for her.

'Julia,' he said. 'I'm sorry I laughed. I shouldn't have done – I can see that now.'

She paused for a moment without looking round then continued into the bathroom without a word, closing the door and locking it behind her.

R

At eleven o'clock that morning, gazing across the drowsy Kentish countryside from his office on the seventh floor, Robert made a sudden decision to take the rest of the day off work. He had a reliable staff and was, to a large extent, his own boss. He would go back home and spend the afternoon preparing the putting green. Alison would be there alone. She could take lunch with him under the buddleia tree . . .

He made the necessary arrangements and an hour later he was back at Birch House, driving into the large empty garage, rejoicing that Julia had in fact gone off to Croydon. He'd been fairly sure that she would; she took these engagements very seriously. He peered at himself in the driving mirror, smoothed his moustache, popped a Polomint into his mouth and went indoors.

The kitchen was deserted and as he stood there, wondering where Alison was, gazing at her apron behind the door, he heard the faint drift of music somewhere in the house. At first he thought it must be from the radio in her room but as he went into the hall he realised that it was coming from the drawing room. It was Mozart's Concerto for two pianos in E flat major, a record he had recently acquired. He opened the door very slowly and stood on the threshold, amazed by what he saw.

Alison was alone in the room, reclining in his big leather armchair with her shoes off and her stockinged feet, ankles crossed, resting on the coffee table. Her eyes were closed, and on her lap lay Robert's blue pyjama jacket, one sleeve hanging down to touch the carpet. Her right hand, loosely holding a needleful of blue cotton, rested among the folds, and a thimble on her middle finger caught a ray of sunlight from the French windows and flashed like a diamond. On the floor beside her was a work-basket, open to display neat rows of coloured cotton reels.

Robert was enchanted. He stood there for several seconds, watching her face. The scar was turned away from him, her three-quarter profile unblemished. There was a little smile on her lips and she looked incredibly young, relaxing there so peacefully, her toes moving gently to the rhythm of the music. He felt he should creep away, then bang some doors to make his arrival known, but he couldn't deny himself the exciting intimacy of the situation.

'Alison?' He raised his voice above the music.

A visible tremor shook her body and her eyes sprang open like a doll's. 'Oh, my *God!*' she cried. In an instant she was sitting erect, her feet on the floor, clutching the mending on her lap, and staring at him with such a mixture of horror and entreaty that he wanted to rush across the room and take her in his arms. 'Forgive me – please,' she said, scrambling to her feet. 'It's just that I'm so fond of Mozart – and I thought I could do the mending and – ' She broke off, shaking her head. 'Oh, God, I'm sorry. There's nothing I can say.'

He wondered for a moment if he should put on a pretence of disapproval but he knew it was impossible. In any case, she deserved his honesty. He swallowed the last of his Polomint and smiled at her. 'Don't worry,' he said. 'It doesn't matter in the slightest.' The second movement drew to a close and in the short silence he said, 'I'm glad you like Mozart. Sit down again and we'll hear the end – this last movement always lifts my spirits – never fails.' He sat on the settee, motioning her to resume her place in his chair.

She sat down slowly. 'I really shouldn't –' she said.

'*Shhhh*!' He put his finger to his lips. 'Just relax and let's enjoy it.' Their eyes met, and she smiled at him with such a radiance of affection and gratitude that he had to turn away. The music was so exquisite and his love for her so overwhelming that his emotions were out of control. I love her, he thought wildly. I love her more than anything in the world . . . He closed his eyes and rested his head against the back of the blue velvet settee. Soon they would be having lunch together on the terrace. He would change into his light grey trousers and his favourite sports shirt, a rather dashing green and white check. She would prepare a delicious little meal and he would open a bottle of wine. He knew without a doubt that she liked him. Could she possibly grow to love him?

R

Alison had spread a white cloth on the garden table, and as they sat on the sun-dappled terrace among the flowers and butterflies, eating chicken-and-mushroom flan and drinking *Chablis*, Robert was in such a state of rapture that he hardly knew what he was doing.

'I still feel I oughtn't to be here,' she said, swirling the wine in her glass so that the reflection rocked and glittered on the tablecloth. 'Supposing Mrs Slingsby came back unexpectedly?'

Robert was savouring the chicken. It had a faint flavour of lemon that delighted him, and the pastry she had made seemed to melt in his mouth like warm buttery snowflakes. 'We're free people,' he said. 'Nobody's going to tell us where to eat our lunch, or with whom.'

'But I'm the *housekeeper*,' she exclaimed. 'I really shouldn't be drinking wine with you.'

'You listened to Mozart with me. *And* Haydn. We drank sherry together. Lunch and a bottle of wine is quite a logical progression.'

She leaned back in the cane chair and gazed at him with a tender, half-mocking little smile. The dress with the yellow irises fused into the dazzle of flowers behind her, so that she seemed to be glowing in a sea of blossoms. 'But what,' she asked softly, 'would be the logical progression from this?'

He felt as if the blood were rushing to his cheeks, flaming in his forehead. 'I don't quite know,' he said unevenly, 'but whatever it was I'm sure it would be quite irresistible.' She's *flirting* with me, he thought. Holy Christ, she's actually *flirting* with me! Is it the wine, or does she really mean it?

'I'll get the dessert,' she said. 'I've made some raspberry ice cream.'

'Later. Let's drink our wine.' If she went into the house, the spell might be broken.

She took a sip, then looked up to watch the butterflies and bees that hovered around the spiky purple blooms above their heads. The scar on her cheek was thrown into harsh relief by a flash of sunlight through the leaves, just as it had been on the day he met her, under that same tree.

Suddenly, surprising himself, he asked the question he had wanted to ask ever since that day. 'Alison, how did you get it – that scar? Don't tell me if it upsets you, but –'

'Of course I'll tell you,' she said, as calmly and easily as if he had asked her where she bought the dress she was wearing. 'It doesn't upset me – not any more. It was four years ago – it all seems like a dream.'

'A nightmare, I should have thought.'

She nodded. 'I was teaching in North London and I was going back to my bed-sitter after a parents' meeting. It was pretty late and I saw a coloured boy coming towards me – tall and thin, he was. He looked like an Indian or a Pakistani. There was no one else in sight but I wasn't really nervous.

148

People are people and it's just bad luck if you meet the wrong type. This chap was whistling to himself – hands in his pockets – he looked perfectly harmless.'

'You're telling it very well,' said Robert. 'I'm feeling quite breathless.'

She smiled and went on: 'He walked past – didn't even look at me, and then I heard footsteps behind me and a man yelled out, "*There's one! Get him!*" I looked round and two men came running out of a side street – white men – drunk by the look of them. One was waving a bottle and he hit the boy across the head with it while the other bloke knocked him down and started kicking him. That's when I knew I'd got to "have a go".'

'Alison – for God's sake –' Robert felt a cold sweat break out on his forehead.

'It was hopeless, really. I just lashed out at them with my handbag – that's all I could do – but luckily the Indian boy managed to get up and run away while they were busy with me.' She drained her glass and Robert filled it up again, spilling wine on the cloth.

'The man with the bottle broke it against the wall and – well, I won't go into the gory details. I woke up in hospital.'

'Did they find the bastards?'

'Never – not so far as I know.'

'God – you *shouldn't* have –'

'Yes, I should. They could have killed that boy. And I'm all right – I've learned to live with it.'

'But they might have killed *you*, damn it!'

'They didn't – that's all that matters. You can't worry about what *might* have happened.'

That's what Nicola had said. She was quoting Barry. 'You were magnificent.' He drank his wine, the glass trembling. 'You know damn well you were.'

'It was instinct – you'd have done the same. You know – jump in the river if a child's drowning. You can't help it.'

'Some people can help it quite easily,' he said. 'No trouble at all.'

'Well, you asked me, Robert, and there you have it.'

'You called me Robert!' He gazed at her incredulously. 'So I did!' She smiled.

He leaned forward, gently touching the scar for a moment – a channel of softness between two ridges of firmer flesh. He wanted to press his lips against it, to run his tongue along that groove. For him, her scar was intensely erotic; he had always found it so. He put his hand on her arm. 'You should be proud,' he told her. 'Every time you look in the mirror you should be proud.'

'Thank you,' she said. 'You're very sweet.' He saw that her mouth was unsteady. 'But that's what we're here for, isn't it – to stand up against brutality – to help each other?'

'Alison,' he said. 'I think I'm falling in love. In fact I know I am.'

'Me too,' she replied. 'Isn't it beautiful?'

R

Robert dug out the final trowelful of earth for the ninth hole and threw it into the bucket. Alison was standing beside him, close to his elbow. 'Me too,' she had said. It seemed impossible. If I wasn't so damned stuffy, he thought, I wouldn't be out on this damned lawn, making a bloody putting green. I'd be in bed with her, drowning in her soft breasts, devouring every marvellous atom of her . . .

He stood up, straightening his back. 'I think that's the lot,' he said. 'We only need nine holes on a lawn this size – don't you agree?'

'I'm sure you're right.' She kicked the box of accessories gently with the toe of her white sandal. 'Shall we put those little plastic cup things in – and then we can fix the flags. I'm dying to see if I can beat you.'

'We have to fix the numbers on the ground before we can play,' he said. 'You know – the places to start from.' He turned to look at her and she was gazing at him with such an expression of tenderness and pent-up laughter that he dropped the trowel on to the grass and took a step towards her. 'Alison – oh God –'

Her arms were around him before he knew it, her lips on his, and then he was kissing the scar, as he had yearned to do, kissing her eyes, her mouth, her hair. It seemed to him, then, quite natural to be standing under a willow tree on his own lawn (no, Julia's lawn) kissing Alison as he had never kissed anyone in his life. Her lips were parted under his, her body pressing closely against him, and he was trembling with a fever of love and desire he had only known before in his dreams of Nicola.

'Let's go indoors,' he muttered at last, breaking away from her.

She smiled at him and nodded, leading the way towards the house. As he followed her, his heart thudding wildly, he wondered if she was past the menopause, or on the pill, and what the hell he ought to do about it. He had no contraceptives in the house; he hadn't made love to Julia for years. As he walked beside her, worrying about it, she gave a little lamb-like skip, as she had done on the day she came for her interview, and he let out a sigh of relief. I can ask her, he thought. We can talk about everything quite openly.

He overtook her and held her hand. 'If ever we can – if you'd have me,' he said, 'I want to marry you.'

Her fingers tightened on his. 'Marriage doesn't matter – not at our age. But it's early days yet – you hardly know me.'

'I know you very well – and the more I know, the more I shall love you.' With her, he could express his feelings more easily than ever before.

When they were half way up the stairs the telephone rang.

'I'll get it,' said Alison. 'I won't be a minute.'

'No – leave it – let it ring.'

'We can't. It might be Mrs Slingsby. Don't forget I'm on duty!' She grinned at him over her shoulder as she turned.

'Oh, Lord – I suppose so.'

He stood on the staircase, leaning against the wall as she hurried to the drawing room. The sound of the phone, echoing through the quiet house, blasted away his joy and even dulled his sexual excitement. When the ringing stopped he watched for her to appear, prayed that she would be smiling, telling him gaily that it was only the butcher, or some such trivia. But when she came running across the hall and stood at the foot of the stairs, her face was anxious.

'It's for you,' she said. 'A call from Sheffield. It's Ivy Jones's sister and she says it's very urgent. I'm afraid it sounds like bad news.'

N

'Telephone, Honey-child. Your father.'

Nicola was in the kitchen, washing a lettuce, and she hastily dried her hands on the damp kitchen towel and hurried to the hall. What on earth did he want? She wasn't going back to Birch House, that was certain . . .

Freddie went back to the typewriter in the living room while Nicola took the call, and the steady thump of the keys in the background helped to calm her nerves.

'Hello, Daddy?'

'Darling – are you all right?'

'Great, thanks. What's up?'

'I'm afraid I've got some bad news, pet. It's Ivy – she's had an accident – a very bad fall. She's in hospital and her sister phoned me up to say she's asking for us all the time –'

'I must go to her,' cried Nicola. 'Daddy – *please* – I must go to her!'

'Yes, of course. We'll drive up to Sheffield straight away – tonight. When can you be ready?'

'*Now*! I'm ready now! Oh, Daddy – will she die? I couldn't *bear* it!' She had a mental picture of Ivy standing at the cooker making Welsh rarebits for them both, smiling and chattering so eagerly that her top teeth sometimes came away from the gums.

'She's got some kind of internal injury but I expect she'll pull through. Poor old Ivy – I'm glad you want to go.'

'Of course I do – I *love* her.'

'I'll pick you up at the Post Office in half an hour. We'll be in Sheffield by nine with any luck. Bring what you need for the night – I'll book an hotel.'

'Daddy – just one thing?'

'Yes, darling?'

'Mother isn't coming, is she?'

'No.'

'That's all right then. See you.' She rang off and went into the living room where Freddie was hammering doggedly away at Cut-Throat-Connie.

When she got into the Rover at the Post Office Nicola noticed a difference in her father. She didn't know exactly what it was but his face looked somehow rounder and pinker, as if he had just come back from a holiday abroad.

He never talked much when he was driving through heavy traffic and after the first greeting they hardly spoke until they reached the motorway. She had looked forward to seeing him again, but now he seemed like a stranger. She glanced at him, sitting stiffly at the wheel, driving so differently from Barry who lounged and smoked and talked, even held her hand and fondled her thigh. Yet oddly she felt safer driving with Barry than with her father, leaning slightly forward and staring fixedly ahead.

At last she saw that the middle lane of the motorway, snaking away into the sunny distance, was almost clear of traffic, with the nearest car a long way ahead. 'Can we talk now, Daddy?'

'Of course.' He gave her an anxious little smile. 'Try not to worry about Ivy – she might be much better by the time we arrive. I phoned her sister to say we were coming.'

'I never wrote to her, you know. I said I would but I never did. If she gets better, I'll write to her every week – I'll never, never miss.'

'Of course not.'

'It's all *mother's* fault. If she hadn't sent her away it would never have happened.'

'I thought you didn't believe in thinking of what might have happened. Isn't that what Barry says?'

She was disarmed by his friendly reference to Barry. 'Did you like him? He said you'd had a good talk in the pub.'

'Yes – I like him a lot. I don't like his politics but I'm sure he's sincere – he really wants a better world for everybody.'

'Yes, and for *everybody*, not just for himself. I don't see why you don't like that. Unless it's because you might have to give a few things up!'

'We won't talk about that now, Nicola. Some other time. It's a terrible shame about Barry losing his job.'

'*What*?'

'Oh – I'm sorry – I thought you'd know –'

'But he loved it there. Whatever happened?'

Her father was silent. In the slow lane a line of lorries trundled in weary procession, one of them belching fumes that filled the car as they passed it.

Nicola repeated urgently, 'What *happened*?' Her father's grim face alarmed her.

'It was a put-up job, Nicola. And I don't care who knows it. Your mother fixed it with Mr Cartwright – he complained about the way his car was serviced. I don't believe Barry did anything wrong at all.' His face seemed suddenly thinner and sharper. 'It was your mother who planned it. She told me.'

'But *why*?' Nicola felt an icy coldness in her stomach, a clamminess in her hands, clenched tightly in her lap.

'It's partly his politics – she wants you away from him because of that. But mostly to punish you, I'm afraid –'

'Punish me? Why? For leaving home? For throwing that glass? What have I *done*?'

'Don't blame yourself, pet. Your first mistake was being born a girl. She wanted a son, you know – you were meant to be Nicholas. And I've never really loved her, so it's my fault, too – I shouldn't have married her. I admired her in many ways but I never loved her. I know that now.'

'I hate her. I've *always* hated her. It's awful to say it but

I'm glad I can tell you – I feel much better.'

'It's not your fault – she's an evil woman, Nicola. It's no use pretending any more. I can understand you leaving home.'

Nicola's fury against her mother was calmed by a great sense of relief that her father had at last been honest with her. She felt as if she had grown in maturity, achieved a new status. He had spoken to her as a sensible, sensitive human being, not as a child, and she felt for him a depth of sympathy and understanding that was quite new to her. It suddenly seemed ridiculous that he should fancy her; Sally was a fool.

'It makes us better friends, somehow, talking about it,' she said. 'I'm awfully glad.'

He glanced at her with a sorrowful little grimace. 'It's a relief for me as well, pet. Pretences are so painful.'

'I've wanted her to die,' she said, warming to confession with a kind of eager relish. 'I've often thought how lovely it would be if she was *dead*!'

He did not reply but she saw the tension in his jaw. I bet he feels the same, she thought. I wonder he hasn't left her ages ago.

'Perhaps her father was to blame,' he said. 'An impossible man – hard and cold and sadistic.'

'Do you mean she takes after him?'

'I'm afraid so.'

She thought, What about *me*, then? Supposing I take after *her*? The notion disturbed her but she soon dismissed it. She was sure she had nothing in common with her mother. Nothing at all . . .

They drove in silence for a while, a steady purring seventy. In the fast lane occasional cars went whizzing by.

'Poor you,' she said at last. 'You have her all the time. I don't know how you stick it – specially without Ivy.'

'Mrs Laurie is a lovely person,' he said. 'She makes it easier. I know you'll like her.'

'You've told me that before, but I shan't be there to find out, shall I? I'm not coming back while mother's there.' He said nothing and she went on, 'Daddy, she can't get away with doing that to Barry. You've got to tell the garage – get him his job back.'

Her father was silent, staring at the road ahead as it rushed under the gleaming white bonnet.

'Well?' she went on. 'You *will*, won't you?'

'Yes,' he said at last. 'I'll go and see the manager as soon as we get back.'

'Promise? I've known you to wriggle out of things.'

'I promise,' he said.

They were passing a sign announcing a Service Station. 'Let's have some food at those knives and forks,' she cried. *Those knives and forks* was a childish name for the motorway cafeteria.

'Can we spare the time? What about Ivy?'

'Just a quick little snack – I'm famished. And I want the bog.'

Over on the left reared a dark forest and, above the treetops, streamers of blue-grey cloud were massing around the sun, preparing for a spectacular sunset. Her father swung the car into the slow lane, and as he drove into the Service Station she thought of Barry and longed to be with him again, driving about in the M.G., eating in cafés, being his girl. Now that Helen had gone she felt a growing confidence that all would be well, that one day they would be married, with beautiful children, and live happily ever after.

R

Sitting opposite Nicola in the crowded cafeteria, their table littered with other people's dirty plates and cups, Robert watched her pouring tomato ketchup over her chips and couldn't understand how he had ever lusted for her. She seemed to him now quite unappealing; adorable as a daughter, but certainly nothing more. Her hair was in strands. Her face was even paler than usual and there were two red pimples on her chin. She was wearing a sloppy grey jersey over a white T-shirt and the sleeves were too long, half covering the backs of her childish hands as she tackled her plateful of sausages, baked beans and chips. Poor little scrap, he thought, how will she face the end of her affair with Barry? But surely at her age she would soon get over it, find someone else more suitable.

'How about the hairdressing?' he asked her. 'Have you found a job?' (Anyone less like a hairdresser would be hard to imagine.)

'Not yet. I'm going to try Sevenoaks. If it wasn't for your rotten Tories and all this unemployment I'd have found something easily.'

He was eating a ham salad and as he carefully cut off a limp brown frill from the lettuce he knew that he must try to get her back to Birch House, away from Station Road.

'Nicola,' he said urgently. 'Come home! You'd like Mrs Laurie – I *know* you would. And your mother's out so much –'

She looked up at him in wide-eyed amazement, a chip poised on her fork. 'You don't understand!' she said. 'I've got to be with Barry. I *love* him!'

'But are you sure it's going to last? You're so young, darling.' He couldn't betray Barry's confidence, only try to prepare her.

'Of course it's going to last. I'm not like Sally, you know – always wanting somebody different. I'll *never* want anyone but him. *Truly*!' She put the chip in her mouth.

'Well, why not play it cool for a year or two – see how you both feel?'

'Play it *cool*?' She swallowed, choked, coughed. 'Haven't you *ever* been in love? Don't you know what it *feels* like?'

He said nothing and realised with a shock of panic that Nicola, at sixteen, probably loved Barry as deeply as he, at fifty-four, loved Alison. 'I'm sorry,' he said at last. 'Of course you can't turn your emotions on and off like a tap. It was a silly thing to say.'

157

She nodded, scooping up baked beans with her fork and flashing him a friendly, forgiving smile.

He suddenly wanted to tell her about his love for Alison and would have done so, but for the fear that she would feel shut out, an encumbrance. Facing rejection from Barry, she would need Robert's support as never before. He must bide his time, coax her back and wait for her to discover Alison's qualities for herself. He longed with all his heart to be at Birch House; it was almost unbearable to be travelling in the opposite direction.

Nicola was saying, 'Anyway, I love it at Freddie's. You'd hate the muddle but I think it's a smashing place to live.'

'Barry said it was a bit of a madhouse.'

She grinned. 'Did he? Well, I suppose it is, but Freddie never goes on at me – I feel so nice and free.'

Reaction against Birch House, he thought. And that's my fault as well as Julia's. I must never 'go on at her' again . . . He knew that Ivy's fall, whatever the outcome, had brought him and Nicola together in a totally unexpected way, opening up a new world of empathy between them. It was a gift beyond price and he prayed that when they arrived in Sheffield Ivy would be well enough to hear about it and rejoice for him.

R

'We haven't got anything to *give* her,' cried Nicola, as Robert drove into the hospital car park. 'We ought to have some flowers or grapes or something – and all the shops are shut.'

'She won't mind that – it's us she wants to see.' Robert's head was aching again. He wasn't used to long-distance driving and his neck and shoulder muscles were knotted with tension. He switched off the headlights and gazed at the glinting cars, the dark hospital building with its rows of bright windows, the ribbons of a faded sunset behind the chimney pots.

'But we *must* have something to take her,' persisted Nicola. She looked distraught.

On an impulse he opened the glove compartment and rummaged among the maps and cassettes. 'How about this?' He took out her copy of Keats's poems. 'She'd love that if you don't mind parting with it?'

'Course I don't.' She opened it and leafed through the pages. 'Where did you find it? I haven't seen it for years.'

'In the utility room. She'll be thrilled if she's well enough – nothing she'd like better. Come on, we'd best go in.'

As they were crossing the car park towards the hospital she stopped and looked up at him, her face white and tragic in the half light. 'Oh, God – I'm frightened!' she said.

'I know – so am I.'

She reached out and took his hand. Her fingers felt cold and thin and he grasped them tightly, praying – more for her sake than his own – that Ivy would be all right.

N

'She's rather poorly, I'm afraid. I can only allow one of you in at a time – and only for a minute. But she's certainly perked up since she knew you were coming.' The nurse was thin and plain with ginger hair and tired brown eyes.

Nicola looked at her father anxiously. 'I think my daughter should go in first,' he said. 'She knows Miss Jones better than I do.'

Nicola's heart was thumping as she followed the nurse down the quiet ward. Some of the patients were asleep, some reading, others staring wearily into space.

Ivy was propped up on pillows at the far end of the room, and at last Nicola found herself looking into the face she had known and loved for as long as she could remember. Only now it was a different face – thin and drawn and paper-white, the eyes feverishly bright in their network of wrinkles. She was wearing a blue bed-jacket that Nicola had knitted for her years ago.

'Miss Nicola!'

'Ivy! Darling Ivy!' Nicola stood nervously by the bed, wanting to hold her in her arms but afraid to touch her. The nurse had gone to attend to another patient.

'Is – your father – here?'

'Yes – he'll come and see you in a minute. Look, I've brought you this – my old school Keats. I thought you'd like it.' She put the book on the bed, but Ivy did not appear to see it. She was staring towards the door, her knobbly fingers clutching at the bed-cover.

'Where is he?' she gasped. 'I want to see him –'

'He's in the waiting room.' Nicola was hurt and embarrassed. 'It's lovely to see you, Ivy. I've missed you terribly.'

'And I've missed you.' She glanced vaguely at Nicola, then back to the door. 'I've missed your father, too. Is he all right? Where is he?'

'In the waiting room. Don't worry, he won't run away.'

'I want to see – him – now –' The tears were running down her cheeks.

The nurse came hurrying over and put a kindly hand on Nicola's shoulder. 'You'll have to go, dear. And your father had better wait a while until –'

'No – *no*!' Ivy's anguished wail rang through the ward.

Nicola walked away, feeling on the verge of tears herself. It was obvious that Ivy didn't want to see her – only her father. And she didn't want the book.

In the waiting room her father leapt to his feet. 'How is she? Could she talk to you?'

'Yes, but she wants to see *you*, Daddy – she doesn't want me.'

Her father shook his head. 'Poor old girl. I've seen the Sister – they think she'll be all right in a few weeks.'

'You'd better go to her – she's crying for you – that's what

160

it looked like.'

Nicola stood at the door, watching her father make his way down the ward, a tall, hesitant figure in his navy-blue blazer and grey trousers. The nurse met him half way, spoke to him and escorted him to the bed. Ivy's arms went out to him as he approached and Nicola went back into the empty waiting room and burst into tears.

R

'Oh – I'm so glad you've come,' gasped Ivy. 'I said to the nurse "I know he'll come," I said – ' She reached out to him as he sat on a chair beside the bed.

He took her hands in his. 'You're going to be all right. The Sister told me you were doing fine.'

'Are *you* all right?' she said. 'Is madam still with you?' She looked much older, shrivelled, vaguely demented.

'Oh, yes – life goes on, you know.'

'Not for me, sir. There's been no life for me since I left. I'd never have had this fall – I was crossing the footbridge to get a card for your birthday. I'd never have gone over that bridge – all those steps – but it's a beautiful shop – sells nothing but cards. And now I won't be able to get one – ' Her lips quivered and she broke off, gulping with emotion.

'Ivy – you mustn't worry about a card.' She was obviously in a highly nervous state, perhaps not well enough to receive visitors. She was staring at him helplessly and he went on, 'You'll soon be all right. How are you liking it up here? Lovely air, isn't it?'

'I'm lost, sir,' she said, 'lost without you. You were my life – you understand me, don't you?' Her hands in his were twitching, bony, hot.

'Not really – it was Nicola, wasn't it?'

'No – it wasn't her – it was you. I've got to tell you – you won't be angry with me?'

161

'How could I be angry? Of course not.'

'I've wanted to say it – all those years – but I never could.' She glanced furtively round at the other beds. The nurse was sitting at a table in the middle of the ward, writing in a book.

He looked down at their joined hands, wanting to break free, yet finding it impossible. She was shaking visibly and he saw Nicola's Keats quivering on the bed-cover.

'It's hard to say it – but I might not have another chance.'

He nodded, his heart beating heavily. He felt that he knew what was coming.

'I love you,' she whispered. 'I've loved you for years – I've got to tell you now – before the nurse comes. I'll do *anything* for you – work for you – go anywhere –'

'Oh, Ivy – what can I say? You know how much I appreciate what you did for us. I'll never forget you – never.' He gently withdrew his hands and folded them together on his lap.

'I'm glad I told you,' she mumbled. 'I had to – I've always wanted to. When you feel like that – you have to say it.'

'I don't know what – I feel very – touched.' His cheeks were burning; he knew he must be blushing like a schoolboy. There was a difficult silence and he blew his nose to cover his confusion. If only he could express himself, show his sympathy and gratitude. But no words came and he put away his handkerchief and looked down at his hands.

Ivy said at last, 'What's the new woman like?' Her voice, in spite of her frailty, had a bitter edge.

'She's nice. Very good. No complaints.' He had a mental picture of Alison's secret smile, her eyes, the soft swell of her breasts . . .

'But she's not so devoted as I was? Not so particular?'

He shook his head. 'Of course not. No one could ever be like you.' Oh, God, the sadness of all this . . .

'When I'm well again, I'll come and visit you,' she said. 'Take a holiday.'

'That would be marvellous, Ivy. And you're going to be well again very soon. Just take things easy.' He couldn't look at her. His eyes were fixed on the Keats, and he thought of Nicola, giving her book so graciously, only to be rejected.

'Nicola will love to see you when you come,' he said. 'She really misses you.'

'That may be so,' said Ivy. 'But she's got a boyfriend now. It's *you* I'm thinking of –' She began to cry, a succession of choking sobs that brought the nurse hurrying down the ward.

'You'd better leave,' she murmured to Robert. 'I'm glad you could come – she's been talking about you all day.'

Robert got up from the chair and Ivy began to cry out in agitation: 'Don't go – don't go – stay a bit longer –'

Robert hesitated but the nurse motioned him away. He waved briefly and hurried towards the waiting room. He had to be back at his desk on the Friday, which meant he must leave the next morning. He was glad he would not be able to visit her again; it was altogether too painful, too embarrassing. He had always known, of course, that she was very fond of him, but *love . . . ?* It was tragic, preposterous. Thank heaven he would soon be speeding south down the motorway, back to Alison.

R

The hotel was grand and impersonal. It was the only one in Sheffield which had been able to offer Robert two single rooms at a moment's notice. The lounge was almost deserted when they arrived from the hospital that night, a large room thickly carpeted in a pattern of red and gold leaves and furnished with luxurious brown velvet chairs. From the adjoining bar, through an archway, came a buzz of conversation, an occasional shout of laughter, the lilt of piped music.

Robert and Nicola sat in a corner under a reproduction of a Canaletto in a huge gilt frame. Her eyes were puffy with crying and the spots on her chin looked fiercer than ever.

163

She had left her grey jersey in her room and sat there in her white T-shirt and blue skirt. Her nipples showed large and pink through the thin cotton but he was no longer excited, only embarrassed.

He was drinking whisky, Nicola hot chocolate. There was a childish rim of foam round her lips as she put down the empty cup and lolled back in her chair, looking moody and depressed.

'You've got to remember,' said Robert, 'that Ivy just wasn't herself. She's probably had all kinds of drugs pumped into her. You mustn't be too upset.'

'Well I bloody am upset. She didn't want to see me, did she? She didn't care about me – but she cared about *you* – she wasn't too ill for that. I needn't have *come*.'

'But you wanted to see her, didn't you?'

'Not if *she* didn't want to see *me*. I don't know what I've done to her – it must be because I didn't write. I *should* have written.'

Robert drew a deep breath. 'Nicola – there's something I must tell you. It'll help you to understand – and not to feel guilty.'

She looked at him glumly. 'What?'

'It's confidential – I know you'll keep it to yourself.' Her eyes opened wider; she was obviously intrigued by the promise of a secret. 'Ivy thinks she's in love with me,' he went on in a low voice. 'She told me tonight. I'd no idea of it – never occurred to me. But she says she's felt that way for years.'

'Golly!' Nicola's eyes were now bright with interest.

'So it's easier to understand, isn't it? Why she was so inconsiderate. Love can make us very selfish – it seems to bring out the worst in people as well as the best.'

'I sort of guessed she had a thing about you,' said Nicola. 'That last evening – in her room – she went on about how good you were. It was sweet, really.'

Robert felt an upsurge of sorrow and affection. 'Well, that's the story, pet. A very sad one.'

'But she's so *old*,' said Nicola. 'I didn't know people felt like that at her age.'

'You'd be surprised. And she's not all *that* old – I think she's sixty-seven.'

Nicola leaned her head against the back of the brown velvet chair and stared at the ceiling in silence. At last she sat up and looked at him thoughtfully. 'I wonder if that's why mother gave her the push?'

'Heavens, no! She couldn't have known – *I* never knew. Ivy was always so proper – never a word out of place.'

'Maybe she gave herself away somehow.'

The idea of Julia sacking Ivy on account of jealousy seemed not only ludicrous but totally incredible. He couldn't imagine her caring one jot about it, even if she did suspect. But if it *were* true it would certainly make her more understandable, more human. He felt he wanted it to be true, but of course he would never know. Anyway, what did it matter? His marriage was over. But he mustn't let her guess about Alison until he was ready to make the break; their eyes would betray them if they weren't extremely careful.

'Anyway, thank you for telling me, Daddy. I feel a lot better about it now.' Nicola got up and reached for her bag. 'I'm going up to my room. It's so gorgeous I want to be in it. I'll watch the telly in bed.'

'If you came back home you could have a set in your room,' he said. 'And I've made a putting green on the lawn – I could teach you.'

She smiled and shrugged. 'Good night. See you at breakfast.'

'Good night, pet. Eight o'clock – we've a long drive.'

'Don't you think we ought to visit Ivy again tomorrow?'

'Can't be done, I'm afraid. I've got to get back. Besides, she isn't really up to it.'

'Oh, well – I'll write to her.'

She sauntered off across the vast carpet, her bag slung carelessly over her shoulder, one shoelace trailing. It was remarkable how quickly they had come to accept one another, to communicate. He felt sure they had established

165

a rapport which would be lasting.

Alone in the lounge he began to think of his future. He was determined to leave Julia and persuade Alison to go away with him, but as soon as Nicola learned about Barry she would probably come straight home, in spite of Julia, and it would be up to Alison and him to comfort her and make her happy.

When the day finally came to leave Birch House, Julia's reaction was easy to foretell. She would only care on account of her reputation but that would be enough to incense her. He could imagine the gossip among her friends: '*Robert Slingsby's gone off with the housekeeper . . .*' She would be enraged beyond endurance. And yet he was no longer afraid of her. Alison had made him feel strong and free for the first time since his marriage.

N

'Could you drop me off at Woolworth's,' said Nicola as they arrived back in Grassley that afternoon. 'I need some writing paper.' It wasn't true – she could always get paper from Freddie to write to Ivy – but she didn't want her father to take her to Station Road. If he went inside and saw the mess and smelt that garlicky-fatty-orangey smell he might get very difficult about her staying. Especially if Freddie gave him tea in one of those cracked old mugs with dirty handles and stains inside. He was so fussy about cleanliness. And besides, Barry might be there, as he had no job; there could even be a chance to make love that very afternoon.

She watched the Rover purr away down the busy High Street, its chromium flashing in the late afternoon sunlight. Poor old Daddy, she thought, he's got nothing lovely to look forward to, like I have – just the misery of being with *her* . . .

She set off for Station Road, running and bumping into people in her eagerness to be with Barry again.

R

Julia was waiting in the hall when Robert arrived home. 'How was your mercy dash?' she said. 'I'm sure Ivy must be feeling better for seeing you?' This was one of those times when he simply could not tell whether she was sincere or not. It might even suggest that she had known about Ivy's unseemly devotion.

'She's very poorly but I think she'll be all right. I could only see her for a few minutes.' He put his suitcase down and wondered where Alison was.

'I hear you took Nicola. That was nice for you.' Now he could see the cynical twist of her painted lips as she stood facing him in her grey silk suit. Was she going out? It was hard to tell; she always dressed so carefully. 'How's she managing?'

'Quite well, it seems. She's happier than she ever was at home.' He knew he should go straight round to Barry's garage as he had promised, but he couldn't face it that afternoon. In any case it would soon be closing time. He would definitely go on Saturday morning. 'It was a long drive,' he said. 'I'd like a cup of tea. Where's Alison?'

'*Alison*?' It was only then that he realised what he had said.

'Yes – Mrs Laurie.' He felt his cheeks burning. 'I call her Alison – it's more friendly. You ought to do the same.'

'You are *not* to call her that. She is *my* servant and I forbid it.'

'But *I* am not your servant, Julia. And there is nothing you can forbid me to do. Please remember that.'

She took a step towards him and her long neck was flushed beneath the pearl necklace. 'Oh, yes there is. I can forbid you to dig holes in my lawn to make clock golf. And I *do* forbid it.'

'It is not clock golf. Clock golf requires a single hole in the middle – that's how it got its name.'

'There's no need to be insolent. In any event, Bernard has filled in all the holes and re-turfed them. He was just as appalled as I was.'

Robert was trembling with rage but he was determined to keep his equilibrium; Alison might appear at any moment. 'I'll put the kettle on,' he said, turning towards the kitchen. 'I need some tea.'

'What, no whisky?'

He looked at his watch. 'It's twenty minutes to five,' he said coldly. 'Incidentally, where *is* Alison?'

'Mrs Laurie is cleaning Nicola's room. I'm turning it into an office – I need somewhere to work –'

'But what about your father's old study? You could work in there.'

'That room is locked and will remain so. I've had the bed moved out of Nicola's room and ordered a desk and a filing cabinet. It will suit me very well.'

'But you can't do that,' Robert exploded. 'She might come back. I was trying to persuade her to.'

'I will not have her back. It's as simple as that – *I will not have her back*.' She leaned against the kitchen worktop, staring at him fixedly, her eyes like glass. He knew that she was totally devoid of compassion – for Nicola and for himself. Possibly for anyone at all. She was some kind of psychopath, without charity, without conscience. It must be her father's doing: the way he had treated her, or some inherent streak. He remembered the Alsatian: her grandfather's inhuman cruelty had taken place in that very room . . .

'I wish I could understand you.' His voice was unsteady. 'Nicola hates you, you know. We talked a lot on the journey, trying to make out why you've always treated her so badly – why you're so hard and selfish.'

Julia's eyes narrowed and her lips tightened. 'If she feels like that about me she won't want to come back, will she? She won't require the room in any case.'

'*I'm* here,' said Robert in a low voice. 'I know I haven't understood her as I should but we've suddenly got much closer. I only wish you could do the same – make a real effort to break down this terrible antagonism –'

'Now I can see why you're so concerned about her room,' said Julia. 'You want her back so you can pursue your unhealthy little attachment. You admitted you were too fond of her, didn't you? Quite a confession.'

'That's a thing of the past.' He took the electric kettle to the tap and could hardly hold it steady.

'A thing of the past? It was only last week as I remember it.'

'What's this – the third degree? You'd have made a fine S.S. woman, wouldn't you?' He turned from the sink, still trembling, and as he did so the door opened and Alison came in.

She was wearing the dress with the yellow irises, and she hurried towards him, smiling. 'I'll do that, Mr Slingsby. How was Miss Jones?' She was taking the kettle, her scent around him, her soft hand brushing his.

'Thank you – I think she'll be all right – we could only see her for a few minutes.' He was aware of Julia watching him with her cold, snake-like concentration.

Alison plugged in the kettle, reached for the teapot, opened the canister of tea. Every movement of her body excited his nerves like a caress.

Julia said curtly, '*I'll* make the tea, Mrs Laurie. Mr Slingsby and I have things to discuss.' She gave a nod of dismissal and Alison retreated, catching Robert's eye with a momentary gleam of alliance as she closed the door.

Alone with Julia again, he did not look at her. 'What do you wish to discuss?' he asked harshly.

'Our daughter. She has chosen to live with this boy and his mother against our wishes. She has forfeited her right to call this house her home.'

'But supposing she breaks up with Barry? That's what you *want*, isn't it? That's what you've plotted for? Or did you only want to hurt her – losing him his job, making him seem irresponsible? I think you're so deranged you don't know what you want.' The kettle began to sing, an undertone of comfort in the malevolent silence.

'Deranged? It's *you* who's deranged – driving to Yorkshire for five minutes with a servant. What a fool she must think you! And what a fool Mrs Laurie must think you, as well. She must be laughing at you behind your back – calling her Alice –'

'Alison.'

'Oh, I'm *so* sorry – Alison. People of her quality don't like familiarity, you know. It's so patronising. They much prefer a straight master-servant relationship.'

'Do you think so?' He remembered the packet of contraceptives he had bought in Grassley after leaving Nicola, and he put his hand in his blazer pocket and touched the paper bag while he stared into Julia's stormy face. 'Perhaps you're right,' he said. 'Would you like some tea?'

'No thank you. I must see how she's getting on with that room.'

When she had gone, he sat on a stool, waiting for the tea to brew. The next time Julia left the house, he thought, would be the signal for his tryst with Alison. It was painfully ironic that they would be making love in the bed that had so recently been Ivy's.

N

There was no sign of the M.G. when Nicola turned the corner into Station Road. So Barry was out! A tin can lay glinting in the gutter and she kicked it viciously, sending it clattering across the street. Ivy's rejection had wounded her deeply and she needed Barry more desperately than ever. Two black children who lived opposite were sitting on their doorstep and jumped up with friendly shouts to kick the can, obviously thinking she was playing with them. It seemed there was no end to human misunderstandings . . .

The familiar thump of the typewriter greeted her as she opened the door of Number 27 and she flung her haversack down in the hall and went into the living room. Freddie carried on typing, pausing only to say, 'Hi, honey – everything all right?'

Nicola threw a bundle of dirty washing off the sofa and flopped among the clutter of old papers. 'Where's Barry?' she said.

'What d'you mean?' Freddie stopped typing and looked round. Her hair was wild, her face greasy. She was wearing her old kaftan with a blue pinafore apron on top.

'I mean what I say. Where's Barry?'

Freddie swung right round on the swivel chair. 'What's wrong, Nick? You look all in. Barry's at work, of course. Where else would he be?'

So Freddie didn't know. And she must not give him away. 'Sorry,' she said. 'I'm tired – I was forgetting it's so early.'

Freddie stood up and pulled the sheet of paper out of the typewriter. She looked at it for a moment and then tore it up and threw the pieces at the waste-paper basket. Some went inside and the rest scattered over the floor.

'What's wrong with *you*?' said Nicola. 'You look all in yourself.'

'Can't write today. It's a load of rubbish.' She rubbed her eyes and smiled, as if to rid herself of the problem. 'How was your old nanny? She must have been thrilled to see you.'

'Yeah.' Nicola would have liked to tell Freddie all about it but it was her father's confidence and she felt she must keep it to herself. 'The best thing was talking to Daddy,' she said. 'We talked like we never did before. I really felt easy with him.'

'That's marvellous. What did you talk about?'

'My mother mostly. He actually said she was *evil*! And he understands me leaving home. It made me feel better to hear it from him.'

'Yes – you don't feel guilty any more.'

'That's *right*. And it was great for him as well – talking to

171

me like that. We really had a ball. God, I'm sorry for him – going back to *her*. It must be hell.' She sighed. 'Is there any wine? I'd simply *love* a glass of wine.'

Freddie laughed. 'Red or white?'

'White please – if it's cold.'

'I've a bottle of *Muscadet* in the fridge. It's a good idea, honey – I need some myself. Connie's been a pain today. Wouldn't do anything I wanted.' She paused in the doorway. 'I don't think Barry'll be in for supper. He said he was going out with his mates from the garage. But we can do without him, can't we?'

Nicola leaned back her head, remembering the night he had made love to her in front of the television. 'No,' she said. '*I* can't do without him. Sometimes I wish I could.'

N

Freddie poured the last of the *Muscadet* into Nicola's glass. They were sitting on the rug playing Scrabble.

'I've got five I's and a B, and a Q without a U,' said Nicola. 'It's hopeless.'

'Don't moan about your letters, honey. Change them and miss a turn if you don't like them.'

'*Like* them? How could I bloody well like that lot? And I've changed them twice already.' Nicola was not much good at Scrabble at the best of times.

Freddie put down 'ridge' with a flourish and Nicola saw that her B could make it into 'bridge'. She was leaning forward to add the letter when there was a ring at the doorbell.

'Who can that be?' said Freddie. She got up and looked anxiously round the room. 'Put that empty bottle under the sofa,' she said. 'It doesn't look too good at half past five. And tidy up a bit if you can.'

Nicola was feeling light-headed with the wine. She kicked

the bottle out of sight, but that was all. She was more concerned with putting her B down and adding up the score. She listened with half an ear to Freddie at the front door. 'Do come in,' she was saying. 'We're playing Scrabble. I hope you'll excuse the muddle – I've been working to a deadline this week and I haven't had much time to –'

Nicola looked up, pushing her fringe out of her eyes, and her heart lurched when she saw the familiar figure of her father behind Freddie in the doorway.

'Daddy? What are *you* doing here? What's wrong?'

'Nothing's wrong, darling – don't worry. I came to bring something for Barry's mother.' He took an envelope from his blazer pocket and handed it to Freddie. 'A cheque towards Nicola's keep,' he said. 'She's happy with you and I'm grateful.'

'You're very kind – there's really no need – she's no trouble.' Freddie stuffed the envelope into her apron pocket, and Nicola wondered how much her father had given her; probably quite a lot. She could think of nothing to say to him in front of Freddie and she took another letter from the Scrabble bag. It was a U which gave her the chance to put down 'quip' on a double word score and boost her total by thirty points.

'Do sit down, Mr Slingsby,' Freddie was saying. 'Here – let me tidy that chair – the sofa springs are rather on the wane, I'm afraid.' She lifted a pile of paperbacks and a cardboard box from one of the armchairs and dropped them on to the floor. Nicola watched her father's face and his expression of mingled horror and amazement was suddenly too much for her; she broke into a torrent of helpless laughter and collapsed on the rug. 'Oh, Daddy,' she gasped. 'Your face! If you could only see your *face*!'

'What's wrong with my face?' His hand went up nervously to touch his cheek, his moustache.

'You're upset by the muddle, aren't you?' said Freddie. 'It's not surprising really. I'm afraid I haven't had time to –'

'It's just that he's so *tidy*,' broke in Nicola. 'If he puts a couple of pencils on the table they have to be lined up dead straight.' She grinned at her father affectionately. 'Don't they, Daddy?'

'I'm made that way.' His cheeks were crimson. 'It's nothing I can help.'

'Of course not,' said Freddie. 'Do sit down and I'll put the kettle on. You'd like some tea, wouldn't you?'

'That would be very nice, thank you – if it's no trouble.'

Freddie, in her sloppy mules, slithered off into the kitchen and Nicola watched her father sit down gingerly in the greasy armchair, adjusting his trouser knees and folding his hands in his lap.

'I'm glad you came,' she said. 'Freddie's a darling – you mustn't pay any attention to the mess. She can't help that any more than you can help being tidy.'

'I hate to think of you in a place like this,' he murmured. 'It can't be healthy.'

'Of course it is. I love it – really I do.'

He shook his head, looking round the room with an anxious frown. 'How are things with Barry?' he said. 'Any news of another job?'

Nicola put her finger to her lips. '*Shhhhh*! For God's sake don't say anything – he hasn't told her yet. She doesn't *know*!'

Freddie was standing in the doorway. 'She doesn't know what?' Her face was cloudy.

'Nothing,' said Nicola, turning to the Scrabble board. 'Nothing important.'

'Tell me, please. I heard you say "He hasn't told her yet." Do you mean Barry?'

'I'm sorry,' said Robert. 'It was my fault – I didn't realise –'

'If it's my son you're talking about, would you just *tell* me please – before I get angry.'

'Barry's lost his job,' said Nicola. 'It was –' She was going to say: It was my mother's fault, but she caught a warning glance from her father and said, 'It was a terrible shame – he loved it there.'

'What happened? Cutting down? Or didn't they like his

politics?' Freddie looked close to tears.

'I don't know exactly,' said Nicola. 'But please don't say anything – let him tell you himself.'

Freddie nodded 'It's funny that I should be the last to hear. I'd have thought he'd *want* to tell me about it.' Her bottom lip was quivering and Nicola longed to comfort her.

Her father did it for her. 'I saw him in *The Star* the night it happened,' he said. 'He hated the thought of telling you and Nicola – he was worried in case he'd been careless when he serviced someone's car. But he hadn't – I'm sure of it. He was the victim of a nasty plot. Nicola, you'll tell him, won't you? He mustn't have any doubts about himself.'

'Course I will. And you'll go and see the garage?'

'Yes – on Saturday morning.'

Freddie was running her fingers through her hair, bleary-eyed with hurt and bewilderment. From the kitchen came the shrieking of the kettle. 'I'll go and make the tea,' she said.

R

Out in Station Road Robert took a series of deep breaths to free his lungs from the smells of Freddie's house. He had walked to Grassley through the Park, leaving Alison with Julia upstairs. Julia was joining a theatre party in Croydon that evening and going to the Cartwrights' for supper afterwards. She expected to be back after midnight, she said. So tonight was the night. Drinks with Alison in the drawing room, an intimate little supper, and then . . . He had decided to walk to Station Road with the cheque to pass the interminable couple of hours before Julia would drive away and leave them alone together.

Now, striding down the street, he could not forget that appalling house. The tea had been almost undrinkable: the milk was slightly off and the handle of the mug was encrusted with some unsavoury substance that had probably been there for months. Nicola had been brought up so carefully, educated at that spotlessly clean and well-ordered convent; it was unbelievable that she should be happy in such squalor. As for 'Freddie' – those hideous clothes, the plastic bangles, the dirty old slippers . . . But he had liked her face. It was honest and lively and oddly endearing, in spite of her blotchy skin and dishevelled hair.

Robert was approaching the entrance to the Park when an open sports car screeched to a halt beside him. Barry was at the wheel, his face bronze and bright in the evening sunshine.

'Hi – Mr Slingsby!'

'Hello Barry – I've just been to see your mother. What a nice warm-hearted person she is.'

'Yeah – she's great.' He switched off the engine and smiled at Robert, his eyes narrowed against the sun. 'So you've been *in*, have you? Seen our grotty set-up? Bit of a far cry from that plushy pad of yours!'

'Yes, well – I'm rather fussy, I'm afraid. Nicola always said so. But if she's happy, that's all that matters. I hope she'll be able to stay?' He knew she could not live at home again unless Julia changed her attitude, and that seemed out of the question.

'Oh, she will. Mother likes having her – they get on fine.'

Robert went up to the car and placed his hand on the door, leaning close to Barry. 'I'm going round to the garage on Saturday morning,' he said in a low confidential tone. 'See if I can get you re-instated. I'm afraid you've been the victim of a nasty frame-up, Barry, and I'm going to do all I can to put matters right.'

Barry frowned, shading his eyes with his hand. 'Really? Oh, well, it doesn't matter now, thanks all the same. I've got something else lined up. I don't want to go back to the garage.'

'Oh? What are you going to do?'

'Scene-painting. I've always had a fancy for that kind of thing – done quite a bit of art work.'

Robert sensed a certain evasiveness and did not question him further. 'Well, good luck anyway. Nice to see you, Barry. And you'll keep an eye on Nicola for me, won't you? I haven't forgotten what you told me – but just a friendly eye, if you wouldn't mind?'

'My mother will, anyway – never fear. She'll be O.K.'

Robert watched the M.G. roar away towards the town and then he headed for home. He would return the way he had come and sit on a seat in the Park for a while. It was a great relief not to be going to the garage; the prospect had unnerved him. He thought ironically that he would be delighted if Barry's workmates found out the truth and came out in sympathy. Nicola was right, of course: strikes against injustice were perfectly defensible.

Now, as he wandered past the children's recreation ground he allowed his imagination to embrace the evening with Alison. Just the thought of her name made his body ache. Soon he would unfasten her dress, uncover her nakedness, possess her . . . His excitement was almost beyond bearing and yet there was an undercurrent of fear. Supposing he was unable to please her? Supposing she discovered that she cared for him less than she had thought? He sat on a seat near the swings and watched a group of children playing in the mellow sunshine. Childhood was the best time – happy and carefree and uncomplicated. If only one could lead one's adult life with the simplicity of a child . . . But of course it was impossible; there would always be money to worry about – money and sex and other people's greed and duplicity.

At last it was time to go; Julia would be sure to have left for the theatre. As he crossed the field that led to April Avenue he caught a glimpse of Birch House, the flash of a window through the trees, and his heart began to beat with painful force. Please God, he thought, let me do everything right. Please God . . .

R

'Mrs Slingsby went off about half an hour ago,' said Alison. She was working in her garden, leaning on the long rake, resting her chin on her hands. She looked up at Robert with a comical little smile.

'So the mice can play!' he said. 'Come and have a drink in the drawing room.'

'I'll just change my shoes.' She leaned the rake against the wall with a gesture of happy abandonment. 'I *must* have the right shoes for the drawing room.'

He saw that she was wearing old sandals and that her legs were bare. 'You aren't going to bother putting any stockings on, are you? Tights or anything?'

She shook her head and their eyes met. She held his gaze for a long breathless moment and he saw her colour rise. He would have kissed her then, out in the warm summer air by the kitchen window if he had not caught sight of Bernard in the shrubbery, sucking his pipe and trundling his wheelbarrow.

'What shall I be pouring out for you?' said Robert.

She grinned. 'Scotch on the rocks, if you please, sir.'

'Oh – a whisky girl! I'm glad.'

'I've a bottle in my room, as a matter of fact. I usually have one before I get the dinner. Sometimes there's a concert on Radio 3 and I love a drink with my music.'

How sad it was, he thought, that she should have been drinking alone in her room while he did the same downstairs. And then he realised that he could say it aloud to her. 'Isn't it sad that we should have to drink alone,' he said. 'Me with my Hi-Fi, you with your radio. Every man needs a woman to drink with.'

'And vice versa,' she said. 'If she's a drinking woman, that is. I gather your wife doesn't care for it?'

'It would make no difference if she did. I can find no pleasure in her company. None whatsoever.' Alison said nothing. She looked at her feet and smoothed the soil with the toe of her sandal. He went on, 'But *you* – I should want to be with you whatever you drank – or didn't drink. As it is, I hope we're going to have a great many whiskies together in the years to come. And doubles every time!'

'I hope so too.' She gave him her radiant smile but her eyes were anxious and he guessed that she was thinking of the problems that would have to be solved before such times were possible. 'I'll go and change my shoes,' she said.

R

Alison had put on a pair of white high-heeled shoes that flattered her slim brown ankles. She looked remarkably young, relaxing with a whisky glass in her hand, leaning back her head on the dark blue velvet. The dress with the yellow irises had buttons down to the waist, pearly little buttons with gold rims, and sitting beside her on the settee Robert could hardly stop himself from trembling.

He remembered Dick Benson asking him at an office party: 'Are you a tit man, Bob? Or a leg man?' Robert had been embarrassed, standing near the girls from his department, but he had managed to answer with a smile: 'Tits for me, Dick, every time.' Soon he would undo those pearly buttons one by one, lay bare her breasts and bury his face against them . . .

She was telling him her arrangements for dinner. 'There's a beef casserole in the oven,' she explained. 'It's cooking very slowly with wine and mushrooms and plenty of sweet basil, and we can have it whenever we like. It won't spoil.'

'Say, two hours,' said Robert, his voice unsteady.

She smiled. 'I've a fresh green salad in the fridge and a rather special chocolate mousse with rum.'

179

'I love the way you talk about food,' he told her. 'It's very erotic, you know.'

'Food is meant to be erotic – and so is drink.' She raised her glass and took a sip.

'I want most desperately to kiss you,' he said, 'but Bernard is still out there and we can't very well draw the curtains, can we?'

'I gather he's – in the other camp?' Her comical smile was there again.

Robert nodded. 'I'm afraid so. We shall have to entrench ourselves and fortify our ramparts.'

'I like the sound of that,' said Alison. 'My ramparts are in the direst need of fortification.'

'Mine too. Shall we begin by having another drink?' He took their glasses to the cocktail cabinet and as he crossed the room it seemed that his happiness was almost beyond bearing. The carpet felt as soft as a cloud and the wallpaper was quite devoid of demons. He turned to her with the bottle in his hand and told her about the screaming faces, pointing out the section of the pattern that had so often disturbed him.

'I can see what you mean – oh, *yes* – how ghastly! But it's only the way we look at it. See it as a leaf and a twist of petals and there's nothing but beauty. It's like that with so many things.'

He refilled both their glasses and as he carried them to the settee he glanced out of the window. Bernard was standing on the lawn, quite close, treading down the turf that covered one of the putting-green holes. His eyes were shadowed by the brim of his deer-stalker hat but Robert, pausing with the glasses in his hand, felt sure that he had been looking into the room. He saw him take the pipe out of his mouth, spit effusively, and plod away towards the apple orchard. Prying bastard, he thought. My house isn't my own with him around. And then he remembered that it was not his own in any case.

'I'm going to get our putting green fixed up again,' he said, setting down their glasses on the coffee table. 'I'll dig out all those holes and tell Bernard to leave them alone. All the stuff's in the utility room – I thought she might have slung it in the dustbin.' He raised his glass. 'But don't let's talk about her. Here's to *us*!'

Alison's ferny scent seemed to embrace him and draw him to her, so that he reached out for her hand and clung to it. 'Alison – you make me new. You make me strong and alive – you give me hope and happiness when I thought I would never have it again.'

She leaned forward and kissed him gently on the lips. 'Darling Robert. This is only the beginning. Just you wait and see what we can do for one another.'

They sipped their whiskies in silence for a while and then he said, 'I'd like you to know that I've never made love to anyone but Julia – and not for many years. She didn't want it and neither did I.'

'How come you didn't find – consolation?'

'Nobody seemed right. And I'm shy with women – always have been. I can't seem to communicate. Until I met you.' One day he would confess to her about Nicola. One day . . .

She said, 'I wish I could say that I've never been with anyone but Jack, but I'm afraid it isn't true. A year or so after he died I imagined myself in love with one of the masters at the school where I taught. Very good looking but that was all – he didn't want me any more after – this.' She put her hand to her cheek. 'I might have known he was that kind of man. I must have been out of my mind to get involved with him.' She finished her drink and smiled. 'Shall we go?'

'Yes please.'

She got up and held out her hands, pulling him to his feet. 'Robert – there's something I must say.'

'What?' Oh, God – had she guessed about Nicola? Had Julia told her?

'I don't want you to think I'm unconcerned about the way I'm behaving towards your wife. Don't think it doesn't bother me that I'm employed by her – trusted – and calmly go to bed with you while she's out at the theatre –'

'Alison – don't – ' He was still holding her hands, the warmth of her fingers throbbing through his nerves.

'Just a minute. It *does* bother me – very much – but believe me, I wouldn't do it if I didn't feel it was – well – *right*.'

'It *is* right. Oh, Alison, it *is*! She's given me nothing but misery all these years – the kind of misery you read about in the papers, see in films. I didn't think it could happen to ordinary people who only want to be peaceful and contented.'

She smiled. 'With me you shall be peaceful and contented. I promise.'

'I know.'

They went out of the drawing room and walked slowly across the hall, their arms around one another like young lovers, looking into each other's eyes, stumbling and smiling.

'If the phone rings *this* time,' he said, 'we shall pretend we didn't hear it.'

'I agree with you.'

'Your casserole smells delicious.'

'It will be extremely delicious.'

'And so will you,' he said.

Suddenly she broke away from him and leapt ahead, chuckling softly. In a moment he was after her, running and slipping up the blue-carpeted stairs, reaching out for her skirts, laughing and gasping with pleasure and excitement.

N

When Robert had gone, Freddie prepared a quick supper of fish fingers, chips and peas. She ate with *The Guardian* propped up in front of her. 'Excuse me reading,' she said to Nicola. 'I'm going to London tomorrow to see my publisher and I like to be up to date with the book reviews.' She seemed to have got over her distress about Barry; she never let things worry her for long. 'I'm planning a new book,' she went on. '*Connie at the Zoo*. Fur and feathers flying right and left. I'm thinking of winding up the series with this one. Connie can be eaten by a polar bear while she's a tabby cat. I must find out if polar bears *do* eat cats.'

'Does it matter?' said Nicola, giggling.

'Of course it matters. Everything's got to be authentic.'

'But Connie turns into a cat – *that's* not authentic!'

'No, but it's a different ball-game. I'll explain to you one day.'

'How much did Daddy give you?' said Nicola, feeling that Freddie was on the defensive and that this was a good time to ask.

'You little sauce-pot! I'm not telling. It was a lot though – he's very generous.'

'He always was. Still, he can afford to be.' She got up to clear the table. 'I think I'll phone him if that's all right. I want to see if he'll meet me in the Park for a talk.' She thought how lovely it would be to walk with him under the trees, to tell him about her worries over Helen, how she missed Sally, how lonely she often felt.

'Ring him now, honey. I'm sure he'd love it.'

'If my mother answers I shall just ring off.'

'Poor Nick. I understand.'

Nicola went into the hall and dialled Birch House. She felt apprehensive at the thought of hearing her mother's voice, but the ringing tone went on and on. Everyone must be out, she thought sadly, replacing the receiver. Even the new housekeeper.

She went back to the kitchen. 'Nobody in,' she announced. 'Shall we have another game of Scrabble?'

'Not tonight, Honey-child. I'm leaving early in the morning – making a day of it – and I've got to sort out something to wear. Must look fairly civilised for the "successful author" image.'

Nicola laughed, but only out of politeness. She was deeply disappointed that she wasn't going to see her father. She desperately needed to talk to him.

183

R

'I knew I'd be too quick,' said Robert. 'I'm sorry, sweetheart.'

'Not to worry – it wasn't surprising, was it? And you made amends so beautifully.' Alison stretched her arms above her head with the voluptuous satisfaction of a cat waking up in front of the fire. 'Oh, God – *so* beautifully.'

The curtains were drawn against the evening sunshine – linen curtains that Ivy had made, patterned with pink and yellow rosebuds. The room was shadowed, but light enough for him to gaze at Alison's creamy nakedness as she lay beside him. The bed was much too small for the two of them; his shoulder was pressed against the wall and his feet protruded from the pale green coverlet.

For a while they lay there in silence, his head on her breast, his hand between her moist, hot thighs. He could see the oak table in front of the window, scattered with her books and trinkets and suddenly he remembered an occasion when Nicola was three or four years old. A carnival procession was going by along the Hastings road and she had been standing on that table, with Ivy beside her, watching the procession from the window. Beyond the sapling silver birches, and the high brick wall, came the waving flags, followed by the carnival floats, gleaming with tin foil. He remembered the thumping of the drums, the warble of fifes, and Nicola's excitement as she jumped up and down on the table, steadied by Ivy's protective arms. He thought of Ivy in her hospital bed in Sheffield (was it only yesterday?) and he knew that she clung to the hope that one day she might be with him again. If she could have seen him at that moment, naked in her bed with the new housekeeper . . . It seemed there was no end to the misery of human life. And no end to its delights.

Alison sat up, sighing with contentment, and he raised his head to gaze at her pale breasts, tenderly veined with threads of blue, her sunburnt arms, her long dark hair hanging loosely round her shoulders. Letting down her hair had been the first thing he did when they closed the door behind them, a fantasy that had excited him from the first day they met. Then they had lain on the bed for minute after minute of exquisitely protracted caresses. The phone had rung once during that time but they had merely smiled and sighed and kissed more deeply. When at last the moment came for the first delicious thrust, his ecstasy had exploded instantly, as he had feared it would. Next time, he was sure, it would be better.

'How about that casserole?' she said. 'I'm terribly hungry.'

'Yes – and we'll have a bottle of very special wine to celebrate.'

'It seems a shame to get dressed,' she said. 'It would be lovely to go down in our dressing gowns.'

'Lovely – but I don't think we can. We must be very careful.'

'Of course. I was only dreaming.'

'I'll watch you dress. Oh, darling – if only you knew how much I love you.'

She smiled and bent to kiss him, touching his lips at first with little more than a breath and then so deeply that their tongues and teeth and saliva seemed to be fused into an eternity of pleasure.

It was in the middle of that kiss that he heard a knock on the door of the room.

He drew his lips from hers and stared at her in horror, his heart hammering.

'Oh, God,' she breathed. 'She's back –'

'Did you lock the door?' he whispered under his breath.

She shook her head and began to speak but he pressed his fingers on her mouth. If they were silent Julia would think that she was out.

The knock was repeated, more loudly, and Alison started

185

to get out of bed, but it made a creaking sound and Robert stopped her, clutching her arm, desperate for Julia to think that the room was empty. He was trembling uncontrollably and he saw that Alison's arms and breasts were covered with goose-pimples. They stared into each other's eyes, breathless with panic, and Robert felt sure that Julia was no longer there. The landing outside was carpeted, and footsteps could retreat in silence, as they had approached.

And then the door opened. The curtains billowed in the sudden draught and Robert sat up, nerving himself for the holocaust. But it was not Julia who came into the room; it was Bernard. He was carrying a potted pink geranium and he shuffled across to the window and put it on the table, moving a book aside to make room for it. Then he drew back the curtains, admitting a glare of light that made Robert shrink against the wall.

Bernard turned to face them, a gaunt silhouette against the window. He had no hat, no pipe, and seemed a different man – bald and bent, his thin mouth twisted with disgust.

Alison spoke first. She was holding the coverlet against her breasts but her head was high, her husky voice quite even. 'Thank you, Bernard. That's very kind of you.'

He didn't reply but continued to stare at them both as if he couldn't drag his eyes away.

For a long moment, Robert could find no words. His mouth was dry, his body still trembling. Then he said, 'Your job's in the *garden* – you've no right in the house –'

'Mrs Slingsby told me to bring a plant in for Mrs Laurie. Them was my instructions.'

'Then you'll keep this strictly to yourself – my private life is my own affair.'

Bernard looked at Alison's clothes on the floor and then at Robert's on the chair. 'Fine how-do-you-do,' he muttered bitterly. 'Fine how-do-you-do.'

Alison said, 'It's a lovely plant, Bernard. Lovely colour. Now please will you leave us. *At once*.'

He grunted, cleared his throat as if he were about to spit on the Indian rug, and went out, slamming the door.

R

The casserole was indeed delicious but Robert could hardly eat it. They sat at the kitchen table, drinking wine, picking at their food.

'She's put him up to it,' Robert kept saying. 'She got suspicious and set him spying.'

'Couldn't he have brought the plant up in all good faith?' said Alison. 'Found the room was empty – as he thought – and just come in to plonk it down?'

'You don't know Julia like I do. It fits in exactly with her sneaky ways. And how did he know which room you were in? She must have told him. I'm convinced it was a plot to catch us out. I hated the way he was looking in through the drawing room window when we were having our drinks. He probably saw us go upstairs.'

'Well, he might not tell her, after all. I get on very well with him – I always give him tea and cake at four o'clock. And I bandaged his finger last week when he cut it on some glass. If you ask me, I think he'll keep quiet and the whole thing will blow over.'

'Nonsense. He'll tell her in the morning and she'll fire you on the spot. Mark my words.'

'Anybody'd think that was what you *wanted*!' Her face was flushed, her eyes dark with unhappiness.

'Don't talk like that. You know I couldn't *bear* it if you went.'

'Of course you could bear it. We'd keep in touch.'

'Keep in touch! I want you *here*, for God's sake. I can't –'

'Robert! We're quarrelling. We mustn't quarrel. Whatever happens we'll just have to cope with it as best we can. I'll get the chocolate mousse.'

'I don't want any – I'm sorry – I couldn't.'

'Poor darling – why don't you go to bed? Take a sleeping

pill.'

He looked at her tragic face, the large, soft eyes brimming with sympathy. 'I'm sorry,' he said. 'It's awful for you as well – your job and everything. But the thought of you going away is more than I can stand.' He covered his face with his hands, ashamed of his outburst yet quite unable to cope with the situation calmly. 'It was all so wonderful,' he muttered. 'I've never been so happy as I was in your room. Never in my life.'

'You'll be happy again,' she said. 'Have you any sleeping pills?'

'Plenty,' he told her. 'And I feel like taking the whole bloody bottle!'

She got up from the table and stood beside him, putting her arms around him, kissing his hair. 'I know how you feel,' she said. 'If *only* I'd locked the door.'

'You mustn't blame yourself – I should have thought of it too.' He leaned his head against her breast and felt the stirring of desire at the touch of its softness. 'I'll have to go to work tomorrow,' he told her. 'At least in the morning to see how things are going.'

'I know. Try not to worry.'

He slipped his hand under her skirt, caressing her warm thighs, searching beneath the frill of her briefs for the consolation of sexual excitement.

'Come to my room,' she murmured. 'It may be our last chance. But first I must do the washing up – clear away the traces before her ladyship comes back.'

'I'll help you.'

'Right. I'll wash, you dry.'

They stood at the sink together like man and wife, and he knew that she was stronger and braver than he could ever be. He wished it were not so, but the knowledge sustained him as he thought of the misery that lay in store.

R

Robert awoke the next morning with an agonising headache. He had taken two sleeping pills and retired to the bleak four-poster before midnight, afraid that Julia might return earlier than she had said. In Alison's room he had been too tense and anxious to make love, but they had clung together, whispering, kissing, speculating, lamenting.

He had not heard Julia come to bed and now, as she lay there with her back to him, her breathing kept time with the throb of his headache. He remembered that Bernard didn't arrive until ten o'clock each morning; by that time Robert would be in his office, coping with a dozen problems that would have blown up during the last two days. He pictured his desk by the window – the in-tray piled with estimates, statements, memos – and the pain in his head grew stronger. He looked at his watch and saw that it was nearly time for Alison to bring the tray.

He had drawn the curtains when he came to bed but where they joined there was a strip of dazzling sunshine that made him wince and close his eyes. He lay there, trying to relax his limbs but when he heard Alison's gentle knock, his body was shaken by an involuntary spasm and as the door opened he began to tremble.

She came in with the tray, her face composed but with smudges of fatigue under her eyes. She was wearing the same dress, and Robert felt that she had chosen it for him. It was as if she were saying: Here are the buttons you undid, the bodice you opened . . . He felt ashamed to be lying under the bedclothes with Julia; it was obscene that he should be in any bed but Alison's after the previous evening.

'Good morning,' she said as usual, placing the tray on his bedside table. 'Another sunny day.'

She crossed the room to draw back the curtains but

Robert called out: 'Not this morning, thank you – too bright – I've a bit of a head.'

She turned and gave him a secret look of love and sympathy but as she did so, Julia rolled over onto her back and said in a quiet voice, 'Just a minute, Mrs Laurie.' Robert saw that Alison was suddenly tense although she answered calmly.

'Yes, Mrs Slingsby?' She stood patiently in the rosy half light and Robert felt ill with love for her.

'Would you please draw back the curtains?'

Alison hesitated, glancing at Robert.

'*Draw back the curtains*!' Julia's tone was shrill, barely controlled, and Robert raised himself on his elbow, his mouth dry, his heart racing.

Alison went to the window and did as she was told, admitting a blaze of sunshine that transformed the room. Julia sat up and arranged the pillows behind her. Her hair was pinned into the usual flat curls but she was not wearing a hairnet. Her face had the cold, hard whiteness of a plaster cast. The only colour was in her eyes; it was as if the eyes of a statue had been tinted with pale blue laquer.

'Thank you,' she said. 'I want to look at you. Come nearer, Mrs Laurie.'

Alison took a step towards the bed. Her face was taut with anger, the scar very prominent in the glaring light. Robert knew that he should intervene but no words would come. He felt as he had with Bernard the previous night: his mouth was dry, his tongue swollen.

'Robert,' commanded Julia. 'Pass my orange juice.'

He did so and she took a series of long slow sips. His cup of tea was steaming on the tray and he longed to drink it.

Julia finished her juice and then she said again: 'Come nearer, Mrs Laurie.'

Alison remained where she was. 'I must go and see to the breakfast,' she said. 'If you'll excuse me.'

Julia slammed the glass down on the bedside table with such force that she must surely have cracked it. '*Do as I tell you*!'

Robert turned to Julia and found his voice at last. 'What's all this about?' he cried. 'What's got into you? Such *rudeness*!'

Julia did not look at him. She continued to stare at Alison who stood uncertainly between the bed and the door, and when she spoke, her voice was shaking with rage. 'Go and pack your things,' she ordered. 'Do it at once – never mind the breakfast. A taxi is ordered for eleven o'clock and I want you in it with all your belongings. You will never set foot in this house again – never see my husband again. Do you understand me?'

Alison looked at Julia in silence, her lips unsteady, and Julia went on, 'I'm going out at ten and I shan't be back till this afternoon. You've been paid to the end of the month and you won't get a penny more. Now get out! I don't want to see you ever again.' Her voice rose suddenly to a manic screech. 'Get *out*! You're nothing but a *whore*!'

'Shut up,' yelled Robert. 'Shut *up*, damn you!'

'I will *not* shut up. Bernard rang me last night at the Cartwrights' as I told him to. I knew there was something going on – he knew it too. He's seen you in the garden together when I've been out.' She turned to Alison. 'You were after him right from the start, weren't you? All that scent – smiling and simpering. You're a *whore*!' She picked up the tumbler and hurled it at Alison but it missed her and hit the door, shattering into fragments.

Alison put her hand to her cheek, stared wildly for a moment at the glass on the carpet, and stumbled out of the room.

She left the door ajar and in a moment Robert was out of bed, breathless and shaking, but suddenly resolute. 'I'll come and help you,' he shouted after her. 'I'll come and help you pack.' And without a glance at Julia he hitched up his pyjama trousers and followed Alison through the door.

R

Alison was standing with her back to the window, staring round her room as if she were totally lost.

Robert shut the door behind him and locked it. 'Sit down,' he said gently. 'Sit down and listen carefully. I've got a plan.'

She sat on the edge of the bed which was still unmade, her pink cotton nightdress thrown across the pillow. 'I've an old school friend in Epsom,' she said. 'I can stay with her until –'

'You won't need to.' He sat beside her on the bed and took her hand, holding it tightly between his own. 'Pack your bags and get them in that taxi,' he said. 'Get him to take you to Granger Coe – the porter's lodge. The porter there is an old friend of mine – Edgar – and he has a summer house in his garden. I know he'll let you leave your things there till we've got a place of our own.'

'A place of our own?' Her eyes shone with sudden tears.

'That's what I want. If you do?'

'Yes. *Yes*!'

He gripped her hand more tightly. 'Edgar's wife will look after you – give you coffee – but I'll get away as soon as I can.'

He heard the distant splashing of Julia's bathwater and was relieved to know that she was following her normal routine.

'Robert – but where will I sleep tonight? Shouldn't I ring my friend?'

'No – you'll sleep with me. I've got it all planned. I'll go to the office as usual – sort things out as quickly as I can – and this afternoon we'll drive away for the weekend. Maybe longer. I know a lovely hotel in Wiltshire – out in the wilds.'

'Oh God – it sounds too perfect. I can't believe –'

'Don't worry, darling. I can see it all so clearly. I'll write a note to Julia and put it in your apron pocket in the kitchen.

192

Leave it on the telephone table when you go.'

'What will you say?'

'"Gone away with Alison – want a divorce." Something like that. We'll vanish into oblivion – no one will know where we are.'

'Like a honeymoon –'

'Just. Oh, darling –' He kissed her and felt that she was trembling.

'Robert – I hate it all so much –'

'Of course you do. But for me it's the freedom I've always dreamed of. I can hardly believe it.'

'How about Nicola?'

'She'll be all right with Barry's mother. Later we can have her with us for a while.'

'Of course we can.'

He got up. 'And now I must be off – keep to my usual schedule so she doesn't suspect anything. Don't forget that note.'

'No. Apron pocket – telephone table. What about your breakfast?'

'I'm not hungry – I'll have a bun at the office. What about *yours*?'

'I don't feel as if I'll ever eat again.'

'You will. This place in Wiltshire is a gourmet's paradise.' He turned to face her, his back to the door. 'See you at the porter's lodge, then. The taxi man will help you with your luggage. Can you manage?'

She nodded and smiled at him, a quivering uncertain smile that made him feel that perhaps she was more in need of him than he had realised. His headache was now much easier; almost gone, in fact.

As he opened the door she called out to him. 'Robert?'

He turned and saw that the tears were glinting on her cheeks. 'What is it, darling?'

'I love you,' she said.

R

Robert saw too late the glass on the bedroom carpet. A needle of pain shot through his toe and he sat on the bed, cursing to himself as he removed a splinter and saw the blob of blood appear.

The bathroom door was shut – probably locked – and he could hear the familiar sounds of Julia's toilet: the bathwater running away, the clink of her talcum jar on the bath surround. Having exploded into violence and humiliated Alison, she would be content for a while, quietly plotting the next move.

He wiped the blood from his toe with his handkerchief and enjoyed the thought of Julia alone in that great house with no one to sweep up the broken glass, no one to prepare her dinner that night. There would be only Bernard. Perhaps he understood what Julia had suffered in the days of Nigel B. Perhaps that was a reason for their odd alliance.

Robert repacked his weekend case (it still contained a few of the things he had taken to Yorkshire) and in his haste he hardly had time for anxiety, but the memory of Nicola so recently hurling a wine glass at her mother was something he dared not dwell on. Like mother, like daughter? No – oh, *no* – it mustn't be like that . . .

He dressed without washing – a thing he hardly ever did – choosing his blazer and not his business suit. Then he took his case down to the car and hurried into the drawing room. He could smell a whiff of Alison's perfume and he wished he could see her again before he left. Their whisky glasses still stood on the coffee table. They had been so concerned with going to her room that they had overlooked the dangers of discovery. It was remarkable that neither of them had thought to lock the bedroom door. No matter, he thought, as he took the writing pad from the drawer in the telephone table, it had brought things to a head. Now he could hardly wait to leave Birch House.

'*Julia*,' he wrote. '*I have gone away with Alison and shall want a divorce. I will return next week for my possessions and hope we can arrange things amicably*.' It occurred to him to say he was sorry for his part in the downfall of their marriage but he decided against it and ended with nothing but his name. He knew she would cause as much unpleasantness as possible but her power was gone. No longer would she be able to undermine his confidence, torment him, destroy his peace of mind. He was free . . .

He put the letter in an envelope, addressed it to Julia and took it to the kitchen, fearful that she might come downstairs at any moment. Alison's apron with the brown and yellow daisies was hanging behind the door and he put the letter in the pocket. By the time Julia found it on the telephone table they would be on their way to Wiltshire. He prayed there would be a room available at the hotel he knew; it was the most delightful rendezvous imaginable.

Five minutes later he was driving down April Avenue on his way to Tonbridge, his headache gone and a smile of wonderment and joy on his lips.

N

On that Friday morning Nicola, half asleep, heard the front door slam. Freddie must be off on her London jaunt. Breakfast alone with Barry, she thought, and decided to go down straight away and get some bacon frying. He had said that he liked the smell of bacon in the mornings.

She put on a clean yellow T-shirt with her jeans and went down to the kitchen. She was surprised to see him already there, leaning against the sink, munching a jam sandwich. He usually stayed in bed quite late if he wasn't going to work.

'Hi,' she said, kissing his cheek. 'Like some bacon?'

He smiled at her but did not kiss her in return. 'No thanks. I've got some work to do on the car. Bit of a problem with the cooling system.'

'Freddie's in London – did you know?'

'Yeah.' He examined his sandwich, opening it up, frowning, and closing it again. 'She was in a rush for her train.'

'Did you tell her you'd lost your job?'

'Yes, but it's O.K. She isn't bothered.'

'Barry – can we talk? I *so* much want to talk.'

'What about?'

'Oh – *everything*. I haven't seen you properly for ages. I want to tell you about going to Yorkshire with Daddy – and Ivy and everything.'

'I've got this job to do on the car – it'll probably take all morning.'

'Shall I cook us a lovely lunch? Bangers and beans and mash – with some red wine?'

'O.K. Great.' He smiled and nodded but there was a moodiness about him that made her feel sick and shaky.

'What's wrong?' she asked. 'You look all edgy.'

'It's the car – I've got to get it fixed.'

'And we'll talk at lunch time?'

'Sure.' He was on his way to the door, not looking at her.

'I'll go to the shops and get some sausages,' she said. 'Maybe we could go for a drive this afternoon when you've seen to the car?'

But he did not reply.

N

The sausages were done to a rich golden brown, the potatoes mashed with butter and seasoned with nutmeg. Nicola had also fried mushrooms and tomatoes and was proud of the appetising lunch she had ready when Barry came in from the car. There had been complications with the cooling system and it was after two o'clock by the time he finished. His face was running with sweat and his blue shirt was daubed with black grease.

Nicola had changed into a summer dress, white with pink polka dots. She had gathered a bunch of white roses from the rambler in the back garden and arranged them in a vase on the table. While Barry scrubbed his hands at the kitchen sink, she poured two glasses of red wine, thinking how nice it must be to come in from a hard morning's work to find such a delicious-looking table.

'Hope you're hungry,' she said. 'Look what I've done for us.'

'Yeah – great.' He was busy with the nail brush and she knew that he had not even glanced at the delicious plateful that was waiting for him. It was the car, of course; he was obsessed by it.

'Have it while it's hot,' she urged, sitting down and raising her glass. 'Cheers. To us!' This was their usual toast.

'No wine for me,' he said, slumping down at the table and picking up his knife and fork.

'Because of driving? A glass or two wouldn't matter.'

'No, it's not that. I don't feel like it.'

'Why not?'

'Oh, Nick – haven't you guessed? Do I have to spell it out?'

'Spell out what?'

'It's over between us. I'd have thought you knew.'

She stared at him dumbly, her heart pounding. He put down his knife and fork and went on gently, 'I'm sorry, Nick. Honest. We had some great times but it just doesn't work – you and me. You know damn well it doesn't.'

She couldn't meet his eyes and looked at the food that lay in front of him untouched. The tomatoes ran together into a blaze of red and she felt as if a burning spiral of terror were mounting up inside her. It rose into her throat and suddenly exploded on her tongue. 'It's because you can't *fuck* me, isn't it? That's why! Because I'm no good in bed? I suppose you'll be having it off again with that bitch Helen –'

'Don't you *dare* to call her that!'

'*Bitch! Bitch!* That's what she *is*!' She stood up, clutching the back of the cane chair.

'I love her, if you want to know,' he cried. 'And she loves me. I'm going down to Brighton this afternoon – moving in with her. That's why I had to have the car ready. She's got me a job at the theatre – painting scenery – helping out. So don't you dare say a word against her.'

Nicola stood for a moment, stupefied with anguish, and then she picked up the chair and slammed it across the table, sending their lunches flying, the plates, the wine, the flowers.

Barry leapt to his feet and stared in horror at the débris. 'You're mad,' he cried. 'You ought to be in a loony bin. Thank God I'm leaving – thank God I'm getting away from you!'

Screaming with rage and misery, Nicola fled from the kitchen and raced upstairs to her room. She flung herself on the bed, biting the pillow until it tore. Soon she heard Barry's footsteps on the stairs and she rushed to open the bedroom door, standing there sobbing as he came up the attic steps.

'Oh, *Nick*!' he cried, pausing a few stairs below her. 'Nick – I'm sorry – you'll soon get over it – I'm sorry – I shouldn't have said what I did.'

She stared back at him, at the face she worshipped, the brown eyes wide with distress, at his hand on the bannister, the crucifix glinting on his chest. She wanted to plead with him, to tell him she would have an operation to put things right, that she would be able to give him as good a time as Helen could, but no words came.

'You can stay on here, you know,' he was saying. 'Mother'll be glad to have you – specially with me away –'

Away? *Away*? He mustn't go away – he couldn't . . . The spiral was whirling up again, tightening in her head so that she looked wildly around for some way to express her misery and helplessness. The telescope stood beside her on the landing and in a moment she had seized it in her arms and sent it toppling down the stairs. Barry let out a gasp of pain and anger as it struck him, and then he righted it and examined it anxiously to see if it was damaged, running his fingers along the dusty tube.

'*Things* – that's all you care about,' she screeched. 'You don't care about *me* – you only care about cars and bloody telescopes.'

He looked up at her and it seemed that his eyes were full of hatred. 'This telescope belonged to my father,' he said in a low voice. 'If you've broken it I'll never forgive you.'

'And I'll never forgive *you* – going off with that old hag – old enough to be your *mother*. It's *disgusting*!'

'I love her,' he said, not raising his voice. 'Age doesn't matter. That's something you wouldn't understand.' He picked up the telescope and carried it carefully to the top of the stairs, setting it down beside her in its usual place. She caught the familiar smell of his shirt, and his hair touched her arm as he bent to adjust the stand. The thought of him with Helen was more than she could bear and she fled down the stairs, sliding and slithering, half falling, until she reached the hall.

Then she was out in the sunshine, running past the M.G., down Station Road. There was only one thought in her mind as she headed for the park. 'Daddy – ' she moaned, half blinded by tears. 'Daddy – I want you – *help* me –'

N

Nicola did not slacken speed until she reached the park. While she ran she could not think coherently and her thoughts were too painful to bear, so she kept on running although she could hardly breathe.

When she reached the recreation ground she could go no

further and she flopped down on a swing, watching the concrete under her feet swim out of focus as she pushed herself backwards and forwards. The gentle motion was a comfort and soon she looked around her, amazed to find that life was going on as usual. Her father would help her. He loved her. He had implored her to go back home and that was what she would do. The sun was warm on her bare arms and legs, a boy nearby was throwing sticks for a dog and somewhere behind the trees a transistor was playing 'Imagine'. Somehow the sound of John Lennon's voice pleading for peace made her own suffering seem bearable. Yoko had lost her man for ever but Barry was still alive; he might come back to her. Surely he would tire of Helen before long. That was what Sally had said: young men often go for older women but it doesn't last. In the meantime she would have that operation . . .

After a while, watching the dog, listening to the drift of music, she felt much calmer. She set off for Birch House, planning to steal up to her room and wait there until her father came home from work. She remembered leaving an exercise book and some pencils in the chest of drawers by her bed. She would write a long letter to Ivy, all about Barry and Helen and Freddie, about the new understanding with her father which had grown as a result of the trip to Yorkshire. Ivy would be glad she was going home; she had been so insistent that she should look after her father. 'You're all he's got,' she had said that night in her room. Now it was mutual and Nicola longed for him as never before.

She made her way through the leafy sun and shadow of April Avenue until she reached the back entrance to Birch House. The gates were usually open but now they were closed and locked. Undeterred, she hurried to a secret passage through the wall behind an elder tree. Strong roots and shoots had cracked the brickwork, and years ago she had excavated a hole that was big enough to wriggle through. It led into the shrubbery and soon she was pushing past the heavy foliage and heading for the house. She tiptoed along the terrace and found that the French windows were open. With any luck she could reach the staircase through the drawing room without being seen.

As she went in, she was startled by a rustle at her elbow, but it was only the breeze lifting the pages of a writing pad left open on the telephone table, and soon she was safely across the hall and up the stairs. Her legs felt weak and her heart was thumping again, but as she approached her room she let out a sigh of relief. It had always been her sanctuary.

When she opened the door she froze with horror. The room was totally transformed. The bed had gone, the wardrobe, the chest of drawers. A desk had been installed by the window, and sitting there in a green dress, writing, was her mother.

Julia turned round slowly as if she had a stiff neck. 'What are *you* doing here?' she demanded coldly, looking Nicola up and down. 'How did you get in?'

'What have you done to my *room*?'

'I asked why you are here.'

'I've come to see Daddy.'

'Then you can go away again.'

'I *must* see him – *please*.'

Julia put down her pen and turned right round in her chair, facing Nicola with a twisted little smile. 'Your father has gone away with the new housekeeper,' she said. 'He isn't coming back.' Her face seemed to narrow with hatred as she added, 'She seduced him, if you're interested. Your father is a very weak and stupid man.'

'Where is he?' gasped Nicola. 'I've got to see him. *Please* tell me!'

'I've no idea. I should imagine he'll be at the firm this afternoon but it's of no concern to me.'

Nicola knew that she must go at once to Granger Coe. She'd get the porter to ring her father's office and he would come down to see her. She had done it before when she was in trouble at school. Thank God he had left her mother at last! She would beg him to take her with him; he had kept on saying she would like Mrs Laurie.

'Could I have some money for the bus?'

'No you could not. Your father gives you money.'

'I've come without my bag.'

'That's your stupidity, isn't it?' She returned to her writing and Nicola felt the upsurge of a new fury swelling inside her head.

'All right,' she yelled. 'I'll bloody well hitch a lift and you can rot in hell! Damn you – I hope you *do* – I hope you rot in *hell*!'

Julia stood up. 'Get out of my house,' she said with icy calmness. 'Get out and never come back. Never come back – do you hear?'

Nicola turned and fled down the stairs, across the hall, out of the front door. Her legs were shaking so much that she could hardly keep her balance, and the drive seemed never-ending as she ran between the silver birches and the apple trees towards the white gate. Soon she would be on the Hastings road; she could easily hitch a lift to Tonbridge and the thought of being with her father gave her the strength to keep running.

When she reached the gate she groaned aloud with frustration; it was firmly locked with a heavy chain and padlock. What was her mother playing at? Making the house into a bloody fortress? Her first impulse was to race back to the house and out by the hole in the wall but it was a long way round by April Avenue to the Hastings road – half a mile or so – and, more important, there was the possibility of seeing her mother again. She would *never* see her again, *never* . . .

There was only one thing to do: she must climb over the gate. She would hoist herself up by getting a foothold on the hinges. The row of spikes looked menacing, sharp and black against the sky, but they were wide enough apart for her to put her knee between them, stand up, and jump cleanly down onto the pavement.

Bernard's wheelbarrow stood empty nearby and she pushed it into position and scrambled onto it. The gate was about six feet high and she reached up to the top hinge, clinging with her finger-tips and gaining a grip on the bottom one with the toes of her crêpe-soled sandals. Her legs seemed to have no strength in them but after a few moments of struggle she managed to grab the top of the gate and heave herself up, her feet slipping on the top hinge. Now she could see over the top – the people, the traffic. Soon she would be with her father.

'Get *down* from there!' She heard the familiar voice of Bernard behind her. 'Miss Nicola – what do you think you're doing? Get *down*!'

Nicola hated Bernard; he had always been an ally of her mother's. Panic-stricken, she made a frantic effort to get one foot on top of the gate, but her crêpe sole slipped off the hinge and with a howl of fear she fell onto the spikes with all her weight. A searing pain ripped through her chest and she was brutally impaled, her arms and legs dangling helplessly.

Faintly she heard the shouts of the people on the pavement below, and as somebody touched the gate, she was shaken by a new explosion of agony. Her head dropped limply forward and the last thing she saw as she lost consciousness was a stream of blood trickling down the white paintwork.

R

'I think it's the loveliest hotel I've ever seen,' said Alison. They had settled into their room and now they were sitting on the lawn enjoying a cream tea. Their table, with its dark blue cloth and little bowl of yellow roses, was set beside a thick hedge of lavender where three white butterflies were floating in and out like bits of torn tissue paper. Beyond the hedge ran a narrow stream, glittering in the afternoon sunlight. The garden tables were set around the edge of the lawn, and there was no sound but the birds and the stream, the murmur of voices from the other residents and the occasional clink of a cup. Robert had lunched there several years earlier when he was on a business trip to Swindon. He had taken his coffee at that very table.

The long low building had once been a farmhouse. It nestled in a froth of woodland foliage – every shade of green in soft confusion: sage and lime and emerald, silvery grey and dark viridian. The ancient roof, red-tiled and mossy, reminded Robert of the roofs in old Italian towns, but the interior had been luxuriously modernised and furnished in yellow and dark blue.

He was delighted to see that Alison had regained her appetite. She had been unable to eat her lunch at the motorway restaurant but when they emerged into the leafy green lanes of Wiltshire she had gradually relaxed and begun to smile again.

'Have another scone,' he said.

She did so, piling it high with cream and strawberry jam. 'They're heavenly,' she said. 'They melt in your mouth.'

'I told you it was a gourmet's paradise. Just you wait till dinner time!'

She grinned at him with a fleck of cream on her upper lip. 'I hope you don't mind fat ladies,' she said.

'Not when they're called Alison Laurie and have such incredibly beautiful eyes.'

'Oh, Robert! Is it all a dream? I'm frightened of waking up.'

'You won't wake up till Tuesday. After that, I can't promise. But as soon as we find our cottage we'll be able to put all the horrors behind us and start a new life.'

On Tuesday he would take her to *The Five Gables* near Tonbridge where he had already reserved a room for them. Alison was delighted when he told her there was a putting green. 'You see!' she had exclaimed. 'Her ladyship can't do us out of our putting after all!' She always referred to Julia as 'her ladyship' in a tone of voice so placid and roguish that Robert had to smile.

He thought of the disastrous occasion when he had taken Nicola to *The Five Gables* for lunch. He would invite her

204

there again, to meet Alison, and when he found a cottage she could live with them; they would be able to give her a proper sense of security until she could make an independent life for herself. He understood her now, as never before. Free at last from the plague of his obsession, free from his former prejudices against her youth, her socialism, her untidiness, he realised that many of her pains and problems were very similar to his own.

And for this wider vision he knew he had Alison to thank.

She was wiping her jammy fingers on a napkin, smiling contentedly. 'It's so romantic,' she said. 'Nobody knowing where we are. I've never done it before – Jack always insisted on leaving an address in case of emergencies. He said if the house burned down while we were away, he wanted to know about it. Not me.'

'I must admit I've never done it before,' said Robert, feeling that he shared Jack's sentiments. 'But this is a kind of honeymoon. People often vanish without trace on a honeymoon.' He certainly didn't want Julia to know where they were; she would be sure to make trouble if she got the chance.

'Three whole days!' Alison gazed around at the beds of yellow roses bordered with lobelia, the soft sunlit foliage, the doves on the roof of the hotel. 'There's only one word for it,' she said. 'Idyllic. Shall we make some paper boats and sail them down the stream? Have races?'

He smiled. 'And there's only one word for you, my darling.'

'What's that?'

'Perfect.'

N

Nicola opened her eyes to see the sun in a bright sky. She closed them again because the pain was too great.

Later she tried again and saw that it was not the sun but an electric light on a white ceiling. She was in a room, in a bed. And it hurt her to breathe; it hurt her terribly to breathe . . .

She heard a woman's voice from a long way off and saw a face, a pink circle with a blur of white on top. A nurse. She was in hospital.

'Hello, dear. How are you feeling?'

Nicola could not speak. She wanted to ask for her father but her lips wouldn't open.

'You're going to be all right,' the voice went on. 'Doctor says you're a very lucky girl. Very lucky.'

Lucky . . . lucky . . . ?

The face of the nurse came clearer for a moment. It was a young face, smiling.

'Your mother's here – she's waiting to see you.'

Nicola felt a convulsion of agony as she tried to speak. 'No – no –' she gasped. 'Daddy . . .' But the pain was suddenly more than she could bear and the room went black as she fell away once more into oblivion.

R

'There's something I must tell you,' said Robert. 'I don't want to, but I must.'

It was nearly midnight on Monday and they were strolling along a secluded woodland path in the hotel grounds. A warm breeze was rustling the leaves, and the full moon, sailing high, had just been extinguished by a drifting cloud.

She turned to him and her eyes were soft and attentive in the half light.

'What is it?' Plenty of women, he thought, would have protested: 'Not *now*, on our last evening!' or 'Oh, God – whatever's coming?' Alison only took his hand and waited for him to continue.

'I hate to tell you,' he said, 'but I want you to know the worst about me right from the start.'

She squeezed his hand. 'Tell me.'

They had enjoyed a perfect dinner with champagne and lingered afterwards in the moonlit garden over coffee and brandy, listening to the stream, the wind in the trees, the call of an owl. It might have been the wine and the brandy, but Robert felt quite certain that tonight was the time for his confession; he had grown so close to her in every way during the past three days.

'It's about Nicola,' he said. 'I used to have a – a sort of terrible fixation about her.'

'A sexual fixation?'

'Yes – I'm afraid so. It's over now, of course – completely over. It went so quickly – out like a light – when I fell in love with you.'

'Did she ever know?' Alison's voice was low.

'Never – at least I hope not. I couldn't bear it if she knew.' He clung to Alison's hand. 'Oh, darling – I feel so bad about it. Can you ever forgive me?' He was suddenly afraid she might reject him.

'Let's sit down.' She led him to a seat beside the path. 'You'll just have to try to forget it.' Her voice was warm and gentle and he could have wept with relief. 'We all need someone to love,' she said. 'That kind of attachment is probably a lot more common than we realise.'

'I can't understand it,' he burst out. 'I keep asking myself "Why me?". It was nothing I could help – the more I tried to overcome it, the worse it got. I felt so guilty – I *still* feel guilty.' He could not bring himself to tell her about the scene with Nicola when Julia had coerced him into beating her. He knew he should have refused to do it and he was deeply ashamed; there were some things one could never confess to anyone.

Alison interlaced her fingers with his. 'I'm longing to meet her,' she said. 'Why don't we take her out for a bumper meal as soon as we get back?'

'Yes, I'll be ringing her tomorrow to put her in the picture. She'll be delighted I've left Julia, there's no doubt about that. We'll get her over for dinner at *The Five Gables*.'

'I hope to goodness she likes me,' said Alison.

'She'll love you. She'll absolutely love you.'

They sat in silence for a while, then suddenly she turned to him. 'You mustn't feel guilty,' she said. 'It's your marriage that's to blame. Her ladyship again. She's got a lot to answer for. I've never forgotten something Jack said many years ago. He was a magistrate, as you know, and he learnt a lot about human nature in the courts.' As she spoke the moon emerged into a clear expanse of sky, exposing the scar on her cheek with ruthless clarity.

Robert had developed a fondness for Jack; Alison spoke of him in such a kindly, unsentimental way that there was no cause for jealousy. 'What was that?' he asked.

'He said: "The wrong face on the pillow can lead to all kinds of madness." It's always stuck in my mind – so true and so terribly sad.'

'Yours is the right face for me,' said Robert. 'And always will be.' He stood up and pulled her to her feet. 'Come along, my sweetheart – it's past our bedtime.'

'Yes,' she said as they walked slowly towards the hotel. 'And you might have quite a heavy day tomorrow.'